W8-CDT-416

DELTA GIRLS

DELTA GIRLS

A NOVEL

GAYLE BRANDEIS

BALLANTINE BOOKS TRADE PAPERBACKS
NEW YORK

A Ballantine Books Trade Paperback Original

Copyright © 2010 by Gayle Brandeis
Reading group guide copyright © 2010 by Random House, Inc.

Published in the United States by Ballantine Books, an imprint of The Random House Publishing Group, a division of Random House, Inc., New York.

BALLANTINE and colophon are registered trademarks of Random House, Inc. RANDOM HOUSE READER'S CIRCLE & Design is a registered trademark of Random House, Inc.

Grateful acknowledgment is made to Adrienne Rich and W. W. Norton & Company, Inc., for permission to reprint "Delta" from *The Fact of a Doorframe: Selected Poems 1950–2001* by Adrienne Rich, copyright © 2002, 1989 by Adrienne Rich. Reprinted by permission of Adrienne Rich and W. W. Norton & Company, Inc.

Library of Congress Cataloging-in-Publication Data
Brandeis, Gayle.
Delta girls : a novel / Gayle Brandeis.
p. cm.
ISBN 978-0-345-49262-3
eBook ISBN 978-0-345-52179-8
1. Single mothers—Fiction. 2. Migrant agricultural laborers—Fiction. 3. Delta Region (Calif.)—Fiction. 4. Women figure skaters—Fiction. 5. Mothers and daughters—Fiction. I. Title.
PS3602.R345D45 2010
813'.6—dc22   2010012555

Printed in the United States of America

www.randomhousereaderscircle.com

2 4 6 8 9 7 5 3 1

Book design by Carol Malcolm Russo

FOR MY MOM

Delta

If you have taken this rubble for my past
raking through it for fragments you could sell
know that I long ago moved on
deeper into the heart of the matter

If you think you can grasp me, think again:
my story flows in more than one direction
a delta springing from the riverbed
with its five fingers spread

—*Adrienne Rich*

DELTA GIRLS

IZZY

PEARS RIPEN BEST OFF THE TREE.

When I picked beefsteak tomatoes in Illinois, the farm stand owners wanted fat, red fruit. In the Arkansas field, it was easy enough to pop a strawberry into my mouth, my daughter's mouth, when the foreman wasn't watching. But pears you have to pick when they're green and hard. When they're not ready to yield to a thumb, a tongue. They may drive you wild with their scent, but they'll resist your teeth, make your lips and gums burn.

PEARS DERAILED US on our way to a blueberry farm in Washington, a family-run place that supposedly welcomed children and paid a decent wage. I had just left my job as a watermelon cutter in Niland, California, near the Mexican border; my task was to slice the fruit from its vine and hand it to the pitching crew that followed me around the dusty field. They hefted the melon from one man to the next, bucket-brigade-style, until it reached the pickup truck where it was stacked like wobbly cord-wood. My daughter Quinn, meanwhile, sat under a nearby tarp with her third-grade math sheets, face flushed, water bottles sur-rounding her like a packaged moat.

We left before harvesting was finished; I didn't have a con-tract like the rest of the crew, whose broker sent them from farm to farm. As a free agent, it was easy for me to take off, find an-other job. Most small farmers were willing to pay a woman under the table; I only had a problem if they expected something under the table in return. Or if they wouldn't let my nine-year-old homeschooled daughter out on the field with me. I always hoped my dark hair, my skin tan from so much time outside, would help me fit in with each new set of fellow workers, but they inevitably pegged me for a gringa right off the bat. Quinn's pale blue eyes probably contributed to this. The fact that I barely understood Spanish after all my time on the circuit didn't help, either.

I hadn't minded the melon picking—I felt kind of like a mid-wife as I eased the ripe fruit through the thatch of wood wool that protected it from sunburn, as I cut the stubborn umbilical cord, handed the bulky baby over to its line of waiting fathers—but the heat was another issue. A fellow cutter, a pregnant nineteen-year-old, had fallen ill from sunstroke, and I didn't want to risk that with Quinn. Plus the pitching crew made me nervous; I didn't like the way the first guy in line would hover over me as I knelt by the fruit so his crotch would be right in my face when I turned around, didn't like the way the group joked about me in Spanish. I would have felt even more vulnerable if it hadn't been for the knife in my hand.

IT WAS GOOD to be on the open road again, zipping up the belly of California. A car can get claustrophobic when you're parked for the night, when you're trying to sleep with the seat reclined as far as it can go, your whole body aching, your clothes sour, your daughter squirming in the back seat behind you, the air like an oven even with the windows open. But when you're driving and she's sitting beside you and the scenery is changing from desert to mountain to farmland, a mint green twenty-year-old Mercury Zephyr's a fine place to be.

Quinn put her grimy flip-flops up on the dashboard. "How much longer, Eema?" she asked, turning the vents to blow more air on the backs of her knees. Her faded turquoise shorts rippled and snapped around her legs like sails. I had never told Quinn that *Eema* was Hebrew for "mother," had never told her to call me that, but she had been doing it since she was a baby. She never said *Mama,* just *Eema.*

"If we drive straight through, twenty-four hours."

She made a noncommittal sound, then went back to her book and her bag of Funyuns. Quinn and I had fallen into the habit of eating convenience store food on the road, negligibly healthy things we could get for cheap: squishy bread with peanut butter, string cheese, granola bars, jerky, the occasional rubbery hard-boiled egg, tomato juice in lieu of fresh vegetables. Plus a rotating string of treats. The Funyuns filled the car with their bouillon cube tang, and I couldn't help but reach into the bag and crunch a few myself. I had a weakness for junk food, and didn't mind the bit of extra heft it gave my belly, my thighs. My body was strong, if achy, from all the farmwork—my body was there for me; it did what I needed it to do. Might as well reward it with some salt and grease.

WE ENTERED A stretch of I-5 with orchards on both sides of the road; the fruit on the trees was too small to identify as we barreled past at eighty miles per hour, sun flashing between the neatly planted rows like a strobe light. Pistachio, I found out when we stopped at a gas station; a small produce stand in the lot was selling bags of the pale green nuts, along with peaches and corn and wedges of watermelon in tubs of ice.

"Need any pickers?" I asked the woman running the stand, her white hair buffeted by the hot wind. My mouth was dry from the chips, my skin and eyes dry from the summer air. I was tempted to buy some watermelon, even though Quinn and I had glutted ourselves on it for days—we would hijack melons that had busted open in a fall or developed sugar-crack on the vine; back at our campsite after work, we would plunge our hands straight into the sweet, mealy innards. We must have looked like lions feasting on gazelle, pink pulp hanging off our faces, juice pouring down our arms.

"Nah," said the woman, "we use machines. Shake the nuts right off the tree."

I GULPED ANOTHER bottle of water as we continued up the I-5. My whole body felt parched; I found myself wishing we had taken the longer route up the coast just so we could see the ocean shimmering beside us. When we crossed what looked like a river in Stockton, I was ready to rip off my clothes and dive in. Instead, I pulled over to check the air in my tires.

"Is this the Sacramento River?" I asked a guy who was refilling his wiper fluid.

"It's the Deepwater Ship Channel," he said, green liquid glugging sweet through his funnel. "You want to see the river? Go to the Delta." He handed me a laminated map, one made for boaters. As soon as I saw the spiderweb of waterways, I knew I had to check it out.

Over a thousand miles of water twisted through the Sacramento River Delta, the river routed by levees and dikes, creating wetlands and estuaries and little islands that didn't look like islands, a few palm trees parked amongst the willow and oak to remind you that you were still in California. The rich peat soil farmland was so dense with minerals, it was known to combust. Pears grown in the Delta made up more than half the state's crop. Delta water made up more than two-thirds of California's drinking supply.

I didn't recognize the pear trees at first. Highway 160 was a tall levee road; it looked down at the Sacramento River on one side, vast orchards on the other. At first, I thought the farms were level with the asphalt, the treetops shrubs. They looked like giant tortoises hulked on the ground; I had a sudden image of Quinn getting out of the car and leaping from shell to leafy shell, as if they were stepping-stones. I couldn't figure out what sort of fruit grew on such strange stubby plants. Then I turned a bend and could see the length of their trunks, all the empty space between them. I felt a little dizzy, thinking of how far Quinn could have fallen.

WE DROVE PAST grand estates, crumbling canning houses, lots of little wooden markets, orchard after orchard after orchard as the road curved with the greenish river. At some point, we took a small ferry, free of charge, that was pulled across the water by cables; it was big enough for maybe six cars, although ours was the only one to make the three-minute crossing. Quinn was thrilled—she said it felt like we were being transported back in time as we floated to the other side. Time did seem to change in the Delta; I could feel my internal clock begin to slow, start to turn as languid as the Sacramento.

When I saw the sign for the town of Comice, population 472, my breath caught in my throat. The painted green letters were faded on the wooden placard, COM barely readable, but ICE sharp enough to reach inside my body and rattle around.

"I have to pee, Eema," said Quinn. We had just crossed a metal bridge with yellow spires, like a miniature, more industrial Golden Gate.

I pulled into the first driveway I could find. A "Pickers Needed" posterboard was duct-taped on the bottom of a sign that read "Vieira Pears."

"I'll see if they'll let you use the bathroom," I said. Quinn bit her lip and jiggled in her seat. We parked the car in front of a weathered two-story clapboard. To our left, surrounded by old machinery, a large vegetable garden grew kale, carrots, onions, lots of tomatoes in cages, the leaves reaching out through the metal, red fruit drooping down like boxing gloves after a match.

An olive-skinned man who appeared to be in his sixties came onto the porch, wiping his hands on his jeans. His dark hair was slicked back on his head. His eyebrows were bushy, the mustache under his prominent nose thick but neatly trimmed.

"Mr. Vieira?" I asked.

"You got him," he said. His voice had an accent I couldn't quite place. When he walked closer, I could see his face was studded with moles, like a chocolate chip cookie.

"I was wondering," I said, "if my daughter could use your bathroom and you could use me." His eyebrows went up.

"To pick," I added quickly. "If you could use me to pick."

I hadn't thought about asking until I said it out loud. The orchard seemed as good a place as any to stop. We'd save on gas money. We'd be near water.

"How's your back?" he asked after he gave Quinn directions to the bathroom.

"Strong," I assured him, even though it griped constantly.

"Don't normally hire lady pickers," he said, "but we'll take anyone we can get this year."

Rows of pears stretched out as far as I could see, the trees shaggy vases, flaring open to the sky. The air was just on the edge of humid, the river lending a mossy tang. A few barn swallows dipped and swerved overhead, trilling.

He nodded to Quinn as she disappeared into the house. "I can't pay her or nothing." His mustache twitched. "Just make sure she don't get hurt."

I HAD NEVER picked fruit from trees before, except to swipe an orange or two—all of my picking experience had been close to the ground. I hoped reaching up instead of down would help balance my back muscles, give them a chance to flex.

Mr. Vieira led me to the edge of the orchard, set up a ladder, and handed me a canvas bag that looped around my shoulders and tied behind my waist, a cross between an apron and one of those fake pregnancy bellies teachers strap onto teenage girls to try to scare them away from sex. He told me the basics of picking—lift the fruit from the tree, don't pull it. Avoid pears with bruises, sunburn, limb rub. Be on the lookout for thrips, blister mites, red-humped caterpillars, flat-headed borers, pernicious scales. The way he rattled off the pests made them sound like Dr. Seuss creatures, too whimsical to cause any harm, but I knew they were anything but.

If you leave a pear on the tree too long, he told me, it starts to rot from the inside out. It develops stone cells, little places of hardness that feel like grit in the mouth. It starts to get eaten by birds, by bugs. Better to pluck it when it's green, store it someplace cold, let it forget where it came from.

I CUPPED A Bartlett and lifted it until the stem separated from the branch. I hadn't believed Mr. Vieira, but he was right. Pulling left a broken stem, a tired wrist; lifting popped the stem right off. I started to relish the feel of the pears, cool and smooth as I gently raised them and they surrendered their weight into my palm. The branches scratched my arms and the straps of the picking bag bit into my shoulders, made my lower back sway and ache in a whole new way, but my hands enjoyed the work.

Quinn played in the dirt beneath the ladder, arranging dropped fruit into circles. Mr. Vieira had left us to our own devices after he watched me pick the first few pears. "Keep practicing," he said before he disappeared into the orchard. "Work on speed."

"You should pick up your book," I told Quinn. Lucky kid, having a pear orchard for a classroom. There was more shade here than there had been at any of my previous jobs.

Quinn sighed and cracked open the collection of Norse mythology we had bought for a quarter at a library sale in Oklahoma. A wasp flew off the blue cloth cover and circled Quinn's dark wispy hair before it reeled away. I touched the pocket of my jeans to make sure her EpiPen was safe inside.

"Tell me a story," I said, and Quinn started in her halting way, stopping to sound out the longer words.

"'In the beginning was Mus-pel-heim, the world of fire and Nif-l-heim, the world of ice,'" she read. "'When the warm air hit the cold air, a giant named Ymir—Ymir?—was created and so was an icy cow named Aud-hum-bla.'"

Quinn paused, her blue eyes uncertain. "I don't know if I'm saying the names right, Eema."

"You're doing fine." My bag was almost full. The heft of it threatened to pull me off the ladder. "It's the story that matters, not the names."

"'In the world of fire, a man was born from Ymir's foot and a woman was born from his armpit.' Gross!" She stuck out her tongue. "'In the world of ice, the cow licked a stone made of salt; the next day, the stone grew hair, then a head, then a body. An entire man emerged from the ice and stone.' What kind of weirdo story is this, anyway?" Quinn wrinkled her nose, flaky with sunburn. "Men coming out of the ice?"

An angular face started to form in my mind; I shook my head like an Etch-a-Sketch, breaking his features into a flurry of metal shavings. No need to think about him now. Just focus on Quinn, on this work, this new world of pears. Lift, then bag, lift, then bag, sunlight dappling my hands.

KAREN

Lifts were her favorite.

To the average viewer watching pairs in an ice arena or on TV, it looked as if the guy was doing all the work, as if all the girl had to do was look pretty and let her partner bear her up to heaven. But a partner couldn't lift a girl who wasn't lifting herself, too. When she was over her partner's head, his hand pressed into her ribs or stomach or the side of her thigh, she had to harden herself against his palm, his thumb, lift herself away from it. Otherwise she would end up with hand-shaped bruises on her skin, maybe a cracked rib. And that's if she didn't fall.

Karen liked lifts because everything looked smaller, more manageable, from the air. The judges with their score sheets. The television people with their cameras. Her mother in fur boots leaning against the boards. For those few seconds of height, none of them mattered. They were earthbound, finite. She was soaring; she was towering; she was sweetly, briefly above it all. The closest she could get to escape.

NATHAN MAIN WAS different from Karen's skating partner of five years, Brian. Nathan didn't treat her like a princess or a butterfly. He didn't apologize for shoving his hand between her legs during a lift or catching a couple of strands of her hair under his blade during a death spiral. "You can take it," he said, and she realized that she could. Nathan treated her like a woman. A body. Strong and capable, worthy of desire. Her mom, Deena, treated her like a body, too, but a body that needed to be changed, perfected, a body that was never quite right. Platinum dye since eleven, nose job at thirteen, a countless string of diets. With Nathan, it was "Here we are in our skins. What are we going to do about it?"

Karen was nervous when her mom first suggested pairing with him. His latest partner, Tabitha, was recovering from a concussion and a fractured vertebra. Karen's partner, Brian, had gone off to Harvard to study French literature and be surrounded by smart boys. Regionals were only two months away. Part of Karen hoped her mom wouldn't find her a new partner; part of her hoped she could sit this competition cycle out, stay away from the ice long enough to want to get back on, but she knew her mom would never let that happen. Especially not with the Olympics coming up in a little over a year.

"He has the best triple axel of any pairs skater out there," Deena said. "Just think of it. With your jumps, you'd be brilliant together."

Deena had groomed her daughter to be a singles champion, but when Karen was twelve and placed sixth at Junior Sectionals, Deena told her she didn't have the chops to go it alone. "You have the jumps, sweetheart," she said, her voice matter-of-fact, her eyes calm, "but not the pizzazz."

Brian had stellar technicality, enough to get them on the podium of most regional competitions and close to placing at Nationals, but Nathan—Nathan had pizzazz. Groupies followed him from town to town—a few raised "Go Tabathan" signs for the pair, but most held signs like "Marry Me, Nathan" and "Watch Out, Tabitha, Nathan's Mine!" He and Tabitha had placed third in Nationals the previous year, and had done respectably at Worlds. They were considered America's next great hope until he dropped her in the middle of a Detroiter—a lift banned from competition—during a summer tour.

Karen was seventeen, Nathan twenty-two when Deena arranged a private early morning tryout session, the sun just starting to send a hint of itself into the sky. Nathan showed up at the rink in Connecticut on a pale green Vespa in jeans and a tight yellow T-shirt, his skates in a black leather backpack, just as Karen and her mom pulled up in their BMW. He wore a multi-colored knit beanie instead of a helmet, his dark shaggy hair swooping out in tufts. Karen tried not to look at the nipples poking under his shirt. He hadn't shaved in a couple of days; his blue eyes were bloodshot when he took off his sunglasses.

"Not used to getting up so early," he said as he shook Deena's hand. She gave a coquettish shrug that made Karen wince.

"But you're worth it, sweetheart." He turned to Karen, looking her up and down. "You're worth every second of missed sleep."

NATHAN STEPPED ONTO the ice before Karen, which startled her; Brian had always given her the courtesy of entering the rink first. Nathan's hair was a bit flat on top after taking off his beanie, but it streamed up like flames as soon as he started to stroke quickly around the rink. Karen took more-leisurely strokes, waiting for him to catch up with her rather than racing to catch up with him. He held out his hand as he drew near; she grabbed it and he surged ahead, practically ripping her shoulder out of its socket.

"Find your rhythm!" Deena yelled from the penalty box, looking giddy and nervous.

Karen sped up and Nathan slowed down and soon they were

stroking side by side, doing crossovers at the end of the rink, their legs moving in perfect tandem, his left arm behind her back, her right across his front as they held hands. Nathan was taller than her other partners, older. She could feel the difference in the way he held her hand, in his smell of sweat and cigarettes and some sweet musky scent Karen couldn't name, in his physical presence beside her—Nathan was solidly in the world, every muscle. She felt her own muscle fiber pack into something more dense, grounded, as they skated together. She felt a current of power run through them, a bright circuit through their arms and chests. Maybe this could work, after all.

"Show me what you got," shouted Deena.

Karen looked at Nathan with her eyebrows raised.

He winked and said, "Let's blow her little mind."

THEY TRIED A few twist lifts. Armpit holds, waist holds, hand-to-hip lifts, lasso lifts, press lifts. Side-by-side camels, then flying camels. Side-by-side jumps, then throws—first doubles, then triples. She loved the air he gave her when he threw her into a triple loop, loved how he held her lower back when they did a pairs sit spin, how her leg pressed against his when they tried a spiral sequence. *This is how it's supposed to feel,* she thought with wonder as she leaned back into his chest during a spread eagle. With Brian, she always felt as if she were skating with herself, as if she were holding her own hand—comfortable, familiar. Nathan was another creature, maybe even another species. The contrast was invigorating.

"One more lift," her mother called from the penalty box, "and let's call it a day."

This time, Nathan did something with his thumb when she was over his head. A little wiggle between her legs. It caused a zing to go through her body, all the way to the top of her skull. A sudden flood she hoped wouldn't drip down his arm. She almost tumbled off his palm, but somehow stayed upright, her one hand clutching his wrist so hard, it left marks.

"What *was* that?" she asked, still catching her breath. She could barely look at him as they slipped on their skate guards and stepped off the ice.

"I don't know what you're talking about." He shook his wrist. She couldn't tell if he was smiling or smirking.

"Don't do it again," she said, as firmly as she could.

He held her gaze until she flushed and looked away. She could hear him chuckle under his breath as he walked toward the lobby.

"THAT WAS BRILLIANT." Her mom strode up to her. Somehow even in her puffy down jacket, she looked sleeker than Karen could ever hope to be. "Utterly brilliant."

"I don't want to skate with him." Karen unzipped her sweater. Sweat ran down her sides in sheets.

"Nathan brought something out in you, Karen," she said. "I've never seen you skate like that before."

Karen brushed past her and ran to the bathroom, her skate guards clapping against her blades. She peeled her skating dress and tights down her body and sat in the stall, head in her hands. The cool air felt wonderful against her flushed skin. She wished she had worn underwear so she'd have something to throw away. She dabbed at the damp crotch of her tights with toilet paper before she pulled everything back up, the fabric cold and clammy between her legs.

Nathan and her mother were sitting with cups of coffee by the snack bar. The morning figure skating session was about to begin—the lobby was now filled with sleepy-eyed skaters, the diehards who were already skating both before school and after. Some of their mothers kneeled before them, tightening their laces; others stood behind them, tightening their buns. Karen forced herself to smile at the girls who waved excitedly in her direction. She wondered if any of them missed the days when skating was just for fun, when it wasn't about competition, the endless, impossible quest for perfection.

Before she started on the competitive track, rising up the rungs of the United States Figure Skating Association testing system, Karen took classes at a rink that followed the more recreational Ice Skating Institute program. She started at the most basic Alpha level, then moved on to Beta, then Gamma. She loved learning how to fall, how to swizzle, how to glide on one foot, wiggle backwards. Just being on the ice filled her with joy. But then she couldn't pass her Delta test. She could do the three turns, the outside edges, and the bunny hop just fine, but she couldn't seem to get the hang of the Shoot the Duck. Every time she crouched down and tried to lift one leg in front of her like a rifle, she toppled onto her bottom. Her mother got more and more exasperated, especially after Karen failed the test the second time.

"What is wrong with you?" Deena had demanded, her face more fierce than Karen had ever seen it. "If you can't pass this test, you can't move up to freestyle. Do you want to be stuck doing bunny hops the rest of your life? Do you want to be a Delta girl forever?"

At the time, Deena made this sound like a fate worse than death, but looking back, it didn't seem so bad to Karen. What would life be like if she had stayed a Delta girl forever—someone just starting to learn, just moving for the pure joy of it? Someone who skated only for herself, who didn't have to worry about other people's judgment, other people's hands?

She slipped onto a green fiberglass bench next to her mother.

"So," Deena said, not looking up from her clipboard. "We can rent the rink early on Mondays and Wednesdays. Other days, you'll have to skate during club time. Three hours a day, minimum. Even more in the beginning. And we'll have to figure out the dance and Pilates sessions."

"I look forward to it." Nathan smiled at Karen and the anger inside her chest unknotted and dissolved. A sudden weakness filled her limbs.

And, as if she had never said or felt anything to the contrary, she took a deep breath and said, "Me too."

MR. VIEIRA RETURNED, HAPPY TO SEE ME WITH A FULL bag. Now I really looked like a pregnant woman, the pears bulging in front of me bigger than I had ever been with Quinn. He showed me how to untie the bottom of the bag, let the pears tumble into a box. All those green puppies—a prolific litter.

"Might as well give you the grand tour," he said. I slipped the bag off, grateful for the breeze against my sweaty shirt.

It turned out Vieira Pears was actually on its own small island, Comice Island, a three-hundred-acre land mass ringed by wide waterways. Highway 160 crossed bridges to run across its rural edge, leading to the town of Comice on one end, Pecan Grove on the other. Comice was actually pronounced *Co-meese;* it was named for a type of pear, a variety originally from France. Bartlett was king here, though, and just coming into season.

"The water seeps up right through the ground," Mr. Vieira told me as he walked us around the farm. "We don't have to irrigate none."

He showed me trenches they'd dug to keep the island from

getting flooded; Vieira Pears was ten feet below sea level, so water easily saturated the soil and rose into the ditches before it found its way back to the river. The island sank a couple of inches a year as the peat soil settled, so the Vieiras had to keep building up the levees that ringed the island to protect their property. The levees had started out as five-foot mounds of dirt and rocks in the late 1800s, but were over thirty feet tall now, towering over the trees.

"If you don't have to water, what's this?" Quinn moved toward a sprayer.

"That's poison!" I yelled. "Don't get too close!"

Quinn ran past it, covering her mouth.

"It's lime and sulfur," said Mr. Vieira. "We're not using poison no more. But she should still keep her distance. Not so good for the skin or eyes. Or any other part, unless you're a tree."

"You're organic?" I had worked on a couple of organic farms. Less burning on the hands. Less sharpness in the lungs. I should have guessed the Vieiras were organic; when I looked around, clues were everywhere—the shagginess of the grass between the rows of trees, good for harboring pest-eating insects; the skinny red pheromone dispensers hanging from the top branches like broken kabbalah bracelets; the tanglefoot wrapped around some trunks like Ace bandages to keep ants from climbing to the fruit.

"Not certified yet," he said. "Next year. You need three years without the poison before they'll certify you. We're what they call transitional."

So are we, I thought. I watched Quinn twirl between two rows of trees, thankfully away from the spray. I wondered how long she'd be so full of whimsy—even at nine, I could see a subtle swell in her hips. Her belly still looked young, though—wonderfully mushy—and she still had those yummy toddler dimples on the tops of her hands.

"My son's the one talked me into it, wanted to go back to my grandfather's ways. He's in Ag over at Davis, but right now he's up in Oregon doing research. Pear slugs."

I winced, hoping not to see anything slimy on the gnarled branches.

"How long has your family been here?" I asked.

"Since the gold rush—1884," he said. "Straight from the Azores."

Quinn and I hadn't stayed in the same place for more than a few months since she was born. "Your family find gold?"

"Golden pears," Mr. Vieira said, chuckling.

The golden apples in our Norse mythology book granted immortality to the gods. These pears offered a different kind of immortality, it seemed, something to pass from one generation to the next. Hundred-year-old trees that still grew fresh green fruit. Amazing as any legend.

A TRACTOR TRAILER pulled up, driven by a woman, her body bulky and formless beneath her housedress, the iris of her left eye lolling to the side as if the string that usually held it in the center had snapped. Twelve men and seven women, all brown skinned, sat on the trailer around large white bins filled with pears. Many of them held coolers on their laps. They stared at me warily.

Mr. Vieira said something in Spanish; a couple of them laughed, a few more glared in my direction.

"I pay pickers by the bin," he said. "They don't like when anyone slows them down."

"I won't slow them down," I promised, but I could still feel their eyes on my skin after Mr. Vieira kissed the driver on the forehead and she drove them past us toward the barns.

I practiced picking pears without pay the rest of the afternoon, Quinn sitting on the ground beneath the trees as my arms and hands got used to the work, as my shoulders got used to the weight of the pear bag. I worked on increasing my picking speed as the strain settled its steady burn into my muscles. I was starving and exhausted by the time we pulled some granola bars and string cheese from the car for our dinner.

When I asked Mr. Vieira if we could park for the night on his property, he told me we should stay in the bunkhouse. The Vieiras had converted their old horse barn, turning each stall into an individual sleeping area with a swinging half-door. I was hesitant, but Quinn was excited about the idea of sleeping in a barn. Sleeping in the car had gotten old. It had been especially brutal in Niland, where we had camped at Slab City, an abandoned army base that had been taken over by RVers and squatters. There was no charge to stay, but there was also no running water or electricity, and even at night, the temperature often reached over 100 degrees. The one cool thing about the place was Salvation Mountain, a hill that an old smiley guy had covered entirely with paint and adobe as his own quirky tribute to God and love. I'd like to say we found salvation there, but we mostly found sweaty sleepless nights, especially when hipsters from LA came to check out the place and kept us awake with their guitars and bonfires, their smirking sense of entitlement.

The bunkhouse looked clean, but I could still smell the gamy ghost of horses in the air, along with the body odor of workers who must have worn the same clothes several days in a row. Mr. Vieira had offered me and Quinn separate stalls, but I didn't want her out of my sight, not in a building full of men. None of the sorting women lived there, but about half the men on the crew did—most of the rest shared small apartments as far away as Stockton, places where they slept three, four to a room but had a full kitchen. The bunkhouse just had a sink, a mini fridge, a microwave, one small bathroom for everyone. I was uneasy—no locks on the doors; no real doors, for that matter.

We brushed our teeth and changed into shorts and T-shirts for the night; when we got to our cot, I noticed something on Quinn's back. A round green sticker that said "Ripe and Ready." I ripped it off her shirt, my whole body furious.

"Who the hell put this here?" I marched into the aisle between the stalls and held it up high. A man with a deeply creased face smiled and nodded from behind his half-door. "You put this on my daughter?"

He smiled and nodded again.

"You sick fuck!" I threw the sticker at his face, but it fluttered to the ground before it could reach him. "What kind of pervert puts a sticker like that on a nine-year-old girl?"

His smile dropped. Even if he couldn't understand English, I knew he could understand me.

"Don't you dare—don't any of you dare—lay a finger on her again. No finger, no sticker, no nothing!"

"Shit, lady," I heard someone say under his breath.

"Quinn, pack your bags," I yelled. I picked the sticker up off the floor, the back of it encrusted with dirt and dust. Evidence.

WE PILED EVERYTHING into the car and were bumping along the dirt road when Mr. Vieira appeared in the headlights in his striped pajamas, dragging a hose.

"Where are you two headed?" he asked.

"We're leaving." I showed him the crumpled-up sticker. "I found this on my daughter's shirt."

He took the sticker and smoothed it in his palm. "That's for the ripe pears we bring to market," he said.

"My daughter is not a ripe pear."

Quinn laughed out loud but stopped when I threw her a look.

"Let me go talk to the men," he said.

I SAT IN the dark car with Quinn, engine turned off to save gas. The moon was full—it hugged the trees, outlined them like a highlighter pen. Bats darted in and out between the rows, wings snapping like flags in the wind. A white owl swooped and gleamed like some sort of angel. Quinn fell asleep, her dark hair splayed against the window, her legs spread open on the seat. I was glad no pervert was there to see her shorts riding up, a sliver of panties peeking out one leg.

Mr. Vieira appeared, making me jump.

"Jorge didn't know what it said." He leaned into my window. "Forget English—he can't even read Spanish. Just thought she'd like a sticker. Kids like stickers."

"He can't go around sticking things on a little girl's body."

Mr. Vieira shrugged. "Where you gonna go?"

"There's a berry farm up in Washington." The thought of so much road suddenly exhausted me.

"All them berries will be picked by the time you get up there," he said.

"We can't stay here," I told him.

"I need all the pickers I can get," he said.

"I can't take her back to a barn full of men."

He looked off into the distance. "I have an option," he said, rubbing his bristly chin. "If you want some privacy."

"How much privacy?" I looked at Quinn again.

"You have to drive there," he said. "It's on the water."

I forced myself to stay skeptical.

"Let me get my truck," he said. "You can follow me."

We drove through the dark orchard out into untamed fields, up a curved dirt hill. When Mr. Vieira said the place was on the water, he meant it. He pointed to a houseboat down on the other side of the levee, circa 1975, anchored at a small pier. I could hear rustling in the tule grass, sudden flapping of wings as we walked to the edge of the hill, Quinn still asleep in the car. The pear orchard lay in the field behind us, thirty feet beneath us; the trees hulked in formation like kneeling monks. A swath of river lay before us, twenty feet down, shimmering with moon.

"If this levee ever breaks," said Mr. Vieira, "the water would drown every last tree. But if you're in the boat, you'll go sailing right over us. Your own Noah's ark."

A couple of short, puffy sheep trotted over, as if they wanted to get on board. "What are you doing all the way over here, you *batatas?*" Mr. Vieira bent down to say to them. "These are our lawn mowers," he told me. Quinn woke up and got out of the car as Mr. Vieira was hoisting the sheep into the back of his truck to take them back to the orchard; she looked startled by the animals' thrashing and bleating.

I wrapped my arm around Quinn and pointed at the houseboat in the water below. "What do you think?" She nodded, her hair crackling with static electricity against my shirt.

We followed Mr. Vieira down the rickety metal steps to the small pier.

"I have to turn on the generator," he said. "And a guy'll come around to pump the septic in a day or two."

The houseboat was a blocky metal thing, like an old trailer plunked on top of a deck, a large A/C unit parked on top of it. The whole thing bobbed a bit when we stepped inside, and I wondered if I had the stomach to live right on the water.

The interior had a tweedy, earth-tone, Brady Bunch vibe. An olive green cooktop in the small kitchen. A brown dorm-size fridge under the counter. A stacked washer/dryer in the shade of marigolds. The booth in the dinette set that opened into a bed combined all those colors into a nubby weave. The plastic shower liner was the same color as the stove, the toilet the same color as the laundry machines.

Mr. Vieira checked the sinks to make sure they worked. "You probably don't want to drink the water," he said. "Comes straight from the slough."

The bedspread on the double bed in the back offered the only nod to the last couple of decades—a really nice bedspread, deep burgundy with eggplant piping. It smelled a little musty, but looked inviting; I couldn't wait to fall onto it. I wondered if the Vieiras had a similar bedspread in their house. It was hard to imagine—they would probably sleep under something more utilitarian: a navy woolen blanket, maybe a quilt one of their

grandmothers had patched together. I doubted they gave themselves the luxury of high thread counts, luxe fabrics. They probably got the bedspread as a gift and couldn't bear its pretension, so
they shuttled it out to the houseboat to gather dust. "It's a queen's
bedspread," Quinn said. It was the fanciest bed she had ever seen.

I had memories of feather beds in Paris, mints on pillows,
maids coming in the evening to turn down sheets, but I didn't
share those with her. She didn't need to know.

"This going to work for you?" Mr. Vieira said. The generator
was loud; I hoped we'd get used to its whir.

"We really get to live here?" Quinn looked ecstatic. It certainly beat sleeping on a cot in a horse stall or curled inside the
car. Other than the occasional motel, we hadn't had a place with
a real bed in ages. Not a place we could call our own.

"For now," I told her, and watched her face fall when she remembered that this, like every other place we'd stayed, was just
a way station. We were just stopping through.

KAREN

THE ELECTRIC GUITAR MADE KAREN'S HEAD FEEL LIKE IT
was about to burst. Nathan liked to blast his CD collection over
the rink's sound system when they had the place to themselves
at 4 a.m. She complained to her mom, but Deena said that it
would get their energy going while they warmed up. More often
than not, Nathan hadn't slept all night, and he needed Jane's Ad-
diction or Jimi Hendrix to keep him awake. Karen knew he'd
sleep in the afternoon after their three hours of skating, their
hour of joint ballet lessons, their hour of Pilates mixed with
weight training and off-ice lift practice, his wrangling with Deena
over choreography while Karen spent time with her tutor. Sometimes when Karen was going to bed at 9 p.m., she pictured
Nathan just getting up for the night. She wondered what it would
be like to wake up and do whatever you wanted rather than
getting out of bed to eat your twenty grams of protein and hit
the ice.

It was hard to keep her focus with the male voices screaming
through the speakers. Nathan's music was so different from the

songs that usually played during club sessions—the classical pieces and show-tune overtures that made up her fellow skaters' long and short programs, the only music Karen really listened to. One of her friends at the rink had skated to a Muzak medley of "Eleanor Rigby" and "Maxwell's Silver Hammer"; the first time Karen heard the original versions coming through the radio at the vitamin store, they sounded wrong to her. Too jangly and raw.

Deena chose the instrumental version of "Let Me Entertain You" for their short program, something with a little jazz, a little sass. For their long program, though, she chose Wagner—*Tristan und Isolde*. Karen had skated to instrumental Disney tunes with her last partner, Brian; Wagner's dark, intense orchestration was a major shift. "*Isolde* means 'rules over the ice.'" Deena winked at Karen over her cup of coffee.

"That's what *Tristan* should mean," mugged Nathan.

"*Tristan* means 'tumult,'" Deena said, her voice deliberately flat.

"I'll show you tumult." Nathan shook his fist at Deena, and she laughed.

"Plus the judges will take you more seriously now," Deena said to Karen. "They'll see you as more mature."

"And you know what that means." Nathan waggled his eyebrows. "They'll think you're fair game. Fresh meat."

"I'm not eighteen yet," she said. She didn't like to think of herself as meat, but that's what she felt like, slabs of muscle aching on her bones.

"You will be soon enough." He bit his lip, swept his eyes over her body. She smacked his arm and he pretended to swoon.

Nathan had been behaving himself for the most part. A few innuendos here and there. A few temper tantrums. Nothing serious. He had taken to wearing gloves during practice. The feel of his hand against her body was muffled now. She found herself missing the sharpness of his touch.

———

THEY HAD TO condense the arc of *Tristan und Isolde*'s story within a four-and-a-half-minute sample of the opera: Isolde's rage at Tristan for killing her first fiancé; their mutual drinking of a poison that turns out to be a love potion; the flaring of Tristan and Isolde's love; Tristan being slayed by her new fiancé, the king; Tristan staying alive until Isolde arrives, then dying with her name on his lips; Isolde imagining Tristan rising to the heavens, then dying heartbroken in his arms.

Deena didn't want them to pantomime the story, just bring its energy into their movements—anger, then passion, then grief.

"Listen to what Nietzsche said about the opera," she said. "'Even now I am still in search of a work which exercises such a dangerous fascination, such a spine-tingling and blissful infinity as Tristan—I have sought in vain, in every art.'" She put down the computer printout and closed her eyes.

"We'll create that in our own art," she said. "Dangerous fascination. Tingling spines."

"Dangerous." Nathan nodded, smiling slyly. "I like that."

"It's true." Deena turned on the boom box, let the overture swell into the air. "Two different conductors died right in the middle of the production. The original Tristan died weeks after opening night."

"Are you saying this song is going to kill us?" asked Karen.

"It's going to kill the audience." Nathan gave her knee a quick squeeze, sending electricity through her whole body.

IZZY

I DIDN'T SLEEP VERY WELL; I SOMEHOW FELT LIKE AN intruder in the boat. I found myself a touch seasick even though the boat barely moved at all, homesick even though I had no home to return to. Quinn, however, slept better than she had in ages.

In the morning, when we climbed the metal steps back up to the levee to head out to my first real day of picking, my legs wobbled. At the top, I felt as if the ground was bobbing up and down.

"I think we're having an earthquake," I said to Quinn, pulling her away from the edge of the levee.

"Eema," she laughed, "it's sea legs." I was always astonished by how much more she knew than me. "It's fun!" She walked around, weaving like a drunk, her arms out tightrope-style.

I STILL FELT a touch woozy as I drove around the edge of the island, as I joined the rest of the pickers, sat with them and the sorters on the back of the trailer and headed into the orchard. No one said anything to me, but a couple of the sorter women cooed over Quinn and offered her part of their pink-frosted *pan dulce,* which she politely declined even though we hadn't had much of a breakfast—just some dry cereal straight out of little individual boxes.

Mrs. Vieira let us off in the middle of the orchard. There was a huge clacking, like firecrackers, as everyone opened up their ladders. I struggled with mine, but no one offered to help. They already had their bags strapped on, were already reaching into the branches.

I TRIED TO keep up, but those guys could pick fast. Their hands were blurs in the trees. In the time I had spent picking plants close to the ground, I'd never seen anyone move like that—*pick-pickpickpickpickpick,* like a speeded-up tape, all those hands lifting as if in frenzied prayer. I thought I had built up a decent rhythm, but they blew me away. Every once in a while, one of them glared over at me as if he hoped I would die on the spot, but Jorge didn't look at me once. It seemed like he might be afraid of me after the sticker incident; I could see his shoulders hunch whenever I looked in his direction. *Fine,* I thought. *It's better that way.*

It was fine, too, that no one spoke to me or Quinn; we didn't need to talk to anyone but each other. That's how it had been at my other jobs—people all around me, but Quinn the only one who mattered. She had brought a book of math problems into the field. There was plenty of math all around her—a certain number of pears per bag, a certain number of bags per bin, a certain number of bins per trailer. The percentage that went into the gallows box, the percentage that was good enough to sell. She could have worked all of that out, but she preferred the workbook with its floppy yellowed pages.

Eventually she wandered over to the flatbed trailer where the women were sorting. They showed her how to loop a sorting ring around her wrist, check to make sure the good pears were at least two and a quarter inches around.

"Remember," Mr. Vieira said as he wandered by, "I can't pay her nothing."

"I know," I said, my arms aching. My pace had slowed, even though I tried to will my hands to keep moving. The guys all around me continued their frenzied pitch.

"Tell her to look for the big ones," he said. "We wanna win the Big Pear Contest this year."

WE FINISHED PICKING at three, just when the heat started to get oppressive. Every cell of my body was exhausted. I could barely push the gas pedal as we drove to the houseboat. Turning the steering wheel felt like too much work.

STRANGE HOW THE strange becomes familiar, how quickly a new place starts to feel like home. The seasickness, the homesickness, were gone when we stepped into the boat. I knew where the salt was, the silverware with its blue handles. I knew where to keep my panties and shoes. I began to see the same face in the wood grain of the bathroom cabinet every time I sat down to pee. Even the smell of the pillow, at first mildewy and offputting, became suddenly soothing and known, a welcome harbinger to the hard-won sleep I knew would be coming.

Quinn adjusted even faster than me, stacking her books on the top shelf of the closet in alphabetical order the first night, devising a quick system for turning the dinette into her bed. She was proud of the fact that she had figured out why all the closet and cabinet doors slid instead of swung open. "It's so stuff doesn't fly out when you're sailing!" she crowed, even though it was likely we'd never leave the dock. She loved living on a boat—"We're Vikings, Eema," she said. It was better to read about the giant Aegir, ruler of the sea, on a boat than in a car, she insisted, better to be able to smell the water, feel the humid air. She could picture his wife, Ran, outside our window, protecting us from drowning. Their nine daughters were the "billow maidens," each named for a different type of wave. Not many of them lived in the Delta, she told me, just the little ripply one, the gently rolling one. I looked out the window; the wind was stamping patterns onto the water like an old-fashioned metal ceiling—elegant squares and swirls. I wondered if they had special names.

Quinn insisted the Delta, with all its waterways, must be just like the Elivagar, the eleven rivers in Ginnungagap at the beginning of the world.

"This water's probably warmer," I said, my eyes wanting to close, my shoulder blades aching against the mattress. "The Elivagar were frigid."

She perked up. "Can we go swimming?"

"Right now?" I wished I had kept my mouth shut. "I'm so tired, Quinn."

"But the water's right here!"

She looked at me with such pleading eyes, I said, "Fine. Get your suit on. But just for a few minutes."

QUINN AND I lowered ourselves over the edge of the deck. She had wanted to jump in, but I didn't know if the water was deep enough. Quinn's yellow bathing suit was getting too small; mine, a vintage granny suit with a brown and aqua tiki pattern, was a bit too roomy. We'd have to look for good thrift shops in the area.

Quinn let go of the railing first, squealing with joy. The water was surprisingly warm right next to the boat, probably from the generator. When we got outside its reach, there was a big drop in temperature, but it still felt wonderful—it had been a while since I had been immersed, since my entire body had felt embraced. The shower in the boat was barely a trickle, and that was better than any we'd had for a while. We treaded water, splashing each other, noticing the little fish darting around us. At some point, I thought I felt my foot touch the slick bottom of the river, but when I tried to find it again, my toes just moved through watery space. Then the water suddenly rose in a big gentle swell. It felt kind of like how the ground had ballooned under my sea legs that morning, but I was inside the wave, not on top of it.

"There might be a boat coming," I told Quinn. I couldn't think of anything else that could make the water move like that. "We should probably get out."

"Already?" she asked.

"I'm exhausted, sweetheart," I said. "But we can go swimming again soon, I promise."

Pulling myself back onto the deck was much harder than I would have hoped, all the strength wrung out of my muscles. We sat outside for a while and waited for the big ship, but it never came.

THE NEXT MORNING, I could barely lift my arms.

"You'll get used to it," one of the sorters told me when I walked over to hand Quinn a water bottle. Her English was surprisingly good. Her hair was still wet from a shower. There was a large gap between her two front teeth. "My Ernesto said it takes a couple weeks."

Many of the sorters were girlfriends of the pickers. All year or just during pear season, I didn't know. There were a couple of wives, too. Sorting was no easy job, either—you got to sit down, sure, but your arms and wrists were constantly going. Quinn wanted to sort again, looking carefully for the biggest pears. The women didn't mind if she was going slow, but the pickers minded that I was. After a couple of hours, when I had dumped just six agonizing bags of pears into the bins as opposed to their twenty or so each, a group went to talk to Mr. Vieira.

He pulled me aside when they dispersed and said, "I can't afford to lose you, but I really can't afford to lose all of them. They won't pick if you stay on their crew."

I rubbed my forearm, fingers digging deep.

"Why are you so pressed for pickers?" I asked. A cottontail hopped between some rows. Quinn jumped off the trailer and chased after it.

"It's harder to get into the country these days," he said. "Crackdowns at the border. Crackdowns over paperwork once they do get in. You know."

I nodded, trying to keep an eye on Quinn.

"Plus the Lake County pears came in early this year," he said. "Usually the Delta pears are the first on the market. Delta, then Lake, then Oregon, then Washington, then Canada. The crew follows them up the coast. Now they're split in half."

"I suppose you're firing me." I missed the houseboat already. I knew Quinn would miss it even more.

"I'm firing you from the crew," he said, "not from the farm."

Before he could elaborate, Quinn called for me, her voice frantic, and my heart caught in my throat. I ran toward her voice, pear branches smacking me in the face.

She wasn't bleeding when I found her, thank God; there were no bee stings, no coyotes cornering her, no men with stickers. She was simply standing, awestruck, beneath a tree; clear long-necked wine bottles rose upside down from its branches like candelabras. A pear hovered inverted inside the widest curve of each, like a pale green lightbulb. It was one of the most amazing things I had ever seen.

"How'd they get the pears in there?" Quinn peered up at the tiny mouths of the bottles. When the glass caught the sun, I had to shield my eyes.

"They grow in there." Mr. Vieira ambled over.

"Upside down?" I asked. It seemed impossible that gravity would let the bottom of the fruit swell on top like that.

He nodded and pointed out the intricate contraption around

every bottle—netting and string connecting it to the branch above, gauze plugged loosely inside each neck to keep bugs away. They put the bottles over the baby pears right after the blossoms fall off. Only one pear per branch—only the "king," the one with the biggest blossom; the rest they trim away, along with all the leaves around it, so the tree can channel its nutrients into the bottle.

"How do you get the pears out?" Quinn asked.

"You don't," said Mr. Vieira. "You pour booze in the bottles and sell them, pear and all."

"That must be quite a sight," I said, my face still stinging from the branches.

"Eighty bucks a pop," said Mr. Vieira proudly. "*Eau-de-vie,* distilled right here."

I knew enough French to make out "water of life."

"I'll have to try it sometime," I said, even though I never drank when Quinn was around. Which was always. And before she was born, I had only had a few sips of champagne.

"You got eighty bucks on you, you can."

"You should put all your pears in bottles if they make that much money." Mr. Vieira sold his commercial pears for about twelve cents a pound. The ones he sold directly to markets brought in a bit more.

"Too much work." Mr. Vieira tapped one of the bottles. "Besides, we only do it with our Comice trees."

I took a closer look. The pears were rounder than the Bartletts, more squat. Some of them blushed a sexy pink on parts of their smooth skin.

"These need to be picked in the next few days," he said. "You got to be more careful with the glass. Don't want to bruise them pears."

"Or cut yourself," said Quinn.

"Or cut yourself," said Mr. Vieira. "You have to be slower with the bottles. Think you can handle it?"

"Of course." My shoulders felt like they were about to shatter, but I could stretch to work out some of the tension. I hadn't been stretching enough. And I could pace myself.

"We need help in the distillery, too."

"Thank you." Some tears, embarrassingly, sprang to my eyes. Mr. Vieira looked away.

"Gotta go tell them guys they don't have to quit." He turned and walked toward the crew. The light bouncing off the bottles made the back of his plaid shirt shimmer like water.

The woman who had been driving the trailer, the one with the walleye, stepped out from behind a tree, making Quinn jump. She wore another formless housedress, and men's brown corduroy slippers with hard soles. Her hair had a life of its own—short salt-and-pepper waves that rose and fell in uneven tufts.

"Mrs. Vieira?" I had guessed before, but it had not been confirmed.

She nodded and shook my hand. Her palm was dry and callused, like the bottom of a foot.

"It's very kind of you and your husband to let me work here," I said, blinking hard.

She nodded again and smiled. It was a bit disconcerting, not knowing which eye to look into when I smiled back. Without saying a word, she pointed to the tree, then showed me how some of the pears had pulled away from their branches inside the bottles. All we had to do was cut off the string and netting, gently turn the bottle right side up, and set it in a sectioned wooden crate. If the pear was still attached to the branch but looked perfect, we needed to unhook the bottle from its string, tip it slowly so the pear slid down as close to the mouth as possible, and snip the stem off the spur.

The work was slow, methodical, but it still scratched up my arms.

———

"HOW DO THEY know how to do it?" asked Quinn later as we walked through the orchard to our car. "How do all the pears know to grow at the same time?"

"They just do," I said.

"But how?" She touched a trunk as if it could tell her, and I realized I hadn't really thought about it before. It was a remarkable feat of choreography, all the Bartletts in the orchard, in the whole region, burgeoning in sync.

"Maybe they whisper to each other underground," I said. "Like friends planning to wear the same shirt on the same day."

I caught myself, knowing she didn't know what that was like—calling friends, coordinating outfits—but she nodded as if she did. Then again, I had said it as if I knew what it was like, myself. We were both good at pretending we were part of the normal world.

THE PICKERS WERE heading out, too. They kept their distance, but at least they didn't look like they wanted to murder me. Maybe I could practice picking more so I could join them after we got all the bottles down. So many pears would rot without my hands. As we drove around the edge of the orchard, I felt a wave of protectiveness, almost maternal, for the trees. I didn't want all their hard work to be for nothing.

QUINN AND I parked and walked toward the metal staircase leading down to the pier. The Delta breezes were starting to pick up; I welcomed the touch of chill.

Across the water lay the remains of an old pear orchard. The trees had been chopped down and stacked in enormous gray piles all over the field, like some sort of bonfire site for giants. The cows that grazed there were dwarfed next to the huge stacks—they looked like miniature critters, like something that could crawl onto your palm. I felt small looking at the heaps of wood, too. They threw the scale of everything off.

A whiff of the dead wood crossed the water, a dry, dusty scent. I felt a little chill even though the wind wasn't cold. I glanced back at the Vieiras' pear trees, just to make sure they were still there, that they, too, hadn't turned gray and toppled over. It wouldn't take much for the orchard to fail.

I found myself wanting to say something to Quinn about how we were perched on a levee between life and death, green and gray; I wanted to tell her what a precarious edge it was, how easy it would be to slip over to the other side. Then she took my hand before we went down the steps, and I decided to let her believe we were safe.

KAREN

KAREN LOOKED DOWN THE FRONT OF HER RED DRESS as she bent over to lace her skates. Shocking to see skin after years of high-collared costumes, a big swath of it down the front. Not that it was skin, exactly—it was nylon covered with netting; the approximation of skin. The promise of it. A plunging neckline. A daring peek at her shoulder blades.

Deena had finished making the costumes just a few days before Regionals. Karen and Nathan didn't have much time to test them out on the ice, to make sure they could move and breathe with them, that they wouldn't slice up each other's hands.

Paillettes and Swarovski crystals studded the dress like seeds on a strawberry; they had the same intricate pattern, too—whorls and honeycombs that seemed so organic, it was as if the cloth, what little there was of it, had been plucked from some glamorous vine. Deena had farmed out the beadwork, but had done all the stitching herself.

"You'll get them hoping for a nip slip." Nathan walked into the dressing room, and Karen kicked her skate at him. There was no chance of a wardrobe malfunction——the dress cinched her in tight, plus she had tape over her nipples to avoid any poking in the cold. Nathan did, too, beneath his one-sleeved, elaborately beaded unitard. His left shoulder rose from it, smooth and muscled.

Karen's breasts ached beneath the adhesive. Her period had just started, always a bummer at competition time. She wondered if she should follow what some of the girls did and go on birth control pills to regulate her cycle, to plan the pills so she wouldn't bleed during competition season. When she suggested it, though, her mother said, "They'll make you fat." Karen thought that was the end of the conversation until Deena said, "If you diet enough, your period stops altogether. Few elite athletes bleed."

Karen rolled her tights down over her skates, secured the elastic strap underneath. She liked the new trend of wearing tights over skates——they made her legs look longer, the line not broken by a chunky white boot. Her feet looked like Herman Munster's, but that was a small price to pay for slightly more elegant stems.

"You look great," Nathan said as they stood next to each other in the mirror.

"*We* look great," she said. She couldn't help but reach up to his shoulder, rest her hand briefly on his warm naked skin.

THE ONE BAD THING ABOUT THE HOUSEBOAT WAS THE mosquitoes. We kept all the screens closed, but we were still riddled with bites, ones that swelled into fierce pink mounds. The sorter women had told Quinn mud would make the bites feel better; she kept slapping it on herself until she looked like some sort of swamp creature. After her shower each night, I replaced the mud with calamine lotion, but the bites were so bad, she found it hard to sleep. That wasn't a problem for me anymore. Working in the pear orchard, even with the slower pace of the bottles, somehow made me more tired than anything I had done before. Or maybe just having a comfortable bed helped knock me out. Even the whine of the most persistent mosquito couldn't keep me awake.

"Eema!" Quinn's voice managed to pull me out of sleep. She was standing at the edge of the bed. "There's a monster outside!"

"It's just a dream," I mumbled. The houseboat was rocking, as if a barge was passing by. That sometimes happened during the night. And the Delta breezes could get pretty intense.

"No, it's a monster! I saw it!"

"Here, get into bed with me." I lifted the sheets and Quinn crawled in, her whole body trembling in her thin nightgown. The top of her head smelled like sunbaked dirt.

"I'm scared, Eema." Quinn wrapped her arms tightly around my waist, hooked one leg over both of mine.

"Dreams can be scary." I closed my eyes again, felt my body rise and fall with the waves. "It's probably from all the myths you've been reading. Go back to sleep."

"Do you think it was Kraken?" she asked.

Kraken was a Norse sea creature with many arms, like the roots of an upturned tree. He would wrap those arms around ships and pull them underwater.

"It wasn't Kraken." A mosquito whined in my ear.

"It came out of the water and looked at me." Her heart raced against my side.

"Just tell yourself that when you fall back to sleep, you won't dream about it again." I could feel sleep tugging at me, wanting to pull me back under.

"You never believe me." Quinn's words sent a shock through my chest. I wanted to tell her that wasn't true, that she was the only thing I believed, the only thing I believed in, but then sleep closed over me again and sealed me away.

I WOKE WHEN something brushed against the back of my leg. Something bigger than Quinn, who was sound asleep on my other side, wedged between me and the wall. Something hairy. It burrowed in closer, pressed against my back, leaking heat. Was this the monster Quinn had warned me about?

I sat up screaming. So did Quinn. So did the strange man in our bed.

"What the hell?" He jumped out and turned on the overhead light. He was just wearing striped boxers, his legs and chest furred. His hair flopped onto his olive-skinned face; a soul patch sprouted below his lower lip.

"Get out of here, you pervert!" I yelled, kicking at the sheets, my voice both higher and raspier than I thought it could get.

"Wait a second," said the man. "Who the fuck are you?"

"Who the fuck are *you*?" I shouted. Quinn clung to me, shaking.

"This is my boat." The guy looked more puzzled than dangerous.

"No it's not," said Quinn into my shoulder. "It's Mr. Vieira's boat."

"*I'm* Mr. Vieira," he said.

"No you're not," said Quinn. I tried to shush her as I pulled the sheet back up over my nightgown, knees drawn to my chest, pulse still pounding in my ears. I looked at his bushy eyebrows, his generous nose. Relief flooded in.

"You must be the son." My voice had almost fallen back into its normal register.

"Benjamim Vieira." He held out his hand. *Ben-ha-meem.* He looked exhausted. "Ben."

"Izzy." His hand was damp but firm when I shook it. My leg prickled where his leg had brushed against it. "And my daughter, Quinn. We're helping at the orchard."

"I'm sure it's appreciated." He pulled his pants back on, tugged a shirt over his head.

I could feel my cheeks flush. Watching him zip up his fly somehow felt more intimate than seeing him in his underwear.

"I guess I'll head over to the house, then," he said. "Didn't want to scare the folks—they weren't expecting me for another week. Sorry I scared you instead. I honestly had no idea you were there—I was so tired; I just thought the sheets were bunched up."

"At least you're not a monster," said Quinn.

"I try not to be." Ben picked up his backpack.

———

"SO YOU MET my son," Mr. Vieira said as we unhooked more bottles from the tree the next morning. I felt my face get hot again. "Scared the hell out of my wife last night. She wakes if she hears a pear drop—thought someone was breaking in."

"He gave us a pretty good scare, too." I looked at a pear inside one of the bottles. It had grown against the glass; one side of the fruit was completely flat. No one would buy it for eighty dollars.

"Didn't mean nothing by it," said Mr. Vieira. "He just wanted to come down for the *festa*."

I handed Quinn a bottle, which she placed carefully in a section of the wooden crate. She looked serious, nervous. A couple of wasps started to buzz around the bottles and she jumped back, almost knocking the crate over. She hadn't mentioned the monster or Ben's visit all day, but I could tell both were weighing on her.

"Say"—Mr. Vieira reached for another bottle, carefully untying it from the branch—"why don't you come to the *festa* with us? Get out a little. It would be good for the girl to have some *sopa*."

I had no idea what a *festa* was, or a *sopa*. He spread out his arms and said, "Nine thousand pounds of beef!" and I was even more confused.

"Is it a big crowd?" Maybe it would be better to just stay in the orchard, on the boat.

"Only all the Portuguese in the Delta," he said, but that didn't help.

"Can we go, Eema?" Quinn looked so earnest, her eyes bright, her mind not on monsters for the first time all day.

"Do you really want to?" I handed her another bottle. "You don't even know what it is."

"I do, Eema," she said. "I really really want to go."

Mr. Vieira looked at me as if to say *See? I told you.*

"We'll miss the mass," he said, "but if we clean up fast when we're done picking, we might make the parade."

MRS. VIEIRA WAS loading cases of her homemade pear preserves in the back of their silver pickup truck when we drove
back to their house, freshly showered and changed. Quinn had
put on what she considered her best outfit—a plaid dress shirt
and a floral skirt, with green penny loafers; I had thrown on clean
jeans and a black tank top, some worn huaraches, large sunglasses. A slash of lip gloss, which I hadn't done in ages.

Ben came out of the house, carrying another box of preserves to add to the stack. His cargo shorts gave me a good
glimpse of his hairy legs. I blushed as I remembered their tickly
heft.

"So we meet out of bed," he said as he walked down the steps,
and I felt my blush grow deeper.

He set the box in the back of the truck. The jars clanked and
settled inside. "Need anything else, Ma?" he asked. She shook her
head.

He walked over and bent down next to Quinn. "Sorry I
scared you last night," he said.

"It's okay," she said, but leaned hard into my side.

"Don't worry about it," I said. I couldn't seem to look him in
the eye as he stood back up, but I could feel him the way you feel
static electricity, a thick buzz all over my skin.

WE PILED INTO the Vieiras' truck—Mr. and Mrs. Vieira in the
front bucket seats, Quinn squeezed between me and Ben in the
bench seat behind them. The center of Comice wasn't too far
away—just about a mile after crossing the yellow bridge—but
the road was so uncharacteristically full of cars, it took almost fifteen minutes to get there. I stared out the window the whole
time, too embarrassed to look in Ben's direction.

Downtown Comice wasn't much to speak of—just a couple
of blocks of worn brick and wooden storefronts, many of them
vacant, most built by Portuguese immigrants in the late 1800s,

the Vieiras among them. The majority of the Portuguese settlers in the Delta had become dairy farmers, but a few, like the Vieiras, had turned to pears. You could still buy Portuguese sweet bread and wine and cheese and linguica from little shops that also sold Twinkies and Bud Light. The street, normally quiet, was bustling with families and packs of teenagers as we drove slowly past.

We snaked through a residential area filled with small bungalows and neatly trimmed yards, to a large field that had been turned into a parking lot. The crowd didn't seem rowdy, just excited. A couple of carnival rides twirled in a park on the other side of the field, booths set up all around them. Loud music, heavy on the trumpet, pumped through a sound system. Lights poured down on some sort of arena in the distance even though sunset was still hours away.

"Looks like the parade is just about to start," said Ben. "We got here just in time."

THE CROWD BY the cars formed a channel between the park and a low, stucco community center on the side of the field. Everyone was turned toward the park, where a brass band, likely the one that had been blaring over the speakers, had assembled. The musicians began making their way down the aisle of cheering people, playing what was likely traditional Portuguese music. Quinn put her hands over her ears as they drew nearer. They were followed by a couple of cows decked out in garlands, pulling wooden carts full of waving children. Quinn took one hand from her ear to wave shyly back.

"The cows were blessed earlier today," Ben told us. "Along with the cows we'll be eating tonight."

Behind the cows, women in traditional Portuguese outfits— colorful patterned scarves around their heads, equally colorful shawls over their white blouses, and wide colorful skirts—carried huge baskets of rolls. They tossed the bread to the crowd. I caught one—light and airy—and gave it to Quinn.

"The bread was blessed, too," he said.

Quinn took a big bite, scattering crumbs down her shirt. "It just tastes like normal bread," she said, disappointed, as if blessed bread should taste like magic. *Eat it all up,* I wanted to tell her. *We need all the blessings we can get.*

A group of girls were next, ranging in age from about five to seventeen, wearing poofy, sparkly dresses, velvet capes, and tiaras.

"Beauty pageant?" I asked.

"Different kind of queen," he said.

The girls, it turns out, represented Queen Isabel; in the fourteenth century, she would sneak food to the poor, against the wishes of her husband, King Diniz. One day, Diniz came upon her when she had her apron full of rolls and demanded to know what she was carrying. "Roses," she said, which made him suspicious—roses were not in bloom that time of year—but when he yanked at her apron, a flood of white flowers came tumbling out.

"It's kind of sad," he said, "how much money the families pour into this. Some have the capes hand-beaded in Portugal, thousands of dollars. The *festa* is supposed to be about giving to the community, but these dresses have become a competitive sport."

The girls passed us and Quinn got very excited, waving and waving. An elaborately beaded saint beamed from the back of one teen's purple velvet cape. A little girl's pink satin cape featured a huge chalice and crown embroidered in metallic thread. A huge dove made of countless tiny seed pearls spread its wings across the red velvet backing of another. Some of the dresses had hoop skirts that made the girls look like they were floating down the dirt path.

I found myself worrying about the girls forced to wear these fancy things, their faces fluorescent with makeup; I worried about what they must have endured at home, their mothers coming at them with curling irons and mascara wands, expressions and expectation equally intense. The girls all looked proud and happy to be queens, though. None of them seemed to resent the crown.

When they reached the community center, a young girl walked toward them, holding a dove in a cage festooned with red ribbons. She handed the cage to the smallest queen, who opened its metal door. At first, the dove didn't want to fly out, but the little queen shook the cage until the bird flopped out and flew listlessly into a nearby jacaranda tree.

"It's supposed to be the Holy Spirit," said Ben.

"Doesn't look so spirited to me," I said. Mrs. Vieira threw me an offended look, but Ben laughed, and we finally made eye contact. Just for a split second, but it made something zap in my blood.

"I have to help my parents unload the jam," he said. "Why don't you two go check out the fair before the *sopa* starts?"

THE SNACKS AT the booths were unlike any fair food I had seen before. Fried sardines. Dark red octopus stew. A dish made with pork and clams. Lupini beans. Salt cod. Chestnuts. Quinn looked appalled by most of the offerings, but the sweets caught her eye. Spiced cookies. Fragrant rice pudding. Lemony doughnuts dusted with powdered sugar.

"You should probably have dinner first," I said, but finally relented and let her have one of the doughnuts.

"Save room for the *sopa*." The woman smiled as she handed me the warm pastry. "You might want to go line up now." A line was beginning to snake out the community center door. I handed Quinn the doughnut and powdered sugar immediately spilled down her front. She didn't mind, so I tried not to, either.

On our way toward the line, a guy sidled up to us, the air around him heavy with cologne. "Hey," he said. "Aren't you that girl . . ."

"No." My pulse flared. I grabbed Quinn's hand and we started to walk away.

"You're not the girl over at Vieira's place?" he called after us. "The one trying to pick the other day?"

"Oh." Relief washed over me, sweet as sleep. "Yeah. Yeah, I guess I am that girl."

"Word travels fast," he said, and my ears briefly roared with blood again. I wondered if he picked at the Vieiras', too; I felt embarrassed that I didn't recognize him, that I probably wouldn't recognize most of the pickers if they showed up in front of me, hair slicked back, dress shirts on. He flashed a peace sign and jogged over to the building.

THE SOPA, IT turned out, was a free meal inside the cavernous, wood-paneled hall. Every single item on the menu was donated by the community—beef from local ranchers, vegetables from local home gardens, the pear preserves Mrs. Vieira had canned. Tons and tons of donated food, enough to serve a thousand people. The centerpiece was the *sopa* itself, a beef soup volunteers had cooked in hundred-gallon vats in the community center kitchen. The big hunks of beef were taken out of the soup before serving, sliced, and put on plates. We stood in line and waited as one volunteer put a piece of French bread in a bowl, the next volunteer ladled the soup over it, the next one put a sprig of mint on top, the next gave us a plate with the beef and more bread. The pear preserves sat on every table, along with local butter. The energy felt completely different from that of any of the soup kitchens Quinn and I had visited across the country, taking advantage of free meals at shelters and churches when our funds had run dry. Shame hung in the air of those soup kitchens like bacon grease, a palpable, discomfiting sense of lack, but this free dinner was all about bounty, celebration. Quinn and I found some empty chairs at the end of one of the long tables and sat down to eat; halfway through our meal, Mr. Vieira saw us and waved us to a table a few rows over.

"We've been saving you seats," he said over the din of the room when we carried our plates over to their table. I sat across from Ben. Beef, pink and wet, thickly sliced, fanned out on the plate beneath the curve of his soup bowl; I wished I hadn't eaten mine so quickly—I wasn't sure if it was rude to go back for a second helping. Mrs. Vieira looked around; she seemed happy to see people spreading her preserves on slabs of dense, slightly sweet bread, the crust shellacked with egg white and sugar. Ben smiled at his mother, his mouth full of cabbage. She was chattering away in Portuguese with a woman across the table—I had never heard her husky voice before; I had wondered, in fact, if she was mute. She seemed to understand English—perhaps she just didn't like to speak it.

Quinn finished her meal and asked if she could be excused.

"I don't know," I said.

"My people are good people," Mr. Vieira said. "They won't do nothing to hurt her."

How could I say no after that?

"Just stay where I can see you," I said.

Before I knew it, Quinn was running around with one of the *festa*'s queens, a little girl in an ice blue dress with a rhinestone tiara secured over her sprayed-stiff ringlets, a cape featuring a child saint also wearing a cape, done up in sequins. Every once in a while, I lost sight of them in the crowd and my nerve endings went immediately from zero to panic.

"She's over there," Ben said, and I saw Quinn climbing out from under a table with the little queen. The moisture beneath my arms immediately cooled, and I slumped, weak with gratitude, in the plastic folding chair.

"Thank you," I said, but he had already turned to talk to his dad. I was kind of glad—that way he couldn't see the tears that had sprung when he helped me find my girl.

AFTER DINNER, QUINN and I followed the Vieiras and the rest of the crowd to the arena behind the park.

"Rodeo?" I asked, looking at the dirt ground of the stadium, the guys in colorful outfits on horseback.

"Bullfight," said Mr. Vieira.

"I thought those were illegal." I had no desire to see someone get gored, no desire to see an animal fall to the ground, life draining out.

"They make exceptions for us Portuguese." Mr. Vieira snorted like a bull.

"It's bloodless," Ben assured me. "It's all done with Velcro."

The brass band walked into the center of the stadium; everyone stood as they played the national anthem, then "A Portuguesa." A great cheer rose up afterward, people stomping the metal bleachers so hard, my teeth rattled inside my head and Quinn grabbed onto me for dear life. Then a single trumpet let out a blare, and a man on horseback trotted into the ring to more cheering and stamping. His outfit rivaled the festa queens'——he wore a bright yellow embroidered matador suit with hot pink kneesocks; his horse was decked out, too, with flowers and streamers and feathers.

Quinn grabbed onto me harder as a bull lumbered into the arena. Its horns were topped with leather caps—they looked like adrenal glands capping long, curved kidneys. The bull was massive, its enormous body shimmering with each step, saliva streaming from its mouth in ropes.

"I want to go, Eema," Quinn said into my arm as the bull snorted and barreled across the dirt.

"In a bit," I said. The matador chucked a long streamer-bedecked spear at the bull. Its Velcro tip landed on the Velcro pad strapped to the bull's shoulder and wagged back and forth. The band blasted a short triumphant tune.

"I want to go now!" She screamed so loudly, some people around us stopped cheering and turned to look.

"Okay, okay," I said, and together we squeezed past the Vieiras and the other people in our row and made our way down the bleacher steps, Quinn crying hysterically.

"What's wrong with you?" I asked as we walked through the fairgrounds. "I thought you were having a good time."

"The monster . . . ," she started.

"It's a bull," I said. "A normal animal."

"I know!" she yelled, as if I had said the most offensive thing in the world.

"So what were you going to say?" I asked, but she walked faster so she'd be a few steps ahead of me.

"I'm sorry, Quinn." I ran to catch up. "Whatever I did, I'm sorry."

She didn't say anything, but slowed down enough so we could walk in step.

Ben pulled up in the truck when we got to downtown Comice. "Need a ride?" he asked. My heart started to pound at the sight of him.

It wasn't a far trek back to the farm, but Quinn looked exhausted. "Thanks," I said. We climbed up into the two-row cab. I let Quinn sit in front.

"Where are your parents?" I asked.

"I'll go back for them," he said. "Just wanted to make sure you two were all right. Bullfights can be pretty intense. Even without the blood."

Quinn took a deep shuddery breath. "The food was good, though," she said.

"The best," he said.

"Do you want to go swimming again when we get back?" I asked her. Maybe that could become our evening ritual—a way to cool off, relax.

She shook her head, face clouding again. Of course she wouldn't want to go swimming, not if she thought there was a monster in the water. I touched her arm and was relieved she didn't try to shrug it away.

KAREN

THE NEW ENGLAND REGIONALS WERE BEING HELD AT their home rink—a big advantage. They knew each inch of the ice, could draw upon the energy of all of their practice sessions.

The place felt different on competition day, though. Vendors in the lobby had set up booths full of skating dresses and tights, books and DVDs, lots of jewelry featuring little silver skates. New skaters, new coaches, new parents, milled about, sending their nervous energy into the air. Plus all the groupies had descended.

Karen had seen Nathan's groupies before, but not since they had been skating together. They were ferocious, these girls, running toward him, grabbing any part of him they could reach, pushing Karen out of the way just to graze the sleeve of his workout jacket. She looked to her mom for help, but Deena just smiled and nodded, as if to say *It's good for business. Let it go.* Nathan, of course, was in his glory, signing programs and shirts and bits of cleavage, giving kisses left and right. Finally, Deena stepped in.

"Okay, cowboy," she said. "Save some of it for the ice."

No, Karen found herself thinking, *save some of it for me.*

IN THE DRESSING room, a skater from Hartford cornered Karen as she hung her dresses from a hook on the cinder-block wall of the locker room. She had brought both dresses, even though they'd only be doing the short program today; she wanted the long program dress to soak in the competition vibe. "So," she asked, "what's it like, being with Nathan?"

"Sexy sexy sexy," said a skater from Rhode Island, pulling an elaborate makeup case from her wheeled bag. Her dark hair, like everyone's in the room, was scraped back into a ponytail, glued to her head with glittery gel.

"You would know." A slightly older skater with Cleopatra eyeliner swatted her in the arm.

"So would you," the skater said back, hitting her with the chamois cloth she used to clean her blades.

"Let's take a poll," said a skater from Vermont. "How many of you have been with Nathan?"

Most of the skaters raised their hands. Only Karen and a fifteen-year-old Korean American girl from New Hampshire kept their hands down. Laughter broke out through the room like a rash. Karen was mortified—this was only Regionals. These skaters weren't even the cream of the crop.

"What?" the older skater said to Karen. "You can't tell me you haven't . . ."

"I'm seventeen," Karen reminded her.

"Hasn't stopped him before," chimed someone else, leading to another round of laughter. Some of the women were peeling off their workout clothes, stepping into their competition dresses. She glanced at a breast and shuddered, thinking *Nathan's mouth has been there;* she looked at a hip, and thought of Nathan's hands. She could barely look at her own dress, hanging limp on the wall. Its redness mocked her; so much empty, sparkly passion.

"I THINK YOU should kiss me," Karen said to Nathan as they stroked, hand in hand, around the rink during their practice session.

"What are you talking about, little girl?"

They each did a three turn, started backwards crossovers together, right over left.

"During the number," she said. "At the end. I think you should kiss me."

"Not a good idea." At the center of the rink, they switched directions, switched hands, left over right. Other couples moved around them, blurs in Karen's peripheral vision.

"I'm not so little." It came out more petulant sounding than she would have liked.

"I have too much respect for you to pull a cheap stunt like that," he said, and a sudden giddiness burbled up her spine. Respect. Of course. Those skaters in the locker room, those skaters now holding their own partners' hands as they all warmed up, dodging each other left and right—they didn't have his respect. Their trysts didn't mean a single thing. Just skin on skin. Fleeting. Nothing. That's why he hadn't touched her again—out of respect. When she and Nathan finally got together, it would be total magic. Respect + passion = forever.

"Besides," he said as he lifted her over his head like an airplane, "your mom would kill me."

She looked down at him. "Screw my mom."

"Okay." He grinned. "If you insist."

"Asshole," she said as he let her down. Why did he always have to ruin the moment?

He winked. "Ready for some throws?"

She sighed and let him toss her through the air.

FANS CROWDED THE bottom of the bleachers at the end of the practice session. They hurled teddy bears and flowers and various undergarments as Karen and Nathan stepped off the ice. Karen had gotten a few trinkets from fans when she skated with Brian, but nothing like this.

"What was all the talking out there?" Deena asked as she helped scoop up the loot. Fans reached down, grabbed at Nathan's hair, his sleeve, screaming. He kissed a few hands, picked up scraps of paper covered with phone numbers and doodled hearts.

"Your daughter has quite a mouth on her," said Nathan.

Some of the fans shot Karen nasty looks. As if the only thing keeping them from Nathan was her and her dirty mouth. Karen picked up a stuffed monkey and tried to smile.

"You both need to focus," Deena said, shaking a pair of teal panties in their direction.

"We're golden." Nathan snatched the underwear from Deena's hand and put his arm around Karen. The panties tickled her elbow. "Aren't we, babe?"

He had never called her "babe" before.

"Golden." She felt the sun rise inside her chest.

KAREN AND NATHAN were the third pairs team to skate their short program. The first two teams had a couple of bobbles, one triple that became a double, nothing too cataclysmic. Nothing too exciting, either. Decent scores, but nothing that would keep them in the top slots.

"We'll sail right past them," Nathan said as they stretched in the holding area.

"You better." Deena laughed, but it sounded more like a bark, sending tingles up Karen's neck. Karen's heart did its normal pre-competition hummingbird dance. She took a few deep breaths, told herself, *Just skate, just skate, just skate.*

When she and Nathan stepped onto the ice, the crowd erupted, and Karen's heart threatened to jump out of her dress. As soon as the music started, though, the throbbing settled into her rib cage and her body went into autopilot. The audience clapped along with the jazzy rhythm, squealing when Nathan shook his narrow hips in time to the drums. Karen doubted anyone was screaming for her hips—the little shake always felt awkward to her, like she was pretending to be something she wasn't. Her mother had often said, "You need to get your center lower, Karen. You're too upright. Sink into your knees and your hips will be freer," but it was hard to subvert all those years of being told to reach her spine up to the ceiling.

Karen kept her mouth stretched into a smile. That took more effort than any of the jumps or spins or combinations; her muscles knew the choreography. Only her face felt strained. It was all she was aware of—not Nathan, not the edges of her blades digging into the ice; only the tightness of her cheeks, the set of her jaw. Then, before she knew it, the number was over, and she felt her face relax into a genuine smile of relief. Fans tossed more flowers and lingerie and stuffed toys onto the ice.

"We did it," Nathan whispered as they grabbed hands and lifted their arms in the air.

Not yet, she thought.

IZZY

I FOUND MYSELF LOOKING FOR BEN WHEN QUINN AND I walked from our car to the distillery, when we stopped at the chicken coop and Quinn said hello to her favorite hen, the Araucana she had named Buttercup, the one who laid pale green eggs. The chickens had made Quinn a bit nervous at first—especially the rooster, who she worried might be Vidofnir, the Norse rooster whose crowing announces the battle that ends the world—but after Mrs. Vieira let her gather eggs and fill their waters, she grew to love them, even when they chased her around the coop, pecked at her ankles, pulled at her shoelaces.

I tried not to read too much into the fact that Ben had gone searching for us, that he had given us a ride home—*he just has his parents' generosity,* I told myself. We hadn't talked much in the truck on the way home; he hadn't walked us to the houseboat, just waved from the cab and went back to the *festa.* But I found myself wanting another glimpse of those dark eyes, those furry legs.

Mr. Vieira walked up to us as Quinn was pointing out what

looked like pom-poms of leaves high in the oaks that served as a windbreak for the orchard. At first I thought they were nests.

"Not nests," said Mr. Vieira after blowing into his cup of coffee. "Mistletoe."

I had a sudden image of Ben, of dragging him toward the line of trees, kissing him beneath each puffy-berried plant.

"Mistletoe's a parasite," said Mr. Vieira. "It sucks the life right out of the oak."

I looked more carefully at the trees—they did look a bit peaked, their leaves less robust than they should be in the middle of summer. Kisses can do that, though. Drain you until you're just a pale shell of yourself.

"READY TO CLEAN some bottles?" Mr. Vieira ushered us inside the distillery. The room was cold, to keep the pears from ripening too fast. "You." He pointed to me. "Not you." He pointed to Quinn. She lifted her book to show him that she already had plans.

The bottles were lined up like beakers in a lab, the pears specimens inside.

"Ben went off to get our labels," he said, and I felt a little flutter. *Cool it,* I told myself. *You're not a teenager anymore.* "Printer's over in Rio Vista."

I walked over to the large map of the Delta framed on one of the distillery walls. The complicated maze of waterways and land made me a bit dizzy. Comice Island looked like a tiny pea on a tangled plate of pasta. Rio Vista was about ten miles away.

"So the houseboat is on Paddleboat Slough?" I pointed to the waterway that arced behind the island.

"Sloo," Mr. Vieira corrected me. "You say it 'sloo,' not 'sluff.'"

I couldn't make his pronunciation jibe with the word on the map—I saw *slough* and I heard "sluff" in my head, like "tough," "rough," "enough." Like sloughing off old skin, making way for the new.

"Old steamboats used to come through here." He traced the slough with his finger.

"The water's deep enough for that?" I asked.

"It's plenty deep," he said. "Near twenty feet at the bottom."

The slough was particularly wide by our pier—wide enough for steamboats to use it as a turnaround, but we had the whole stretch of it to ourselves. Ourselves and the barn swallows and egrets and occasional beaver. And occasional hairy-legged man.

"Thanks again for letting us stay," I said.

He grunted and handed me a bottle with a pear resting inside. "We need to get these eighty dollars' worth of pretty," he said.

THE RHYTHM IN the distillery was different from picking, but satisfying in its own way. Pouring cooled boiled water into the slender-necked bottle, clear water into clear glass, made me feel clear inside myself, gleaming and empty. A pale green pear pulsing in the center like a heart.

I eased the soft, flexible brush into the bottle and lightly scrubbed any lingering dirt off the pear and the sides of the bottle. When I turned the bottle over gently to drain it and the pear landed with a soft thud at the base of the neck, I felt a thud in my own body, like Quinn kicking my cervix when she was still inside. I looked at Quinn sitting on a metal stool, swinging her legs, reading *Harriet the Spy* for the thousandth time, and wondered how it was possible my girl once fit inside my skin. She seemed almost back to her old self; she hadn't mentioned the monster once all day.

I rinsed the bottle out once more with the boiled water— water straight from the tap could leave a residue—then set it carefully on a rack to drain. Mrs. Vieira tipped the bottles upright again when they were ready and poured in the eau-de-vie by funnel. The essence of pear filled the room; it took thirty pounds of pears to make one bottle of clear brandy, their fragrance condensed into a singular heady perfume.

Mrs. Vieira poured a bit of the liquid into a shot glass and handed it to me.

I scanned Mrs. Vieira's face to make sure she wanted me to drink it. Mrs. Vieira nodded and tilted her head up sharply to mimic tossing one back.

I took a sip. The flavor nearly knocked me over; it was as if the whole orchard had been boiled down to the very soul of pear. I could feel the alcohol rise immediately to my head, some of it creating a warm channel down the center of my body.

"Amazing," I said.

Mrs. Vieira laughed gruffly and took a sip herself.

"I wanna try." Quinn had put down her book. I wasn't surprised—it would be impossible to focus on anything but the intense scent filling the air.

"It's a grown-up drink," I told her. "You can have some pear nectar later."

Quinn scowled. Mrs. Vieira poured a tiny bit, less than a thimbleful, into another glass and passed it to her, then looked at me with her eyebrows raised.

"I don't know . . ." I started. Quinn scowled at me again. "I guess one little sip is okay."

Quinn took a taste; I searched for a light switched on in her eyes, some chromosomal voice that said *At last; this is what my body's been waiting for all these years,* but all Quinn did was cough. "Strong," she said, to my relief, and passed the rest of the glass back to Mrs. Vieira.

BEN RETURNED WITH long white boxes full of labels. They were self-adhesive, elegant, designed to curve right below the neck of the bottle—the background the same pale green as the pears, the lettering simple and white. *Eau de Vieira.*

"What does that mean?" asked Quinn.

"'Water of Vieira,'" I said.

"Ew," Quinn said to Ben. I was glad she didn't still seem afraid of him. "Like your pee!"

"Hadn't thought of it that way before." His smile loosened something inside me. "It's a play on *eau de vie*. Water of life."

"Did you design the labels?" I asked.

"An old girlfriend did," he said, and I felt a surprising flare of jealousy.

"Hey," he said. "You want to see the old pear crate labels?" Before we could answer, he ran off to the house.

"We drank his pee," Quinn whispered, cracking up, as I started to clean another bottle.

BEN CAME BACK with a brown leather photo album full of labels. The front had a hand-lettered page taped to it: *Vieira Pears Through the Ages!*

"I wrote that when I was about your age," he told Quinn. "I always loved looking through this book."

How would Quinn be different, I wondered, if we had stayed in the same place all her life? If she had been tied to a specific piece of land?

Mr. Vieira had told me it takes ten years to get a viable pear orchard going. Ten years of waiting to see if the roots will take, if the fruit will be big enough, healthy enough. Ten years to get it to stand on its own. Some of the trees at Vieira Pears were ten times that old. Enough to confirm this place could grow a good, lasting pear.

Quinn would be ten next year; it was amazing to see how she had grown, often on sandy, shifting soil, often without much ground to latch onto at all. Somehow, she had flourished. My sweet miracle fruit.

BEN CRACKED OPEN the book. It sent a musty library tang into the air.

"This has always been my favorite." He pointed to a light blue Vieira Pears label that featured a large green pear with a slightly sinister-looking face: pencil-thin mustache, one eyebrow cocked, a smarmy smile showing lots of teeth. The pear wore a flat black sombrero, like the matador's at the bullfight. "I think it scared customers away, though."

"I wouldn't want to eat that pear." Quinn grimaced.

He flipped the page. "This one's prettier," he said. "It's from the forties." The label featured a single pear tree, light beaming off of each piece of fruit. "This one, too." He turned to a gorgeous detailed label with a bird's-eye view of the orchard—including the Vieiras' house, the glimmering slough.

"Who painted it?" I asked.

"My grandmother," he said.

He showed me more labels she had designed—close-ups of pears so lifelike you could almost smell them; women holding pears, looking ecstatic; a donkey with baskets of pears on its back. The colors soothing and vibrant all at once. Her name wasn't on any of them.

"My family stopped using labels in the fifties, when cardboard came around," he said, "and you could print the necessary info right on the box."

"You should resurrect them," I said.

"Sometimes we do." He ruffled through labels of rivers and trees, a pear painted like a baby with one little curl on the top of its head, a large pear on someone's hand, the command *Eat One!* in yellow movie-poster letters above it. "When we approach a new store to sell to, we use a label, a wooden box, the whole deal."

"You should give your grandmother credit," I said.

"I like that idea," he said.

He turned a page to a black-and-white photograph. I recognized Mr. and Mrs. Vieira standing in front of their house, even though they were younger and thinner. Mrs. Vieira was turned slightly to the side, probably so her walleye wouldn't show. Both were beaming. They were flanked by older relatives, the women in black dresses, men in button-down shirts and fedoras.

"This is her." He brushed his grandmother's face. She looked severe, bitter. I never would have guessed she was an artist, especially such a gifted one. Sometimes as I walked past people, I thought about how I could be looking at someone who was the best violinist in the history of the world or the greatest cheesemaker ever and I would never know. I would just see a normal person going about their life; I would be unaware of the brilliance beneath their skin. I looked at Ben and bit my lip, wondering about his hidden talents.

"So you work with slugs, huh?" I asked, trying to derail my thoughts.

"Pear slugs," he said, nodding. "But they're not really slugs."

"Ah," I said, glad to hear it.

"They're the larvae of sawflies," he said. That didn't sound a whole lot better.

"Are they sluggish?" Quinn asked without looking up from her book.

"They are indeed." He laughed. "Slimy green little things. They'll eat the life out of a tree. Fortunately, it doesn't take much to get them off. Throw some dust at them, spray them with a hose . . ."

"If that's what does it for them," I said and immediately blushed. I hadn't used an innuendo in years. I didn't know I was still capable of it. A sly smile of recognition spread across his face.

"Well." I took a deep breath. "I should probably get back to work." It was the last thing I wanted to do, but Ben's parents would be back any moment and I still had a load of bottles to wash. Ben stood to leave, then lingered.

"Have you two had a chance to explore the area much?" he asked.

"Not yet," I said, heart pounding.

"Well then," he said. "We'll have to remedy that."

I told myself not to get too excited.

"Maybe we can drive around when we're done for the day," he said. "I've shown you the history of the orchard. Might as well show you the history of the Delta."

AFTER BEN TOOK off, I held a bottle to the light. The Comice inside, like most pears, had freckles all over its skin, but the specks didn't appear to be on the surface. They looked like they were just underneath, like someone wearing a sheer blouse over a camisole spattered with tiny polka dots. Like the red and blue hockey circles below a fresh layer of ice. Like the past breathing directly under the skin of the present, sometimes so sharply, you imagine it's right there with you.

KAREN

AFTER THE FIRST ROUND OF JUDGING, KAREN AND Nathan found themselves in second place.

Karen squealed and hugged Nathan tighter than she ever had. He hugged back, but she could feel him looking around the rink, not pouring all his attention into her inside his arms.

"Don't get too excited," said Deena. "You still have the free skate tomorrow."

"And we're going to nail it!" Nathan broke away from Karen and raised his hand for a high five. She had to jump to hit his palm. When her skate guards landed back on the rubbery floor, her teeth clacked together.

"We should have been on top after the short," Deena said.

"You like being on top, do you?" Nathan raised his eyebrows at her.

"You know it." She smiled at him in a way that made Karen's stomach clench.

"We should do something to celebrate." Karen stepped in between them.

Nathan waved to someone coming through the stadium doors; Karen realized it was the skater from Rhode Island. "I know what *I'm* doing," he said, and wrapped his arm around the woman, now in a tight ribbed turtleneck sweater, pointy-toed high heels poking out beneath dark narrow jeans, her face still in performance makeup. She laughed and pressed her grown-up body against him, looking straight into Karen's eyes.

KAREN COULDN'T SLEEP that night, even though her mother warned her she needed at least eight hours.

She tortured herself, imagining Nathan with Miss Rhode Island. Were they naked right now? Was her lipstick all over his skin? Had she let her hair come undone, the top of it still crispy with gel, the rest flowing around her shoulders, around his face? Did they do pairs moves together as a joke? Did he lift her, nude, above his head, taking her nipple into his mouth as he lowered her back down? Was that what people did when they were naked together?

Karen hugged a dozen fan-tossed stuffed animals to her chest, comforted by the fact that Nathan had briefly touched their fur.

THE NEXT MORNING, Karen couldn't look at Miss Rhode Island. She tried not to listen as the woman recounted her night, as she talked about Nathan's apartment, which Karen herself hadn't seen, as she talked about Nathan taking her to the "big O"—"and I don't mean Olympics, ladies," she said, to a chorus of locker room "oooOOOoo's."

Karen tried not to notice that Miss Rhode Island was looking in her direction the entire time she spoke, sending laser beams into the back of Karen's neck, trying to get under her skin, rattle her, throw her off her game. She tried to pretend she didn't notice Miss Rhode Island's untied skate lace draped on the floor like a tapeworm, tried to pretend she didn't know what she was doing as she stepped on it with her own skate, slicing it neatly in two with her blade.

IZZY

AFTER I WAS DONE CLEANING BOTTLES, BEN DROVE US to Locke, a tiny town about ten miles down the levee from Comice. It had been founded by Chinese immigrants, farmworkers mostly. One of the first towns built "by the Chinese for the Chinese" in the country, and the only one still on the map. Chinese immigrants were not allowed to own land, so they leased it from George Locke in 1915 and built gambling halls and restaurants and shops along a one-block street, the flat-faced wooden two-story buildings fronted with awnings that shaded the sidewalk, propped up with slender rectangular wood pillars. A few people sat on the second-floor balconies of apartments that used to be rooming houses for pear and asparagus pickers. Not to mention whorehouses staffed by white women. Locke was filled mostly with white folks now—only about ten of the eighty or so people living there were Chinese American.

The town had been named a National Historic Landmark, but it was dusty and neglected-feeling, as if no one cared whether or not it hung around. Many buildings tilted sharply, leading to a general air of precariousness. Then again, maybe I just felt precarious being out in the world, being out with Ben, walking so close beside him the hair of our arms sometimes brushed.

Some of the buildings had been transformed into art galleries and exotica shops, but even those had a shabby, sleepy feel. We drifted into the Dai Loy Museum, an old gambling hall trapped in time, its faded wooden floor violently warped. I felt seasick walking up and down its dips. Tables were set for games of *pai gow* and *fan tan;* sandpaper still adhered to their legs for easy match lighting. The walls were a pale green, the color of old dental equipment.

Quinn ran around, popping in and out of the small lottery room and money rooms, looking at the displays of old cookware and newspapers, racing up the narrow stairs. I trailed behind her, worried the floor would collapse beneath her feet.

At the top of the steps was a small alcove with a metal cot, a thin mattress. A place for a guard to sleep. A small hole was cut out of the wall so the owner could look down at the gamblers, make sure they weren't cheating. Ben pulled up behind me. I felt my cheeks redden.

"The dealers used to put pillows on their stools," he said, looking over my shoulder at the gambling tables below. "If they took a break, they had to carry the cushions with them. It was considered bad luck to leave body heat behind."

Then we're in trouble, I thought, remembering the heat he left in my bed long after he stepped off the boat.

"THAT WAS PRETTY cool," said Quinn as we walked out of the dim museum. "Did you read about the *bok bok* guys? They banged blocks to let people know everything was all right at night."

"Holy shit," said Ben.

"It's not that exciting," Quinn snorted.

"Not that," said Ben. "Isn't that that reporter, from CNN or something? What is she doing in Locke?"

He might as well have poured cold water down my back. I recognized the Asian woman from one of my rare moments of channel surfing, her hair straight and glossy, reflecting light. She and a small group of hangers-on, including a cameraman, walked up the narrow steps to the old Chinese school. Blood started to whip through my veins.

"Do you want to meet her?" asked Ben. "We should go meet her. Maybe we could be on TV!"

"I want to be on TV," said Quinn excitedly.

"I need to find a restroom," I said. "I'll catch up with you in a little bit." I walked quickly, shakily, in the other direction, and ducked into a dusty shop—"Locke Ness: Things Old and Odd." The building used to be the "Victory Club," one of the town's other gambling halls, but now was filled with a funky assortment of ephemera. After looking at mariachi bands made out of seashells and jars full of buttons, I realized I really did need to use the restroom, but when I asked, the woman with flame-red hair behind the counter told me the only public one was in the old schoolhouse. "Or you can use the one at Al the Wop's," she said. "But only if you buy something."

I poked my head out of the store and looked both ways to make sure the news team was not back on the street. The town looked like a movie set, but no contrived movie set could capture the true dinginess of the place, the sadness weathered into every plank of wood. I felt like a movie actor myself as I scurried across the street like someone holding a gun up to her chest.

The restaurant was really named "Al's Place" but everyone called it "Al the Wop's"—the name was even painted on the window—since Al Adami bought Lee Bing's restaurant in 1934 and turned it into the only non-Chinese business in town. It took a moment for my eyes to adjust to the dim light. The ceiling was papered with sooty dollar bills, some new ones standing out like leafy greens. Open jars of peanut butter and orange marmalade sat on every table. Several guys in biker jackets sat at the bar. I could smell decades of beef wafting off the grill, decades of beer and whiskey souring the air.

"Can I use your bathroom?" I asked, panting.

"You gotta order first," the bartender said, looking as if I had woken him from a nap.

I took a quick glimpse at the menu and ordered the cheapest thing—fried bread—before I ran to the restroom in the back of the place.

The bread was sitting on the bar when I returned, thick slabs of it fried on the grill, dripping with oil. I sat down on one of the square black vinyl stools.

"I suggest it with the peanut butter." The bartender pushed a jar in my direction, a knife already stuck inside, covered with greasy fingerprints.

"I put it on my steak," one of the bikers near me said. He and his friends laughed when I winced.

"Try it," the bartender cajoled, looking bored but serious about his command. I spread a layer on one of the pieces just so they'd leave me alone. They were right—the peanut butter melted against the warm bread, silky and delicious. I gave the bikers the thumbs-up, my hand shaking just a little, and they turned back to their own plates.

"How'd you get the dollars up there?" I asked the bartender, my feet jiggling on the bottom rung of the stool.

"Give me a dollar," he said, "and I'll show you."

I dug one out of my pocket, even though I didn't have many to spare.

"Tell you what," he said. "I'll put in a dollar, too."

The bikers next to me chuckled.

He punched a thumbtack through the corner of my dollar, pulled a silver dollar out of the cash register, and wrapped my dollar around it. When he threw the dollars up to the ceiling, mine stuck, but his slipped out and fell right back into his waiting hand.

The bikers whooped.

"Nice." I turned back to my bread.

The door opened a crack and the reporter poked her expertly made-up face inside. My throat went completely dry. Thanks to the peanut butter on the roof of my mouth, I couldn't swallow, either.

"Is that who I think it is?" the bartender said.

"I'll be damned!" said one of the bikers.

I turned away on my stool.

"Come on in!" The bartender's voice was booming and jovial. "Price of admission is just an autograph."

"Small price to pay." She gave a measured anchorperson laugh as she stepped inside. Her heels clacked against the wooden floor. Her perfume wafted over me, a whoosh of air from her rapid gait.

As she shook hands and started to sign her name on napkins and menus and shirts, I slipped off my stool and hurried out the door, looking down as I passed the cameraman. I felt a little bad for not paying, but I *had* given the place my dollar. The bread wasn't much more than that.

QUINN AND BEN were wandering down the street, both still beaming from their brush with celebrity.

"She's doing a story on the Asian heritage of the state," Ben told me.

"She's pretty," said Quinn, "even though she has big teeth."

"Can we get out of here?" I wanted to leave before she came out of the restaurant. "I'm not feeling so great."

"What's wrong?"

I checked Ben's face, but he just looked concerned.

"You smell like peanut butter," said Quinn. She showed me the signature on a tourist brochure: *Dear Quinn, Shoot for the Stars!*

"Let's just go." I grabbed Quinn's hand and pulled her to the car.

I STAYED QUIET as Ben and Quinn chattered away on the way home about an elaborate community kitchen garden in Locke—some of the remaining Chinese residents grew bitter melon, fuzzy melon, winter melon there, plus long beans, Chinese okra, other vegetables I hadn't heard of. When the conversation turned to television news, I felt myself pull into myself even more.

"You better save that signature," said Ben. "It will be worth something someday."

Any energy that I had been sending out to Ben was sucked right back into my own muscles. He must have sensed it; his energy stopped reaching toward me, too. I felt hard and lonely inside my skin, my whole body closed, like a fist.

KAREN

NATHAN LOOKED FLAYED IN HIS RED UNITARD. KAREN could barely touch him during their practice session. Her own dress, which had seemed so sexy, felt like a stupid joke.

"I hope you washed your hands well," she said. "I don't want to catch anything."

"Listen to you, Miss Germophobe," said Nathan.

"I'm sure she at least has HPV," said Karen.

"Someone has their panties in a wad today."

"Someone has seen too many panties," she said.

She wanted to strangle him when he laughed.

MISS RHODE ISLAND and her partner were late coming to the ice for practice. No one in the locker room had been willing to give up a spare lace, so the pair's coach, to Karen's delight, had to buy a set from one of the busy vendors in the lobby and then take the time to relace the boot. Rhode Island shot Karen a hateful look as she skated by in her ice blue dress, holding her pissed-off partner's hand.

Karen wanted to feel a surge of triumph, but she just felt tired. And off balance. She fell after the throw triple salchow and jarred her tailbone. She didn't even attempt the side-by-side double axel. She felt dizzy after the death spiral. She could see her mother lifting her arms in exasperation.

"Get it together," said Nathan. She wanted to kick him with her blade. She wanted to see his red blood seep through the red fabric, drip beautiful red drops all over the pearly ice. Instead, she dug her fingernails into the backs of his hands during their next press lift, and was disarmed when he gave her an affectionate squeeze back.

KAREN TRIED TO catch her bearings, to find her center, as they walked around in their skate guards to keep their muscles loose after the practice session. She snapped her headphones on, listened to *Tristan und Isolde* over and over again, trying to visualize the performance, trying to drown out the other music and the crowd's cheers and gasps as one couple after another took to the ice for their long program. Still, she couldn't concentrate. She looked over at Nathan, headphones clamped over his ears, too, as he lunged and stretched and rolled his head around. As he marked the choreography, lifting his empty hands, tossing a ghost Karen.

She could barely hear the music, even with the volume turned up. All she could hear was the blood in her head. She took a deep breath, rolled down the length of her spine, let all the blood rush to her face. When she rolled back up, she felt lightheaded and stumbled a few steps backwards.

"Come on, Karen, focus, please," her mother said, her voice tight with stress.

Karen closed her eyes. She tried to slow her heart inside her chest, valves flapping, muscles contracting. She tried to imagine herself sitting inside one of its chambers, Nathan in the other one, just a thin membrane between them. She imagined pressing her hand to the wall, feeling his hand pressing back. If they breached that membrane, she thought, it wouldn't kill her. It would just make her heart more open, more whole.

IZZY

WHEN WE GOT OUT OF BEN'S CAR, WE FOUND MR. AND Mrs. Vieira by the chicken coop, shaking their heads. Feathers were everywhere. Blood, too.

One chicken was splayed open, hollowed out. Quinn ran toward it, dropped to her knees, and wailed. The autograph fell from her hand into the dirt.

"What happened?" I asked.

"Coyote," said Mr. Vieira.

Coyotes didn't live on the island; they had to cross the bridge to get to the farm. The image struck me as funny—it made the coyotes seem civilized, somehow, like they should be wearing little suits.

"A coyote ate Buttercup!" Quinn was beside herself. I bent down and wrapped my arms around her.

"On a farm," said Mr. Vieira, "you learn not to name the chickens."

"I know how you feel," Ben whispered to Quinn. "I used to name the chickens, too."

Quinn cried even harder. I pulled her tight, rested my chin on her warm hair.

"I hope you'll feel better soon," Ben said to me, but I couldn't bring myself to look up at him.

"Thanks for taking us." My words felt flat in my mouth. I wanted to be effusive. I wanted to say "Let's do it again!" but I held back. I watched his blue-jeaned legs walk away, past poor eviscerated Buttercup. Strange how something so alive can be so easily reduced to feathers and skin. I wondered if any of her beautiful green eggs had been inside her when she was eaten, if they were now settling, broken, inside the coyote's belly.

I kissed the top of Quinn's head, then lifted the autographed flyer from the dirt and tried to smooth it out. In its short time on the ground, it had grown wrinkled and smudged.

"Do you want to go for a walk through the pear orchard?" I asked Quinn, hoping to distract her.

"The coyote might be there," she fretted.

"We could go back to the boat," I said.

"The coyote could be there, too," she said. "Or the monster!"

"Quinn," I started, but she sobbed so hard, I knew she wouldn't hear me. She picked feathers from the ground slowly, one by one, as if she were performing some ritual, and set them on top of the flyer in my hand. A couple of the words had smeared; now it looked as if the reporter was instructing Quinn to "Shoot the Stars!"

BACK ON THE boat, Quinn curled up in bed, feathers cupped in her palm. I put the signature in the back of the Norse mythology book to try to flatten it out.

"Maybe it wasn't a coyote," she said, her body rocking a little. "Maybe it was the monster that got her."

"It was a coyote, sweetheart," I said. "Coyotes kill chickens all the time."

Quinn had always been practical—she had known I was the

tooth fairy, had never believed in Santa Claus. This talk of monsters was totally out of character for her.

"Why don't you believe me?" Quinn sat up and pulled her knees to her chest. I saw all the scratches on her legs, all the mosquito bites.

"Monsters aren't real." I felt like a broken record. "You should know that, Quinn. You're old enough to—"

"Eema!" Quinn scooted back against the wall, her face a spasm of fear as she pointed to the window, arm trembling.

I turned toward the glass.

"What the hell!" I jumped back, too, fell onto the bed next to Quinn, knocking my head on the paneling. An enormous eye was looking in our direction, a dark bulky head rising partly above the water.

"I told you," Quinn said. "I told you!"

I grabbed onto Quinn as the houseboat bucked. I couldn't make any sense of what I was seeing. It couldn't possibly be real. Was it a movie prop? A robot? But then the huge rheumy eye looked right into me, and what robot could do that? The light swayed over us like a pendulum. All I could think was *Hold Quinn, hold Quinn, hold Quinn,* as if my arms could protect her from whatever was trying to tear our house apart.

The eye disappeared, followed by a spume of water that sounded like someone squeezing a huge fireplace bellows; some sprayed through the window screen, spattering both of us with cold wet drops. Quinn shrieked and scrunched herself into a ball, but recognition flooded my limbs.

"Oh my God." Awe mixed with the fear in my veins. "It's a whale. It's a whale, Quinn."

Quinn raised her head. "What's a whale doing in the river?"

"It must have taken a wrong turn somewhere." I wiped the beads of water from my face. The boat was rocking less now. I stepped over to the window and craned my head out, but the water was still, placid. A pair of herons rustled through the tule reeds, but otherwise there was no sign of life. I looked across the slough at the great heaps of gray tree trunks and imagined the great body gliding underwater, maybe even under our boat, and felt very very small.

"Should we call the police?" she asked.

"No," I said, looking out at the dark water. "Let this be our secret." What could the police do, anyway? The whale would surely find its way back to the sea.

"What if it wants to hurt us?" she asked.

"Whales are peaceful." I hoped I remembered this correctly. "If anything, it wants to play."

"And it's our secret." Quinn snuggled against me, her breath still a bit ragged. Buttercup's feathers fell from her hand, scattered over the bedspread like honeymoon rose petals.

I knew how large secrets could grow within a person; holding a whale inside would be a piece of cake.

KAREN

DEENA GENTLY PULLED KAREN'S HEADPHONES AWAY.

"You're on, sweetheart," she said.

Nathan was already striding toward the ice. Karen ran to catch up. When she stepped on the ice, she immediately fell. She stood and her feet slipped out from under her again. Her hip burned where she landed; her ears roared with blood, with the murmurs of the crowd. Had she forgotten how to skate? Was it all over—could they kiss their skating dreams good-bye? A feeling rushed through her like cold water; she couldn't tell if it was fear or relief.

"Your guards," said Nathan. "You forgot to take off your guards."

He kneeled down and slipped them off her blades, then stood and waved the hard plastic in the air like spoils. The audience cheered.

"They're in our pocket now," he whispered as he set the guards on the low wall that rimmed the rink. "Falling is the best thing you could have done." Karen wanted to believe him, but she felt rattled, stripped naked. She could barely feel his hand as he led her to the center of the ice.

"YOU WERE A zombie out there." Deena looked drained after their program. "Isolde should not be a zombie, Karen. Isolde should be buzzing with life."

Karen could barely remember skating. Her body had done the right moves in the right order—she hadn't stumbled, hadn't fallen, at least not as far as she could recall—but her mind hadn't been in it. Her heart hadn't been in it, either; she and Nathan were still stuck inside their separate chambers there, even as he shoved his hands into her armpits, against her thighs, even as her crotch hovered just over his head. She felt dizzy, breathless, as she let her mother lead her toward the bleachers reserved for skaters awaiting their judgment. A low-rent "kiss-and-cry," only a couple of local cameras trained upon them. She felt too blank to cry, too blank to offer up her cheek, her lips, for a kiss. She sat still and fought to keep her eyes open. When a little girl in a skating dress came over, excitedly, to deliver the next crop of fan presents, a wave of nausea barreled through Karen and she threw up all over the stuffed animals. The little girl jumped back and ran off, crying, leaving bile-soaked teddy bears on the floor. Karen let Nathan usher her out of the rink while Deena stayed behind on the bench, smiling for the cameras, waiting for their scores.

KAREN LAY ON a bench in the dressing room; Nathan draped a wet paper towel over her forehead. None of the women seemed to mind the fact that he was in there with her. Many of them were in various states of undress, their competition dresses hanging down from their waists, breasts bare except for their taped-up nipples, but, to her relief, Nathan wasn't looking at any of them. He was just looking at her, stroking her hair, her arm.

"You sure know how to make an event memorable," he said. "Falling. Puking. What's next?"

"Shitting her pants," said Miss Rhode Island. "If she hasn't done that already."

"That's uncalled for," said Nathan; he looked down at Karen and said, "You want me to kill her for you?"

Even though Karen's head felt like it was going to split open and her stomach gave another lurch, she felt warmth spread through her whole body.

"Nah, just torture her a little." Karen eked out a smile.

Miss Rhode Island turned away in a huff as the other skaters laughed.

Deena breezed into the room, trailing cold air from the rink behind her like a veil.

"Your scores weren't bad," she said, moving someone's skates away to sit on a bench across from Karen's. "Better technical than artistic, no surprise. You're holding on to second for now, but there are still five more teams to go. Including the top ones."

"I think I need to go home." Karen was shivering now with fever.

"If you're lucky enough to medal, you need to get on that podium, sweetheart," said Deena. "You want people to remember your face."

"I really think . . ." Before Karen could finish her sentence, she threw up all over someone's bag.

"Oh, sweetie," she sighed. "Hang in there. I'm going to keep my eye on the competition." She left and Nathan started to clean up the mess. He was the only person Karen knew who could have women fawning all over him even as he cleaned a pukey skating bag. Karen wanted to help, but could barely raise her head. Every few minutes, after each pair's program, Deena poked her face into the locker room with an update:

"She fell on her triple toe."

"He botched the throw."

"You're holding on to second."

"You're holding on to second."

"They weren't together on their footwork."

"You're still holding on to second."

"The seventh-place team was flawless." Her voice was tense. "You're in third. And the team in first is next. Time to say your prayers."

This from the woman who never taught her daughter to pray, who only took her to temple for High Holy Days—their dose of Jewishness for the year. Nathan came over and squeezed her hand. That felt like a prayer in itself—their hands creating the church, the steeple, the whole congregation between their palms.

THE FIRST-PLACE TEAM fell three times and dropped out of the running. The fourth-place team, Miss Rhode Island's team, fell twice, and didn't advance. Karen and Nathan held on to third, by two-tenths of a point.

Nathan kissed Karen's sweaty forehead when Deena broke the news.

"You were lucky this time," she warned. "You can't count on luck when you get to Sectionals."

Karen knew how much hung on Sectionals. If they didn't place in the top three there, they wouldn't get to Nationals. And if they didn't get to Nationals, they wouldn't be on the judges' radar, and they'd be much less likely to get to the Olympics the following year. But none of that mattered at the moment. At the moment, all she wanted was a pillow, a soft, cool pillow, beneath her heavy head.

"God, Karen, your breath smells awful," her mother said as she replenished Karen's lipstick before the medal ceremony. She fished a piece of gum out of her bag and stuck it in Karen's mouth, then gave her a quick kiss on the cheek.

Karen couldn't walk without feeling dizzy, so Nathan carried her out to the podium, like a baby. The cold air was a shock on her skin, and her limbs trembled with fever, but she felt cozy in Nathan's arms, safe. She managed a small wave to the audience after he stepped up, with a huge grunt, onto the third-place platform. The cheers surrounded her like hundreds of arms.

IN THE MORNING, I DECIDED MAYBE I WOULD TELL BEN, after all. He would love knowing a whale was in his backyard.

I looked for him as Quinn and I drove to the distillery, as we walked past the chicken coop and Quinn held her breath, trying to be brave, as I settled into my bottle-cleaning routine. No sign of his dark hair anywhere. Aside from the clacking of the tripod ladders out in the orchard, the occasional crowing of a rooster—tinged, it seemed to me, with grief—it was a quiet day.

Finally I couldn't help myself. "Where's Ben?" I asked Mr. Vieira, trying to sound casual.

"Had to go back to Oregon," he said. "Some problem with the slugs."

I winced, even though I knew the slugs weren't slugs at all.

"At least that's his excuse." Mr. Vieira handed me a bottle to clean. "I think he wanted to get back to that girl of his."

"Girl?" He hadn't mentioned a daughter. Maybe he had one Quinn's age, someone she could be friends with . . .

"His research partner," he said. "Said they talked about getting married—don't know if they set the date."

The bottle slipped out of my hands and crashed against the floor; the pear bounced and landed on my sneaker. Broken glass glittered everywhere.

"Hey," he said. "You owe me eighty bucks."

When tears sprang to my eyes, he handed me a broom and said, "Jesus Christ, I'm only kidding. We always lose a few."

Quinn came over to help me clean up, but I told her to step back. She was wearing sandals.

I didn't want her to get hurt, too.

THAT AFTERNOON, I took Quinn into the town of Comice to distract myself. We were thrilled to find a small branch library on a side street we hadn't visited before—just a single storefront room, with a few battered tables and chairs, a corner by the children's books with puzzles and toys, a couple of computers. And, of course, books. Not a lot of books, but more than we had seen in a while. Quinn took a deep breath, as if smelling a fine wine. More than anything, the scent of a library was home.

"We should look up whales, Eema," Quinn whispered.

"Brilliant idea," I whispered back.

We combed through the stacks; there weren't any books exclusively about whales, but we found a couple of encyclopedia entries, a couple of chapters in books about marine life. After looking at various charts and illustrations, we came to the conclusion that our whale was a humpback. We recognized the long flippers, the grooves beneath the jaw, the bumps all over the flat head that made it look kind of like a giant pickle. Humpback adults were forty to fifty feet long, and around seventy-nine thousand pounds. They were baleen whales—instead of teeth, they had rows of fringed baleen plates hanging from their front jaw like strips of curtain at a car wash, to filter their food. They caught fish using the bubble net method—they'd swim around their prey in circles, blowing bubbles to create a sort of holding pen for the fish, then they'd swoop in, mouths open, and scoop up thousands of fish at once.

"I hope there are enough fish for it in the river," whispered Quinn.

"Me too," I whispered back.

We found a quote from Melville; he called humpbacks "the most gamesome and light-hearted of all the whales . . . making more white water and gay foam than any other."

"See," I said to Quinn. "I told you it was there to play."

I wondered if I had touched the whale with my foot when we had gone swimming, if it's what had made the water rise. The thought of sharing the slough with such an immense creature gave me a dizzy, giddy sense of vertigo, as if the floor were dropping underneath me. I tried to imagine what it would be like to actually swim with it on purpose. I imagined its skin would smell like rubber and oil, that it would squeak like a balloon if you ran your finger across it, that lying on it would feel like lying on a giant inflated inner tube, the kind you use to laze down a river, but with muscle inside.

It made sense to me that humpbacks belonged to a suborder of Cetacea called *Mysticeti*—from the Greek for "unknowable." They remained a mystery, vast and deep, no matter how much we could ever learn about them.

ON THE WAY home, we stopped at a little market to pick up a few groceries.

"Should we blow some bubbles around the peanut butter?" I asked Quinn. She laughed and made a raspberry sound with her lips.

"I think we're almost out of jelly, too, Eema," Quinn said.

"We can get that back at home," I reminded her. We had access to the Vieiras' pear pantries, adjacent to the icehouse. Pear jellies. Whole peeled pears floating in syrup spiced with peppercorn and basil. Thick sweet pear nectar. Chewy dried pears, slices that curled at the edges and looked so much like women's genitalia, I felt a bit funny biting into them. Pear vinaigrette spiked with Gorgonzola. I hadn't eaten a fresh pear yet, but I had the taste of pear in my mouth just about every day.

Sometimes Mrs. Vieira would bring out one of her creations to share with the workers—a pear tart, a little cup of pear sorbet, sausage studded with chunks of pear. I was starting to feel a bit peared out, but it was nice to see what all could be done with a simple piece of fruit. I was glad Mrs. Vieira could show Quinn that flavor meant something more than powdered nacho cheese.

"Are you tired of pears yet?" I asked as we made our way down the narrow aisle, grabbing bags of corn chips, cans of bean dip.

"I'll never be tired of pears. I'm obsessed with pears." She pulled a jar of pear preserves from a shelf, the jelly gleaming like amber as she held it to the light, scraps of pear suspended inside.

I TRIED NOT to obsess over Ben. It's not like we had kissed. He hadn't promised his undying love. He had just brushed up against me in the night. He had just shown me some kindness. No need to feel like my heart was ripped from my chest. At least that's what I told myself all night. Anyway, I had a whale to think about. And pears. And, at work in the morning, the distraction of a new face, even if it was a sour one.

"Hey, Vieira." A tall sandy-haired guy in a yellow golf shirt and ironed blue jeans appeared in the driveway as Quinn and I were getting out of the car. "I hear you're having trouble with labor this year."

"We all are, Roberts." Mr. Vieira didn't glance up from the tractor engine.

"Not me," the man said. "I got myself a robot."

Quinn looked at me, her eyebrows raised. I wondered, again, if the whale was some sort of animatronic creature, if the neigh-

bor had sent it to us to freak us out. Maybe it was possible to create a soulful-eyed robot now.

"You gotta come take a look," the man said. "It's the future of
farming. I'm telling you, Vieira, you won't have to worry about
beaners never again." I thought about the pistachio farms on the
I-5, how they used mechanical shakers. What would happen to all
the workers, what would happen to us, if farmers no longer
needed our hands?

"I got stuff to do." Mr. Vieira busied himself with his wrench,
and the man eventually walked away, shaking his head.

"Can I see the robot?" Quinn asked.

"I don't know," I said. Mr. Vieira was obviously fuming; I
didn't want to upset him more.

"What's a beaner?" she asked. The word made me cringe. I
didn't want to hear it coming out of her mouth.

"Someone from Mexico," I said. "Someone who eats a lot of
beans."

"I like beans," she said.

"I do, too," I told her. "But it's not a good word to use."

"Uptight asshole," Mr. Vieira grumbled. "Thinks he can pick
pears with a robot."

"Why can't he?" asked Quinn.

"Pears are delicate. Bruise easy. Wind knocks a leaf into a
pear, you get a bruise. Wind bumps the pear into a branch, you
get a bigger bruise."

He wiped his forehead with his sleeve. "You need human
hands to pick pears. Robot hands will go right through the skin."

"Maybe his robot will attack him." Quinn sounded gleeful.

"Quinn!"

"I hope so," said Mr. Vieira. "I hope the robot kills that sonofabitch."

"That's not something to joke about," I said.

"Who's joking?" Mr. Vieira went back to his wrench.

I SWIPED A pear bag, strapped it over my shoulders, cinched it around my waist, and practiced picking during lunch, taking Quinn to a quiet part of the orchard where no one could see us. I didn't have a ladder, so I worked on the low-hanging fruit, moving from one tree to another, lifting pears. They had grown considerably softer since the last time I had picked; not ripe, but there was a noticeable difference in how they felt against my hand. They had a more mature heft to them, a sensual gravity, as if they had grown more at home inside their skin. They were starting to smell like their true selves, too—their perfume hung over the orchard, creating its own sort of humidity.

The Vieiras had lost a few more pickers; the workers would get calls on their cellphones while they were up on the ladders, calls from friends saying they could make a few more bucks a box at another orchard down the road. Pickers would hear this and be gone before lunch. I didn't blame them—they had families to support—but the Vieiras were getting desperate. They couldn't afford a robot, not that they would want one. The pears were getting closer and closer to ripeness, closer and closer to rot. I needed to learn to pick faster so I could help them get the fruit to market in time.

I bent my knees softly and focused on moving from my center of gravity, which kept shifting as I added more pears to the bag. *Your belly supports your arms,* I told myself. *Your movement comes from your belly, not your shoulders.* I tried to keep my breathing deep and regular as my arms gained speed. Nowhere near the speed of the other pickers, but it took me a lot less time to fill the fifty-pound bag than it had before.

I lugged the pears over to the tractor trailer, waddling like a pregnant woman, one hand on my lower back. I opened the bag at the bottom, dumping the fruit into one of the plastic bins.

"Hey!" Mr. Vieira saw me. I had been hoping he wouldn't. He strode over, looking pissed off. "That's not your job."

"You don't have to pay me for this," I told him. "I'm practicing. I just want to be able to help out."

He looked embarrassed, as if I had offered to bathe him. "Just don't let the other pickers see you," he said.

"At least I don't have metal hands," I said.

"At least." He rubbed the scruff on his chin.

"Who was that guy, anyway?" I stretched one arm across my chest, pulling it closer to me with my other hand. In the short period of picking, I could already feel the strain in my back. The empty bag hung from my torso like a slack kangaroo's pouch.

"Roberts?" he said. "He owns the orchard across the slough."

"The one with all the dead trees?" I asked, stretching my other arm across my body. He looked at me funny, so I dropped both arms to my sides.

"That's the one," he said. "He has plenty of live trees, too. More acres than me."

"He's not organic though, right?"

"Nah," said Mr. Vieira. "We're the first in the Delta for that. But he'll follow, mark my word. He'll do whatever he can to show me up."

"Like the robot?" I asked.

"Like the stupid bastard robot," he said.

Quinn laughed. "I still want to see it," she said.

"He loves it when I have a bad year," he said. "He don't want to be shown up by no *Portagee*."

"And you?" I asked.

"Kind of sad what a farm does to you." He shook his head. "Makes you want your neighbor to die."

A BARGE GLIDED across the alfalfa fields before us as we drove toward the levee. I knew it was actually in the slough behind the farm, but its rusty bulk appeared to be charging over the land. After the whale, I wasn't sure I could trust my own eyes anymore.

Quinn grabbed her math book and I grabbed an iced tea and we sat on the deck of the houseboat to feel the Delta breezes begin to pick up. The water still churned a bit from the passage of the barge, now long out of our sight, making the houseboat pitch. I stared at Roberts's levee across the slough to keep myself oriented; it resembled a heap of crumbled gravestones. Every once in a while, I could hear rocks plink down the side of it, plop into the water. No trees were planted along its edge, making it look barren, forsaken. A place where a robot would feel at home.

The levee on our side had trees and tule grass and wildflowers mixed in with the stone. Mr. Vieira had been able to get a thirty-year waiver; the state couldn't touch the land, even though they yearned to strip it bare. The state is stupid, Mr. Vieira had told me. The levees become more vulnerable when you cut down the plants, not less. The roots hold the stones in place, keep the two-story mound together. They make it an ecosystem, a tightly woven web, less of a potential rockslide.

I had asked Mr. Vieira if all the dead wood on Roberts's land was cut from the levee, but he said no, Roberts had lost a portion of his orchard to fire blight the year before. "Didn't jump the water," Mr. Vieira told me, eyes twinkling. "My pears were fine."

The birds definitely preferred our side of the slough—more places to perch, more bugs to munch. Egrets, barn swallows, the occasional duck, a constant teeming. Real life everywhere you turned. Even the posts that stuck out of the water next to our pier were sprouting green shoots at the top, like Chia Heads.

"I hope the boat didn't hurt the whale, Eema," said Quinn. "I hope there was enough room for both of them in the water."

"I hope so, too, sweetheart," I said.

Then, as if on cue, we saw the spray. Quinn dropped her book and ran to the railing.

"There are two, Eema," Quinn said. "Look!" The boat started to rock even more.

She was right. There was a second plume of water, a second dark back arcing up, slipping under. This one smaller than the other. Their tails perfect as drawings of whale tails, the edges lightly serrated as if they had been cut by those scissors people use to scallop the sides of invitations.

"It's probably a mother and child," I said.

"Like us," said Quinn.

"Like us." I wrapped my arm around her, and a pang went through my ribs as I thought of my own mother. She was never my partner the way Quinn was my partner, but that moment, I missed her terribly. I squeezed Quinn a bit tighter and brought myself back to the deck, to the whales. The water looked velvety as it cascaded over their backs, as it closed over them when they disappeared into its depths. I wondered how it felt, sheeting off their skin, surrounding them. It looked as if it would feel delicious, but if they were used to salt water, maybe the fresh water was unpleasant. Maybe it was harder to swim through it, no salt to buoy them up. I hoped they didn't have to strain too hard. I couldn't even begin to imagine how much a strained whale muscle would ache. It must feel like grief. It must feel as if the whole world is throbbing.

KAREN

A SIMPLE FLU BUG," HER DOCTOR SAID DURING A house call, "but they're bad this year. Rest, water, you know the drill."

"She has Sectionals coming up." Deena paced around the room. "She doesn't have time to rest."

"If she doesn't rest," said the doctor, "she won't be well enough to compete."

Every fiber of Karen's muscles ached and she threw up anything she tried to swallow, but it felt wonderful to lie down all day, to do nothing but let her body sink into the mattress.

Her mother tried to get her to do Pilates in bed.

"At least some core work, sweetie," urged Deena. "You don't want to lose your core strength."

Karen closed her eyes and pretended to sleep. Maybe she would never get up. Maybe she would become an invalid. Knowing her mom, though, she'd find some way to turn that into a competition, too. She'd coach Karen to be the sickest girl ever. To have the worst blood tests on record, the most gruesome X-rays, the symptoms that only the most highly specialized doctor could diagnose. She was already a little famous for being sick—pictures of her throwing up, of Nathan holding her as they got their medals, had been picked up by different news sources, had rippled out into the national media. But Karen knew that wasn't enough. If she was going to be bedridden, her mom, with the best of intentions, would want her to be like Lydwina, the patron saint of both skaters and the infirm. Lydwina was paralyzed in a skating accident at sixteen; she performed miracles from her bed until her death four decades later.

Karen knew she wasn't capable of miracles. She was capable, at best, of hard work. She knew she'd get back on the ice much too soon, with a throbbing head and wobbly limbs. She knew she'd let her mom push her to exhaustion. But for now, she let herself close her eyes; she let herself drift into true sweet slumber.

DEENA RENTED MORE ice time after Karen's fever broke.

It was 3 a.m. Karen still felt woozy, off balance as she took to the ice; she wanted to ease back into skating, but Deena was impatient. Nathan was, too. Karen told herself to skate well for him, but she couldn't land her triple loop, missed his hand during a run of footwork. Then Nathan's blade nicked the back of her neck during a flying camel. The shock of pain sent her crashing to the ice.

"You could have decapitated me," she said, holding her hand to the cut.

"I didn't," he said.

She felt the blood seep against her palm.

"I could be dead right now," she said.

"Don't worry." He did a backwards pivot next to her. "Your hair will cover the scar."

DEENA DROVE HER to the emergency room, paper towels pressed to the gash. Karen needed five stitches, like a zipper across the back of her neck. She had to take yet another day off of training, a numbing bag of ice like a bolster beneath her. Her neck was tender, stiff, for days—she found herself holding her head up when she should give in to gravity, holding her breath when she should be filling her lungs. She found herself dizzy after every spin and jump.

"You need to pull yourself together, sweetheart," her mother said when she did a double toe instead of a triple. "Sectionals are a week away."

"Don't be a baby," chided Nathan when she begged off on the death spiral, but later he examined her stitches with such tenderness, and looked at her with such concern, it was almost worth the pain.

WHALES ARE BIG," SAID QUINN IN BED THAT NIGHT.

"This is a fact," I said.

"Much bigger than us," she said.

"So true." I loved the smell of her at night, her just-brushed teeth, her earthy warmth.

"But when I start to worry about how big they are, I just remember that story about Hymir and Thor."

"The one where they go fishing?" I asked.

"Yeah, and Hymir catches two whales and he's all excited, but then Thor catches the serpent whose tail can go around the whole world, and it makes the whales seem dinky."

"Small potatoes," I said.

"Hymir's embarrassed," she said, her eyes closed, her voice starting to drift. "All he could catch is two whales."

I hoped we'd have a chance to get back to the library soon. Maybe we could have them special order a book about whales. Maybe they'd even let us get a library card—some libraries allowed that for seasonal farmworkers and their families. I was eager to learn more about our new humpback friends.

Quinn breathed steadily next to me now. I gazed out into the dark water, unable to sleep. The surface barely stirred, but I could feel the whales out there, moving low and large and slow, like dreams simmering in the subconscious, waiting to breach up into the brain.

The large one, the mother, raised her head, just a few inches above the surface, a dark curve barely discernible in the darkness; I hadn't realized how many layers of darkness existed—the darkness of the night, of the river, of her body, all different shades, like the blue of the sky, the sea, blending but distinct. Like the old blank polar-bear-in-a-snowstorm page, but inverse. I knew the bottoms of her fins and tail were white, but they were hidden underwater.

"What are you doing here?" I asked.

An eye, dark in dark in dark, looked toward me, full and indifferent. I wanted her to look at me with hope, with confusion; I wanted her to say "Help me" or "Follow me" or "I'll help you" with that one sloe liquid eye, but she didn't. Her spray briefly caught the moonlight before misting back down.

KAREN

THE EASTERN SECTIONALS WERE BEING HELD IN Oldsmar, Florida. Deena, in a fit of indulgence, bought all three of them first-class plane tickets.

"I don't think of Florida as eastern." Nathan downed his complimentary glass of champagne—only one, Deena had cautioned him. She herself was on her third flute.

"What do you think of it as, then?" Karen took a sip of her ginger ale. The bubbles snapped against her nose. Her seat was next to her mother's and directly across the aisle from Nathan's. If she wanted to, she could reach out and touch his arm. Or his knee, which rose so invitingly inside his jeans.

"Tropical," he said. "Geriatric."

"So you're moving there in a couple of years?" Karen asked her mother with a laugh. She felt giddy, even bold, up in the air, lifting her gold-rimmed glass.

Deena said, "Ha ha," but then fixed her with a glare so potent, Karen barely spoke the rest of the flight.

EVEN IN NOVEMBER, the air in Florida was dense with humidity, like the inside of someone's mouth. Karen's eyelids felt heavy; she wanted to lie down on the tarmac and let the thick air blanket itself over her, but the palm trees that stood sentry outside the Tampa airport warned her to stay upright.

After the first-class plane ride, Karen was expecting an equally swanky hotel, but Deena pulled the rental car into the driveway of a two-story pink stucco building on a street full of furniture stores and cheap souvenir shops. Deena had reserved adjoining rooms; Karen daydreamed about opening the inner door to Nathan's room in the middle of the night, knocking so he'd open his own. If her mother had enough of the little bottles from the minibar, she'd sleep right through anything.

"Get your suits on," Deena said as they lugged their bags up the concrete and wrought-iron stairway. "We can do some water training."

A small kidney-shaped pool sat within a chain-link fence in the center of the parking lot. A couple of kids paddled around the greenish water inside inflated plastic rings. When her mother had told her to pack a swimsuit, Karen had imagined a beach from a postcard, or at least a fancy pool, one with cabanas and plush lounge chairs, waiters carrying fruity drinks.

"Why'd you choose this place?" she asked. Her mother opened the door to their room; it was dark and smelled of mildew.

"It's off the beaten track," said her mother. "No one will know we're here."

KAREN FELT SHY when they emerged from their rooms at the same time, her with a scratchy white hotel towel wrapped around her navy one-piece, Nathan in Hawaiian print trunks that rode low on his hips. He was shoeless, even though the concrete was hot, even though he should be protecting his feet. His chest was smooth, but a wispy path of hair traveled down his belly into his waistband. Karen followed him to the stairway and watched the muscles of his back slide beneath his skin as he sprinted down the steps.

As soon as they went through the gate to the pool, Nathan ran and dove into the water, despite all the signs that warned against it. "What do you want us to do?" he asked Deena when he emerged, water dripping down his face. He shook his head like a wet dog. A couple of drops splashed onto Karen's leg. Water beaded on his eyelashes, darkening them, making the blue of his eyes even more intense.

The kids were still churning around in their plastic tubes, their mother reading a gossip magazine in the area's one patch of shade.

"Try some lifts," Deena said from a rubber-strapped chaise. She looked like a movie star in her gold-toned bathing suit with a filmy leopard print cover-up, gold sandals with a little heel. Big sunglasses, big floppy hat that would make Karen look like a farmer but made her mother somehow even more glamorous.

"You'll have to get in first," Nathan told Karen, who stood on the top step in the shallow end, letting her ankles get used to the surprisingly cold water.

Karen tentatively stepped down to the next concrete landing. Her calves adjusted to the temperature, but the line where her skin transitioned from water to air was freezing. She knew the line from hips to belly would be especially hard to cross. The line from ribs to breasts would be even worse. She took a deep breath and stepped down to mid-thigh.

"Aw, come on," Nathan taunted. "You can do better than that." He dove underwater like a dolphin and swam under the kicking legs of the kids; his head emerged in front of the steps, gleaming, as he crouched in the shallow end.

"I like to take my time," said Karen.

"So do I." Nathan winked, and even though Karen wasn't ex-actly sure what that meant, she had to hold on to the metal rail to catch her bearings.

"Sometimes, though," he said, "you need to just dive in and get it over with."

He splashed Karen's belly. She bent over at the shock of cold. He splashed some more, big handfuls that drenched her shoulders, her hair.

"Stop it," she said.

He stood up, water sheeting down his chest, and wrapped his arms around her—his cold wet body a bracing thrill—then threw himself backwards, carrying her underwater with him.

NATHAN HAD TOUCHED her skin before, but never so much of it. Her legs were always encased in tights, her back covered with mesh. Now their limbs slid against each other underwater, briefly entwining, slick as kelp. Nathan put his hands on her belly and lifted her above the water, the warm air blowing goosebumps across her skin, then tipped backwards and let her tumble on top of him, both of them going under again. They stared at each other for a moment through the greenish water; Nathan smiled and blew bubbles through his nose before they surfaced, their bodies separate now, Karen's nipples embarrassingly hard.

"Quit fooling around," called Deena. "You have training to do."

LIFTS FELT DIFFERENT in the water, harder and easier all at once—an alternation between buoyancy and slog. They tried a few throws, too, the water grabbing onto her legs, dragging her down with its resistance.

"I wish the ice was this easy to fall on," Karen said after Nathan dropped her during a hand-to-hip lift and she had twisted the fall into a dive.

"Ice turns to water when you skate on it." Nathan lifted her again, this time lowering her slowly so her front brushed against his. "Maybe if I skated fast enough, I could turn the rink to water before you land."

"That's the sweetest thing anyone's ever said to me," said Karen, her chest against his ribs. She could feel a hardness in his trunks press against her stomach. It scared her a little, but also made her feel proud, as if she had accomplished something important, something adult. She wished the little boys weren't still in the pool, watching from their plastic rings, their mother's face now poking above her magazine.

"It's true." Nathan laughed, leaning into her. "The blades melt the ice."

She wanted to tell him that she was telling the truth, too.

"You haven't done the lasso axel yet," her mother called from her chaise. Karen couldn't see her expression beneath her large sunglasses, but she could tell Deena was irked. She grabbed onto Nathan's hands underwater and he hoisted her away from him, toward the sun.

IZZY

IN MY DREAM, I TOOK A PEAR AND CLEAVED IT IN TWO with my hands—it came apart easily, cleanly, no rough edges or spilled juice. The center was filled with dark round seeds, like a papaya, not like the typical two or four inside a pear; the scent of pear wafted out clear as day. I handed half to Quinn. She plucked a seed out with her thumb and forefinger, the way she used to lift Cheerios from high-chair trays in diners across the country, and put the dark pearl in her mouth.

"It's sour," she said, and I felt a jolt of fear. Apple seeds are full of arsenic; apples and pears are cousins, if not sisters. Pear seeds are probably packed with poison, too.

"Spit it out," I barked, but it was too late; she had already swallowed it whole.

I WOKE WITH a start, and watched Quinn breathe—the sweetest sight in the world—until the dream lost its hold. I microwaved a cup of Earl Grey and brought it onto the deck to try to enjoy the sunrise. I loved how the water lapped against the boat in the morning, a gentle easing into the day. Birdsong rippled through the air. A light breeze played upon my skin, made me feel a bit more awake, a bit less freaked out. No sign of the whales, but it made me glad to know they were out there, somewhere, big and silent and peaceful. Next time they came back, we would really connect. Next time, they'd be able to tell me something I needed to know.

I set my mug down on the life preserver box, stood and stretched my arms over my head, darts of tightness shooting down my back. I found myself slipping into an old warm-up routine to loosen my muscles, starting with isolations in my neck, shoulders, rib cage, hips, moving into a simple rolling up and down of the spine, side stretches, lunges. It had been years, but my body remembered the whole sequence as if it had been only days. I put my foot up on the railing and bent sideways over my leg, one arm in the air, stretching out my poor neglected hamstrings.

Quinn wandered onto the deck, her hair pillow-frizzed. "I didn't know you could bend like that," she said.

"This is nothing," I told her, so happy to see her alive and whole, unpoisoned. "I used to be a pretzel."

"I used to be a cupcake." Her smile was soft with sleep.

I didn't often let myself think of what I used to be able to do; I felt a sudden wave of loss for my old flexibility, for how easily I could lift my leg over my head or drop down into a split. I took my leg down, put my other foot onto the railing, told myself I could get at least some of it back.

Quinn propped her leg on the life preserver box and bent over it like me. We stretched together for a while, which quickly slipped into dancing together across the deck, copying each other's arm swoops and spins and waltzes. Out of the corner of my eye, I could see our reflections glimmering in the water, moving in tandem across the slough like the mother and baby whale.

THE STRETCHING HELPED. I felt faster, stronger than I had before when I practiced picking over my lunch break. My body felt more integrated—foot and thigh, belly, shoulder and hand, all working together. It wouldn't be long, I hoped, before I could join the rest of the team. Show them how fast a woman could pick.

I thought I had been so stealthy in my practice, but Jorge walked toward us as if he had known where we were all along, carrying the largest pear I had ever seen. He held it out to me on both hands, like some sort of offering.

"I don't need it." I shook my head. My pear bag was almost full.

He nodded and pushed it closer to me. I took a step back. I could smell several days of sweat on his clothes.

"For the contest, Eema," Quinn said excitedly. "The Pear Fair."

He gestured to ask if he could give Quinn the pear. I shrugged, and he set it in her waiting hands. It was larger than her head when she was born.

"Thank you," she said.

"Yes, thanks." I still hadn't completely forgiven him for the sticker incident, but I figured I could at least try to follow my daughter's manners.

Jorge gave a sheepish smile and a little bow, then ambled off, walking as if he had a sore hip.

"We're going to win for sure!" Quinn said, and ran to show Mr. Vieira.

Mr. Vieira stopped pruning for a moment and studied the giant pear as if it were a rare jewel. "This is a beauty," he said. "Put it in cold storage, in its own basket so it don't end up with the other fruit."

Quinn ran off with the pear cupped carefully in her hands.

"The Pear Fair's not going to be the same this year." Mr. Vieira lobbed off a dead branch, let it crash to the ground. "Not much to celebrate, half our crop going to rot."

"How are your neighbors doing?" I asked.

"Don't know, don't want to know."

I wasn't sure I believed him, but he snapped his pruning shears shut and that was the end of our conversation.

BEFORE OUR BREAK was over, Quinn convinced me to walk across the bridge to Roberts's farm. She said she felt like a spy; I felt more like a traitor.

"You're Vieira's girl, aren't you?" Roberts strolled toward us as we came up the gravel driveway. He had replaced the clapboard on his two-story farmhouse with aluminum siding; it made the house look like an impersonator of itself. The air felt different on his side of the slough; maybe it was the pesticides in the air. My throat started to burn.

"My daughter wanted to see the robot," I said.

"You've come to the right place, then." His face beamed so brightly, my heart softened a touch.

He led us back to the orchard. A few workers, a couple of whom I recognized, were up on ladders, busy picking. So he still needed some human hands, after all. The trees were still full of fruit—it looked like he was having trouble getting enough pears picked in time, too.

"My pride and joy," he said, pointing toward a tractor. "They're not even on the market yet—I'm a test case."

"That's not a robot," said Quinn.

"The robot's in front." He led us to a contraption sitting on a platform attached to the nose of the tractor. Quinn looked disappointed; she must have been expecting something from a sci-fi movie—a person-shaped machine with electronic eyes, arms like air-conditioning ducts, a tinny voice that said things like "At your service" in a vaguely British accent. This just looked like a tall red desk lamp. It even had what looked like a small white shade, be it an upside-down one, fanning out at the top—more, perhaps, like the collar on a postsurgical dog.

Roberts pushed a couple of keys on the computer mounted on the platform; the machine whirred as it rose and lowered from its hinges, the white cone swiveling like a head.

"The robot's reading the tree now," he said.

"Like a book?" Quinn was excited again.

"More like the sight on a gun," he said.

I flashed on an image of Roberts and Mr. Vieira, pointing rifles at each other.

"How does the robot know where the fruit is?" Quinn asked.

"Difference in temperature." He turned the monitor so we could see it. The pears glowed like red upside-down lightbulbs. "It can pick a fruit every eight seconds."

"People are much faster than that," I said. Even *I* was faster than that.

He pushed another few keys, and the top of the machine sucked a pear into it like a vacuum, filling the monitor with red. The camera must have been inside the cone. It turned its head down and dumped the fruit into a plastic crate. I could see bruises all over its skin.

"Robots will revolutionize the fruit industry," said Roberts.

"If you want a bunch of banged-up pears," I said.

"*Hasta la vista,* illegals!" Roberts said, as if he didn't hear me. "Too bad Vieira can't afford one."

"Speaking of whom," I said. "We should get going. I need to get back to work."

He rubbed his hands on his ironed jeans. "Vieira pay you enough over there?"

"I do all right." I found myself wondering if Roberts would offer me more money, wondering if I would consider taking it.

" 'Cause I could use some help around here," he said, rocking on his heels. "The house could use a lady's touch. Hell, *I* could use a lady's touch."

The way he tilted his hips forward made the hair on my arms squirm.

"I hear they have robots for that." I grabbed Quinn's hand and we headed for the bridge, headed back to the low-tech peace of Comice Island.

WE SAT ON the porch of the distillery that afternoon, putting the finished bottles into their individual cardstock boxes, slapping on the pale green labels. I felt self-conscious looking out at the picking crew, a white woman sitting in the shade, doing easy work, while the brown men climbed ladders, strained backs, dug arms through punishing branches. Felt dirty, disloyal, for having gone over to Roberts's place, for having entertained a job offer from him, even for a fraction of a second. I thought of all we could lose: the houseboat, Mrs. Vieira's pear jelly, the place where Quinn had felt more at home than anyplace else I could remember. Not to mention Ben. Not that he was around. Not that I had ever had him to begin with.

Quinn smoothed a label, a bit cockeyed, onto a box. What would a yuppie who paid eighty a bottle think if he knew a nine-year-old girl with dirt under her fingernails had packaged his eau-de-vie?

"I'm going to go pick," I told Mrs. Vieira. "You need me there more than here."

She nodded and peeled the back off a label. A mosquito flew onto it and got snagged, like flypaper.

"I'll stay here, Eema," said Quinn, "if that's all right."

I looked at Mrs. Vieira. She nodded as she picked the mosquito off; it left a speck of blood—maybe her own—on the sticky backing. She pressed the label, blood and all, onto the waiting box.

THE PICKERS DIDN'T look thrilled when I joined their crew, strapping a bag over my chest, cracking open a ladder, but they didn't complain, either. I even noticed a few looks of surprise, a few grudging nods of respect, when they saw how fast I could move my hands through the trees. We fell into a silent but companionable rhythm—climbing, picking, dumping fruit into bins, the foreman occasionally calling out to speed us along.

When the workday was over, one man came up to me, shook my hand with his rough palm, and said, "Not bad, *guera*." It sounded like *wayda*. The two syllables gave me a start at first, but I was grateful for the compliment.

Mr. Vieira walked toward us, looking very serious, Quinn tagging behind him.

"The ice people are coming." Mr. Vieira pointed his finger, seemingly at me, and my heart froze in my chest.

"Like the ice giants?" Terror flashed over Quinn's face.

"I-C-E," he said. "Immigration and Customs Enforcement."

I saw the relief in Quinn's eyes; momentary relief flooded my own body, but the workers around me started to bristle.

"We need your paperwork," Mr. Vieira said. "ID and social at the very least. Birth certificate, passport, whatever you have."

"We already showed our paperwork," said Carlos, an older, sharp-featured man from Jalisco, who translated Mr. Vieira's words for the rest of the group. "You have our paperwork on file. From the broker."

"ICE needs to see it again," said Mr. Vieira. "Make sure everything matches up."

Tension rippled through the group; I could feel it creep back into my own limbs.

"Why you lookin' so worried, *guera*?" said Carlos. I guess that had become my new nickname. White girl. "You're homegrown. You're golden."

I couldn't bring myself to speak.

"It don't just hurt you," Mr. Vieira told us. "You have fake papers, I get fined. Your ID don't match your social, I get fined."

"And we get deported," said Carlos before speaking in Spanish to the rest of the group. A few of the men started to complain loudly. One threw his hat at a tree, knocking a couple of pears down.

Quinn looked up at me, full of confusion. I rubbed her dark hair to try to reassure her.

"I don't want to lose none of you," said Mr. Vieira. "I can't afford to lose none of you. But if your papers don't add up, you should do us both a favor and vamoose."

Carlos looked at him, uncertain how to translate.

"Leave," said Mr. Vieira. "Get out of here. Find another job."

"Do we have to go?" Quinn whispered, leaning against my side, as Spanish ricocheted around us.

"I don't think so," I said. "At least I hope not."

"The ice giants were banished by Odin, remember?" whispered Quinn. "They had to go somewhere like Antarctica. Someplace even the gods couldn't go."

THAT NIGHT, I pulled my paperwork out from the envelope in my glove compartment. Everything looked good. Nice official Social Security card. Stamped, notarized birth certificate. No one should want to dig any deeper. No one should be able to tell I was born hundreds of miles from the town neatly typed on the page.

KAREN

THE POOL WATER TURNED HER HAIR A PALE GREEN. Karen kind of liked it—it made her feel like some sort of mythological creature—but Deena freaked out. "It will clash with your red dress," she said. "Thank goodness I brought an extra bottle of bleach."

The scent made her eyes sting, but Karen enjoyed her mother dyeing her hair, fingers raking expertly across her scalp. It reminded her of when she was younger, and Deena did her makeup for her before a competition or skating show; it always felt like a sacred anointment, a blessing. As difficult as she could be as a coach, Deena's hands were so tender when they smoothed the foundation over Karen's forehead, when she kissed Karen's lips with a Revlon tube. Karen loved the concentration on her mother's face as she defined her cheekbones; it wasn't the same tense concentration as when she stared at Karen from the stands or the penalty box. Karen could barely stand to look at her mother's face then. But when she applied makeup, her face was soft, open. Karen could tell her mom liked the feel of her skin beneath her fingertips. And Karen loved the smell of makeup, even the taste of it when she bit down on her greasy red lips. It was a little whiff of being a woman.

Karen taught herself to do her own makeup when she was fourteen—Deena didn't trust her at first, especially with the eyeliner, but Karen had a steady hand, and Deena eventually relinquished her job. Karen wasn't prepared for how much she missed her mother's fingertips, but she was too stubborn to let her know, and she knew Deena was too proud to say anything first.

BY THE TIME they had to leave for their practice session, Karen was back to her usual platinum brass. She wished Nathan had been able to get a good look at her green hair, but he was holed up in his own room, getting ready. Maybe, hopefully, thinking of her.

She wanted to hug him, to feel the same wet closeness, when they met again on the landing outside their rooms, but his track-suit—blue with white stripes down the side, matching her own—somehow felt like a barrier. He might as well have been wearing armor.

Karen tried not to worry about how distant he felt as she sat in the back seat on their way to the rink, Nathan in the front with her mom. She tried to remind herself how she loved competitions away from home. She loved being able to look out the window of the rental car of the moment and see new trees, new storefronts, new faces. She usually didn't get to explore the new place much, but it was enough to know it existed, that people lived lives there that didn't have anything to do with skating, didn't have anything to do with her.

She wondered what she would do with her day if she didn't have to skate. She had looked longingly at all the glossy tourist brochures in the tiny hotel lobby—places where you could pet alligators, places where you could see wax movie stars, pick real oranges. She had brought a handful up to her room and unfolded them like treasure maps on her bed after her mom had passed out. But maybe if she had a whole day, she'd just want to go to the ocean and watch the waves; better yet, she'd bring a book with her and disappear into its pages. She couldn't imagine anything better. Unless Nathan was lying on a towel beside her.

Nathan's dark hair flared through the hole in the headrest before her, as if straining toward her hands. When she brushed it with her fingertips, though, he flinched and leaned forward. *He didn't know it was me,* she told herself. *He must have thought it was the wind sending chills down his neck.*

AS MUCH AS she loved new towns, new rinks made Karen nervous. What was the consistency of the ice? Would there be any rough patches, any divots? Would her blades feel happy on the surface? Would the dimensions of the rink be the same so they wouldn't crash into the boards or get swallowed up by too much open space? Would they be able to hear their music over the sound system?

Every ice rink smelled different and the same at the same time. There was the comforting scent of the cold, sweet, and almost chemical, like chlorine; there was the rubber flooring that gave off a whiff of gymnasium, or maybe preschool; there were the varying scents from the snack bar—coffee and frozen pretzels, sometimes popcorn, sometimes hot dogs. This particular rink smelled like Gatorade or Mountain Dew, as if someone had painted the walls with a vaguely medicinal, fluorescent yellow drink.

Skaters in workout clothes milled through the lobby while coaches signed registration forms. Karen stood to the side as Nathan wove through the crowd, giving too-long hugs and kisses everywhere he turned.

"Hey." A short freckled girl around her age, wearing a bright red tracksuit, walked up to Karen. "I saw you barf on TV."

"Oh my God, that was on TV?" Karen felt her face grow hot.

"It was awesome," the girl said, twisting her long black hair into a knot. "You're my hero."

Karen blushed more deeply.

"Isabelle." The girl extended her hand. Karen could feel Isabelle's bones shift inside when she shook it. "I'm from New Hampshire, skating with my cousin. First year in Seniors. We're not going to win, but it's just fun to be here, yadda yadda yadda. And we get to go to Disney World tomorrow. Wanna come?" Isabelle asked, snapping her gum.

"I don't think my mom would let me," Karen said, heart racing. It had been a long time since another skater had wanted to spend time with her, had wanted to talk to her about anything other than Nathan.

"You're in Florida!" Isabelle flung her arms out and Karen could see her Pilates training; the spontaneous, reckless gesture came from the very center of the girl's body. "That's what you do when you're in Florida! You go on the teacup ride. You go to Never Never Land."

You go from rink to hotel room and back again. You train every single possible second.

"Then I'll kidnap you," the girl said, unfazed. "No one should miss the Happiest Place on Earth."

Karen looked over at Nathan and caught him looking back at her. If she didn't know better, she thought she could almost see some jealousy in his eyes. *I'm allowed to have friends, too,* she told herself, and turned back to Isabelle. She could still feel his eyes on the back of her head; she shook her hair to show him how much fun she was having without him.

"SO WHO'S YOUR little girlfriend?" Nathan asked as they stroked around the rink. His grip seemed especially tight.

"Just a skater," she said. "Just Isabelle."

"You like her better than you like me?"

Karen thought he was joking at first, but his jaw was clenched.

"It's different," she said. Isabelle and her cousin were laughing across the rink, doing some sort of goofy footwork that probably wasn't even in their program. Karen did a three turn and inhaled sharply, waiting for Nathan's palm to jam itself into her solar plexus, push her toward the roof.

NATHAN SEEMED ESPECIALLY charged up during the short program; there was an intensity in his eyes, in his hips, that almost scared her. Karen could barely look at him as she skated; she had to force herself to keep her own movements strong. The audience ate it up, though. And they seemed to like her, too. People in the stands threw flowers and stuffed animals tucked inside barf bags with her name written across the waxy paper. Karen was embarrassed at first—she could barely look up and wave to the crowd—but Isabelle ran over and helped her pick up the presents.

"How cool is that?" she asked, waving a penguin in Karen's face. "No one else gets their loot in barf bags. You, my friend, have arrived."

The fact that Isabelle called her "friend" was more exciting than any thought of arrival.

Nathan shot Isabelle a look, then grabbed Karen's arm and pulled her over to the kiss-and-cry.

THEY ENDED UP in fourth after the short program, and that was by a hair. Isabelle and her cousin were second to last; Karen wondered if they'd regret their Disney trip, but they didn't seem bothered in the least. Isabelle, in fact, was thrilled by the fact that she had received a couple of flowers, even though they looked ripped from larger bouquets meant for other people.

Deena scooped all the gifts into a couple of large Saks Fifth

Avenue shopping bags that still smelled of the cosmetics department.

"You'll need to step it up in the free skate," she said. "Fourth
won't get you into Nationals."

"Only I can get us into Nationals," Nathan said to Karen.
"Don't you forget it."

KAREN FUMED ON the way back to the hotel. She wanted to
kick Nathan's seat until he yelped, pull his hair until tears sprung
into his eyes. He was unusually silent as they drove past palm
trees and bright pink storefronts and women showing their
shoulders to the sun. Deena was quiet, too. Karen knew they
were both mad at her, for whatever reason. For finding a friend.
For not getting them into first place right off the bat.

The humidity made Karen's body feel twice its usual weight
when they got out of the car. She was ready to slog through the
heat up to her room, bury herself in a book for a couple of minutes before it was time for more Pilates practice, when Nathan
grabbed her arm.

"What?" She whipped around to face him. The dense air jiggled, nearly viscous, against her skin.

"I'm sorry for before," he said. "If I was a jerk." He corrected
himself. "*When* I was a jerk."

Something inside Karen unknotted, but she tried not to let it
show on her face.

"This is a big deal, this competition," he said.

Karen was about to say "I know," but he kept talking.

"I know I shouldn't take my stress out on you," he said, "but
my dad is in the hospital, and I let myself get all wound up . . ."

Karen hadn't thought about Nathan having parents before,
especially not sick ones. He hadn't said a word about them; as far
as she knew, they had never been to any of his competitions. She
couldn't imagine him as a baby, a boy. He seemed like someone
who had always been twenty-three. Who would always be

twenty-three. Who had sprouted fully formed, clad in spandex, from the center of a rink. It was strange to imagine an older version of Nathan out there somewhere, a compromised version, his head pressed against a scratchy hospital pillow. Strange to think that somewhere she had a father, too. At least someone who had donated sperm; she was a turkey baster baby, her mother had told her, bred to be a skater. From championship stock, just like a show dog. She might as well have sprung from the ice, herself.

"It's okay." She was pleased to see his face soften, his breath release. And even though she didn't, not really, she said, "I think I understand."

THEIR FREE SKATE felt different this time. More emotional. When Nathan, as Tristan, died at the end, a wave of real grief crashed over Karen. She had never seen Nathan as vulnerable before, as mortal, even in all their months of fake dying. Now, seeing his eyes closed, his body quiet against the ice, she knew, knew in her bones, that someday he would not be in the world; even with his occasional jerkiness, this seemed a fact too horrible to bear. As she died in his arms as Isolde, she had to swallow down the urge to sob. A few tears escaped anyway, trailed into her ear, dripped against Nathan's face.

"I see I got you wet," he whispered as they stood and bowed to thunderous applause, and even though it was kind of a gross thing to say, it was a Nathan thing to say. She put one arm around him and squeezed tight as she waved to the audience, happy to feel his heart thumping against her shoulder.

"THAT WAS AMAZING." Isabelle ran up to them as they walked to the kiss-and-cry, still wrapped around each other. "Total goosebumps." She held out her arm to show them her pale stippled flesh.

"Thanks." Karen tried to keep her voice calm, crisp; she

didn't want to upset Nathan by seeming too excited to see Isabelle.

"Do you want to go check out Kennedy Space Center with us?" asked Isabelle. "It's just a couple of hours away."

Karen could feel Nathan's body stiffen. "I better not," she said. "We have training to do."

"What training?" laughed Isabelle. "You just finished competing! You should let yourself have some fun."

"We're going to Nationals," Karen said, even though they hadn't received their scores yet. "But that's something you wouldn't know anything about, now, is it?"

Isabelle looked as if Karen had just slapped her in the face, but Nathan pulled her closer, so for a moment, it felt like a decent trade-off.

"Fine," said Isabelle. "Have fun with the asshole."

Karen wanted to chase after her, to say *Wait,* to say *Nathan's not so bad,* to say yes, she actually did want to go the Kennedy Space Center with them, but Nathan kissed the top of her head and it felt like an air gun, like something nailing her into place.

IZZY

FROM THE PIER THE NEXT MORNING, I COULD SEE A TENT set up in the field, not too far from our car. The dark green dome looked like a giant brussels sprout rising from the earth. I didn't want to go past it and whoever was potentially staking us out inside, but there was no other way to get to the car, get to work.

"Let's tiptoe," I told Quinn. "They might be sleeping."

She grabbed my hand and we crept forward like cartoon spies, Quinn stifling giggles.

The tent door unzipped with a loud metal whine when we neared the car; we both jumped back, my heart pounding wildly. I was relieved when a sleepy-eyed woman with blond dreadlocks emerged, sunburn across her freckled chest. She was probably around thirty-five, maybe a bit older. No camera or gun, as far as I could tell. Her breasts hung low beneath her tank top. Her Indian print wrap skirt was coming undone; there was a large gap at the slit. I tried not to look at the slice of pubic hair it revealed next to her sturdy thigh.

"So this is the women's camp." She walked over to introduce herself. Her accent was thick, Australian, and I couldn't quite make out her name. It sounded like *Absadee.* Her handshake was firm and enthusiastic.

"Absadee, like rhapsody?" asked Quinn, clearly entranced.

"You could say that." She smiled and shook Quinn's hand. Quinn winced at the hard squeeze. "Are you a poet?"

"No." Quinn looked embarrassed, as if the woman had asked if she picked her nose.

"You have the vocab," she said.

It's because of me, I wanted to say as Quinn beamed; *I bought her all those books.*

"I'm a poet myself," the woman said with pride. "Abecedarian."

"ABC what?" I was glad Quinn asked. I had never heard the word in my life.

"All my poems follow the alphabet. Just like my name—A-B-C-D-E."

"That's how you spell your name?" Quinn's mouth was wide open. Abcde nodded.

"I bet your teachers were confused," I said.

"Nah," she said. "I was Abbie back then. Changed it to Abcde when I started publishing."

"I'm Izzy," I said. "This is Quinn."

"*Z* and *Q,* great letters," she said. "Ten points each in Scrabble."

"Except you can't use proper names," said Quinn.

"True," said Abcde.

"And there's only one *Z,*" Quinn said.

"We'll have to play sometime," said Abcde. "I can tell you're a worthy opponent."

I suddenly felt possessive of our boat, our game, a travel set with tiny magnetic letters. "Our board is missing a few tiles," I said.

"Just makes it more of a challenge." Abcde shrugged. "A lipogram."

A lipogram sounded like a medical procedure, or an envelope filled with globs of fat, but before I could ask what it really was, Quinn asked if she could touch Abcde's hair. I tried not to feel jealous as Abcde bent down and Quinn reached out to pet the thick woolly ropes.

"Are you from Australia?" Quinn asked when she took her hand away.

"Perth," said Abcde, stretching back up.

"What brings you here?" I asked, wanting to break the smile between them.

"A beautiful California." Abcde swept her arms out to take in the pear trees and the river and the heat of the day. The hair in her armpits was almost as thick as the hair on her head.

"ABC," Quinn said with a grin.

"Exactly." Abcde winked. "Actually, I'm teaching at the Squaw Valley Community of Writers later this month." She slid her ribs from side to side, like isolations at the beginning of a dance class. "I flew in early to explore the Golden State."

"How'd you end up here?" I gestured to her tent.

"I heard about the Delta and had to check it out," she said. "Delta is the letter D, you know."

"In Greek," said Quinn.

"Exactly." Abcde smiled. "Couldn't pass up an alphabetical place."

"Alpha, beta, gamma, delta . . ." Quinn rattled off.

"*D* was actually a hieroglyph before it was a delta," said Abcde, and Quinn looked so eager for the knowledge, it made me want to weep. "A pictogram for a door, or perhaps a fish."

"The letter *D* does kind of look like a fish," said Quinn, rapt. I shot her a look to make sure she wouldn't say anything about the whales.

"Anyway," said Abcde, seeming to suddenly remember I was there, "I just stumbled upon the farm last night. They said I could set my tent back here—other women around and all." She winked at Quinn.

"How long are you planning to stay?" I asked. Not long, I hoped.

"Don't know," she said. "Thought I might hang around a couple of days. Heard they need some help picking pears."

"It's hard work." Her arms looked too soft for picking. She'd be full of scratches within five minutes.

"I'm up for it," she said. "A poet's got to use her body every once in a while."

Her muscles would be screaming within half an hour. Less.

"Besides," she said, "it's good to be in the dirt. Most of America is a bit clean for my taste."

"A Bit Clean." Quinn was grinning. This had become a game for her.

"Automatic soap dispensers at the airport, even. That white spurt—it's like some stranger ejaculating in your hands."

"Ew," said Quinn. I hoped she had no idea what that really meant.

"Ew, indeed," said Abcde. "Cleanliness is not next to godliness, as far as I'm concerned. Dirt is where life comes from— what could be more divine than that?" She pinched some soil from the ground and rubbed it over her heart; specks of it tumbled down the front of her shirt.

"A Bit Crazy," I whispered to Quinn, who tried not to laugh.

I SURREPTITIOUSLY CHECKED Abcde's nails as we walked over to some trees at the edge of the orchard. They were short, boxy—bitten, maybe. That was good. Long nails could break right through the skin of a pear. Another reason there aren't many women pickers, Mr. Vieira had told me.

I had always kept my nails short, but they used to be polished, usually a clear opalescent sheen, each nail a gleaming oval, like its own tiny ice rink. My hands used to be smooth as pears, carefully manicured, kept in soft gloves at night, slathered with lotions. Now they were callused and scratched and caked with dirt, and I loved them because they did work that mattered.

"I should give you some pointers before you start picking," I told Abcde, glad to have a chance to boss her around a little.

It actually felt nice to be in the role of the teacher, to tell her about lifting, not pulling, about limb rub, about sunburn, about what size pear to pick, what to leave on the tree; I was glad to know I had gained some useful skills in my short time there, ones I could pass down to others, especially others who seemed to think they knew it all already. We practiced on a tree at the edge of the orchard. She was a willing but sloppy student, her face determined, but her hands tender, easily tired. "Arms be courageous," she said to herself under her breath. "Don't endanger fruit."

I WAS WORRIED—and, to be honest, a little hopeful—that the other pickers would tear Abcde to pieces. They had accepted me reluctantly, and that was only over time, as my picking improved. She moved through the branches slowly, ploddingly. Plus there was the whole ABC thing. But for some reason, the other pickers were happy to welcome her to the team. Maybe because she spoke Spanish. Maybe because she didn't wear a bra. Maybe because a few more pickers had left in the wake of the ICE paperwork, and everyone knew the more pears picked, the better, even if it was by a weirdo Australian poetess. I'm sure it also helped that she wasn't getting paid.

"You should probably stay off the ladder," I told Abcde as we joined the crew in the field. "Your center of gravity is low."

"Goddess hips," she said, nodding. She stared up at the tree and took a deep breath, steeling herself for the work.

I cranked my ladder open. I was glad to climb up it, to be able to look down upon her fuzzy, befuddled head. Everything always felt more manageable from high up in the air.

ABCDE SURVIVED THE morning shift a little worse for wear—
some of the scratches on her arms looked fierce and swollen and
she was clearly exhausted—but to her credit, she didn't complain. When lunchtime came around, Quinn and I went off for our
own picnic, as usual, but Abcde chose to stay and eat with the
other workers.

I spied on them later, after I left one of the porta-potties in
the middle of the orchard. From behind a tree, I could see Abcde
sitting on the ground with the pickers and sorters. They were
heating flour tortillas over a small fire they had made with old
pear branches between two rows of trees. Blisters and brown
spots broke out over the pale discs like some sort of disease, but
the toasty scent made my mouth wet. Everyone was laughing and
speaking in Spanish, including Abcde, as they spooned beans
from a plastic container onto the tortillas, drizzled on salsa from
another container. I hid behind a tree and watched. I wished I understood more Spanish; I was familiar with a few words like *án-
dale* and *más*—"faster," "more"—words I heard every day in the
orchards, but I never would have been able to join a conversation
like Abcde. Her Australian accent made Spanish sound like a new
language entirely, but everyone seemed to be able to understand
her. I wondered if she spoke alphabetically in more than one language.

The Vieiras weren't around the fire, but when they spoke
Spanish, it sounded different, too. The Portuguese pronunciation
was more nasal, their vowels longer; a few of their words were
different. When they were with the workers, though, everyone
still understood each other. Even the ones who spoke Mixtec,
Mayan, Zapotec at home. Quinn and I were the odd men out as
far as Spanish was concerned.

"Hey, what are you doing back there?" yelled Abcde. I hadn't
done as good a job of camouflaging myself as I had hoped.

A couple of sorter women yelled and gestured for me to join
them. Most of the men glanced over at me, then looked away.

"No, it's okay," I said with a wave, and went back to join Quinn and our lunch of cheese and crackers and pear preserves.

"DO YOU WANT to hear one of my poems?" Abcde asked later, after we were back to picking.

"Sure," I said, even though I didn't, not really.

"I have one about fruit," she said. "That would be most appropriate, given the setting." She stood still for a moment, took a deep breath, then recited the poem from memory:

"Apple brownbetty cures depression.
Eat fruit generously; hunger is just
kindling, lurking minutes north
of pleasure. Quit rationing;
start tasting unlimited varieties,
wanting x-tasy, yumminess, zest."

My mouth watered in spite of itself.

"Do you have more?" asked Quinn, who was sitting beneath the tree doing word problems.

"Hundreds," said Abcde.

I started picking faster; it was clear she wasn't going to start working again anytime soon.

"Can I hear another one?" Quinn stood, as if to hear the poetry more clearly.

"Coming up." Abcde took another deep breath and intoned:

"All bodies create desire.
Especially fleshy girls
have instant juju. Kissed
lips may not obey propriety;
quiet rustlings spawn
tempestuous undulations,

vault wild x-tasy,
yawning zippers."

"That one?" I glared at her. "Not so appropriate."

"You used 'x-tasy' twice," said Quinn, unfazed.

"More times than that." Abcde winked at me and I felt a little sick. "*X* is a big challenge—there's only so much you can do with it."

"Xylophone," said Quinn. "Xerxes."

"Not always easy to fit those in a poem." She was smiling.

"A Big Challenge," Quinn said.

"You better get back to work," I said to both of them. The foreman was walking toward us. Rather than chew Abcde out for not picking, though, he said something in Spanish that made her laugh, and she said something that made him laugh in return. He patted her on the shoulder and she started to gather pears again in her awkward, plodding way.

"YOU WOULDN'T BELIEVE the stories these guys have," said Abcde after the foreman was out of sight. "What they have to go through just to get here."

"I want to know," said Quinn, and Abcde began to give us the litany, thankfully not in alphabetical order.

Jorge had five children. He made enough during the harvest to live comfortably with his family the rest of the year in Guatemala. Back home, he was a carpenter and musician, but he couldn't find enough work to make ends meet.

Hector came from Michoacán to look for his father, who had left to find work over the border and disappeared. He never found his father but he did find plenty of work. He hoped to bring his mother and sister up soon.

Tomas carved birds out of fallen pear wood. He sent them back to his family in El Salvador, who sold them to tourists at marketplaces.

Vincent had a wife in Jalisco but also had two children with Estrella, one of the sorters.

Several of the sorters were from the Delta area, daughters of former pickers. Most of the men had come from somewhere else; a few of the women had, too.

Gertrudis's husband was ill with pancreatic cancer; she crossed the border to find work so they could afford his medical bills. She hoped to bring him across for better treatment when he was up to the journey.

Evalina came because her parents had wanted a better future for her, their only child.

They came hidden under onions, under rice, under piles of blankets. They came stuffed into the trunks of cars, packed into the backs of trucks, holding on for dear life atop speeding box-cars. They came through guard dogs and sirens, rivers that rose up to their ribs. They came through desert, through blisters and dehydration and hunger. Some of them had to try two, three, four times, before they made it across the border. Some of them had Social Security cards of those who had come before, who had become legal but had to go back home; some of them had fake cards; some had the cards of dead men and women. Some had worked at farms where there were no porta-potties, no drinking water. Where they were beaten. Some knew people who had died of heatstroke in the fields. Some had worked for farmers who docked so much of their paycheck for food and housing, they had nothing left to send home to their relatives. Some had worked for farmers where no housing was offered, so they slept behind bushes on flattened cardboard boxes. The Vieiras' horse stable was the cushiest place some of them had lived this side of the border. Some were legal but had been detained anyway, sent to a center where no one read them their rights, where they weren't allowed to make any phone calls, where they were let go after two months and no one told them why they were released, why they were even held to begin with.

"We're lucky, aren't we, Eema?" Quinn had abandoned her

word problems in the face of these bigger, more human problems. If a train leaves Oaxaca at fifty miles an hour, how many people will still be on top by the time it reaches Nogales?

For all the nights we had to sleep in our car, for all the uncertainty and confusion of our lives, we were a lot luckier than I had let myself realize. "That we are, sweetheart," I said. When I looked at the men a few rows away, picking their hearts out, I felt a wave of admiration, a wave that felt very much like love. I found myself wanting to climb all their ladders, give them all hugs, tell each of them how glad I was they were there.

KAREN

Dᴇᴇɴᴀ ᴛᴏᴏᴋ ᴋᴀʀᴇɴ ᴀɴᴅ ɴᴀᴛʜᴀɴ ᴏᴜᴛ ᴛᴏ ᴅɪɴɴᴇʀ ᴛᴏ celebrate their second-place finish. A supper club that had been around for a while, with curved red leather banquettes and flickering chandeliers and a guy in a tux playing frantic classical music on a shiny black baby grand. She even let Karen order whatever she wanted, although she told the waiter "No, thank you" when he brought over a basket of rolls, insisted on vinegar only on the salad, cut the fat off the edge of Karen's steak, and let her eat only a fraction of her buttery mashed potatoes.

"Here's to Nationals." Deena raised her glass of champagne and clinked Nathan's flute before tapping it against Karen's glass of diet ginger ale. "Hell, here's to the Olympics in a year!"

People at a few tables around them clapped politely. Deena beamed in her black strapless dress like some sort of beauty queen. She had given Karen a new dress for the occasion, too—a sundress, smocked at the top, yellow with tiny little flowers, like something a five-year-old would wear. Karen tried to put the competition smile back on her face.

"I have a proposal, Mr. Main," said Deena after everyone around them had turned back to their own conversations. "I think you should move in with us." She swatted Nathan's leg with a napkin.

Karen couldn't imagine Nathan living across the hall. The thought made the mashed potatoes rise up in her throat.

"You won't have to worry about rent," said Deena. "And it will be easier for the two of you to train." Deena was just about done turning the garage into a Pilates/dance studio, complete with mirrored walls, a ballet barre, and a harness for practicing jumps. It made Karen feel a little claustrophobic to think that she could do everything but skate without leaving her house. And her mom had even been looking into artificial rink surfaces for the backyard.

"We could train all night long." Nathan met Karen's eyes, but she quickly looked away, blushing.

"Now, now." Deena swatted Nathan's leg again, this time with her hand. Karen was dismayed to see her mom's breasts jiggle in reverberation, even more dismayed to see how much Nathan seemed to enjoy the sight. Karen's own breasts were pressed even flatter than normal by her dress; the smocking dug uncomfortably into her nipples, already chafed from the adhesive.

"This is what we've been working toward, sweetheart." Deena cupped Karen's face with her hands and Karen felt a sudden, unexpected rush of love for her mother.

"Thank God you didn't find a way to screw it up," said Nathan. Karen slumped back against the booth as Deena and Nathan clinked champagne flutes once again.

THE HOUSE FELT different with Nathan in it. His male scent seeped into the furniture, sent its musky pheromones into the air.

Karen found herself wishing they had a cooler house—something sleek and modern, full of sharp edges. Not a stodgy

Cape Cod with pleated lampshades, etchings of hunt scenes and carriage rides, her great-grandmother's dishes displayed in the china cabinet. The guest room with its chenille bedspread and fleur-de-lis wallpaper didn't feel like the right place to keep Nathan. He should have a leather headboard, dark walls, recessed lighting. He should have satin pillowcases, strange metal sculptures, a bear skin on the floor. Still, she liked to poke her head into the room when he was downstairs to see his clothes shucked all over the rag rug, breathe in his mix of sweat and cologne and hair gel.

She found herself keeping her own bedroom door closed, only coming out if she was fully made up, wearing something other than ratty pajamas. She chewed breath mints before going out to brush her teeth in case they crossed paths in the hallway. She found herself posing when he walked into a room, trying to look studiously, sexily casual when she felt anything but, her leg draped over the arm of a chair as she read *Jane Eyre,* her bottom raised just a little as she lay on the floor, doing math problems. She found herself sitting across the breakfast table from him at 3 a.m., both still groggy over their egg white omelets, and thinking *This is what it would be like if we were married.* Sometimes she wondered if he thought the same thing when his eyes met hers and he winked, when he ruffled her hair as he walked by, when he chose to come home with her after their evening skate session rather than disappear to wherever he disappeared to at night.

Deena seemed more "on" with Nathan around, too, wearing high-heeled slippers with her cashmere robe, touching his shoulder as she walked past him. At least her mom and Nathan seemed to get on each other's nerves. Deena was putting together a new short program for them, a jaunty one to "If My Friends Could See Me Now" from *Sweet Charity,* and she could often hear the two of them arguing over the choreography as she finished up her homework for the night. They were keeping *Tristan und Isolde* as their free skate—"no need to mess with perfection," Deena had said after they received 6.0s at Sectionals—but their synthesized hip shaking had, in Deena's words, grown stale.

"I don't think anyone's buying it," Karen heard Deena say to Nathan. "She doesn't have the right oomph in her hips."

"I'll give her some oomph," said Nathan, and Karen felt a little thrill.

"Hold your horses, lover boy," said Deena. "She's still seventeen, remember?"

"Just for another couple of months," said Nathan, and Karen had to walk in circles around her room to get all the excitement out of her legs. When she heard footsteps on the stairs, she held her breath, wondering if she should open her door, wondering if she should let Nathan know she heard him, wondering if she looked too much like a little kid in her thermal shirt and plaid pajama pants. But by the time she poked her head into the hallway, Nathan's door was already closed.

OUR DAYS STARTED TO HAVE AN EASIER RHYTHM ONCE I knew the other workers' stories.

They must have felt the shift in me. They didn't say anything, but some of them started to offer me bites of their breakfast as we rode out into the orchards on the backs of the trailers—egg burritos and *pan dulce,* toast with peanut butter, pieces of banana, sips of thermos coffee. Sometimes the foreman tossed a box of doughnuts into the back and we jokingly fought over the maple bars. Otherwise, we didn't talk much, but it was a companionable silence. We looked out at the rows of trees as they went by, noticed the different patterns that emerged, the dizzying uniformity of rows that you could look at forwards, sideways, diagonally, the spaces between them regular as gaps on a peg loom, pears blinking everywhere, growing heavier by the day, waiting for our hands.

———

MR. VIEIRA HAD tried to recruit local high school kids to beef up our numbers, but working at McDonald's in Rio Vista was much easier. You have air-conditioning in McDonald's. You don't have to lug hundreds of pounds of fruit.

"Them high school kids will eat our pears," Mr. Vieira had said, "but they won't lift a goddamn finger to get them off the tree."

"I'll pick your pears," Quinn told him, but he just ruffled her hair and told her she'd have to wait a few more years. Still, when she found some decent ones on the ground, she put them in the sorting bin.

THAT EVENING, WE sat on the deck and slapped at mosquitoes as we ate some pear bread topped with slabs of jack cheese and potato chips. My muscles rang like glass bowls with exhaustion, but my mouth enjoyed the mix of sweet and salty, soft and crisp.

"Maybe we could build a gentle robot," said Quinn. "One that could pick pears but not hurt them."

"That would be a cool thing to develop." I peeled a potato chip off the top of the cheese and crunched it alone. "As long as it doesn't replace people, just helps more pears get picked. Maybe that will be your claim to fame, a gentle pear-picking robot."

She looked pleased by that idea. "What's your claim to fame?" she asked, tossing bits of bread to the ducks paddling by.

The question made sweat break out all over my face. I wiped it away and said, simply, "You."

KAREN

That thanksgiving, deena broiled some skinless turkey breasts, sprayed butter-flavored Pam over green beans with slivered almonds, cooked raw cranberries with Sweet'N Low, and smushed some boiled cauliflower to resemble mashed potatoes.

"Couldn't we have some real Thanksgiving food?" Karen pushed the white goop around her plate, stirring up its old-sock smell. It was 4 p.m. but already dark outside, the sky lumpy with rain clouds.

"We can't afford you getting carb bloat so close to Nationals." Deena took a decisive bite of turkey. She was already on her third glass of wine; maybe her fourth.

"Nationals is still two months away," said Karen. "I could work it off in plenty of time."

Deena turned to Nathan. "Karen has a fat face, don't you think?"

"I hadn't thought about it." His mouth was full of cranberries, red and glistening, like entrails.

"As slim as she is," Deena said, "people look at her face and know it wouldn't take much for her to balloon out."

"It's my face, Mom! God!" Karen dropped her fork on her plate. "What do you expect me to do about my face?"

"I thought the nose job would help," Deena said, as if she were talking to herself. "But it only accentuates the problem."

Karen turned her head away from Deena's boozy scrutiny. The rain was hammering against the windows, drops bouncing off the back patio, a mad frenzy. Karen tried to imagine it turning to snow, blanketing everything in pure, quiet white.

"It's probably just baby fat," said Nathan, and tears stung Karen's eyes

"If it was baby fat," said Deena, "it would have been gone by now."

"Well, happy Thanksgiving to you, too." Karen threw down her napkin and stomped up to her room.

WHEN SOMEONE KNOCKED on her door an hour later, Karen assumed it was her mother, attempting an apology. She swung the door open, shouting, "What?"

Nathan jumped back. His sweater sleeves were rolled up, a bit wet at the edges; he must have been helping clean the dishes, unless he had put his hands outside to feel the rain. "Sorry," he said. "I can come back later."

"No, no, it's okay," she said, and he stepped through the doorway.

He had never been inside her room before. She hadn't pictured it like this—her with red puffy eyes, in old sweats, him with low-fat gravy spattered on his chest. When she had pictured it in her mind, they were dressed up like they had just gone to a ball, her hair swept up (which he would let down), pearls wound around her neck (which he would unclasp, his bow tie hanging crooked, like a door on a bad hinge). He was sitting at the foot of her bed, as she had imagined, but she couldn't bring herself to sit next to him. She sat on her desk chair instead, facing him, their knees close to touching.

"Do you want to come visit my dad with me tomorrow?" he asked.

"He's still in the hospital?"

"They moved him to a permanent care facility." He looked down, bunched her pink comforter in his fist.

"I'm sorry," she said, flashing on Nathan as Tristan, dead on the ice.

"His body was bound to give out eventually." He shrugged and yanked the bedspread, making all the stuffed animals on her pillow fall over.

Maybe his dad was an athlete and had trained too hard, she thought. Maybe he was like her mom, someone with a promising career who blew her knees out and had to retire too early.

"Sure, I'll go." She inched her leg forward, let it briefly graze his. A blue bolt of static electricity zipped between their feet.

He stood, his hair rising in places from the shock; she was tempted to rest her head against his stomach, let her hair stick to his sweater. Part of the comforter still poked up where he had grabbed it, like a little tent. The satin edge of her inner blanket was exposed by the headboard; it looked racy, somehow, as if her bed's underwear were showing.

"We should go in the afternoon, after weight training." He walked to the door, chest more puffed out than before.

"Cool." She hoped the word sounded casual, grown-up, coming from her mouth.

"By the way," he said from the hall, "there's nothing wrong with your pretty little face."

When he was out of sight, she toppled onto her bed and breathed in the heat his body had left behind. The rain on the roof sounded like fans stomping their feet on metal bleachers, waiting for their star to return.

IZZY

WE WOKE JUST BEFORE DAWN TO A HORRIBLE CLANG-
ing.

"What is it, Eema?" Quinn clung to me.

"Maybe it's the guy here to clean the septic tank," I said. We
had been in the orchard when he had come before—it was hard
to imagine that would be such a loud job, but I couldn't think of
what else the racket could be. I sat up, hands over my ears, and
looked through the window. A small Coast Guard boat floated
nearby. A few people dangled pipes into the water and banged on
them with metal sticks, like a demented kindergarten music
class.

I stumbled out onto the deck. "What's going on?" I asked.

A woman held up her hand to get everyone to stop their
clanging. "Sorry to wake you," she said. "We're from the Marine
Mammal Institute. We're trying to drive some whales back to
sea."

"We saw them." Quinn appeared next to me, blinking the
sleep from her eyes.

"When?" the woman asked.

"Over a week ago," I said.

"And you didn't report it?" She looked incredulous.

I shook my head.

"You would have been the first," she said. "We received our first sighting yesterday."

I felt a little surge of pride that the whales had waited so long to show themselves to anyone else, but when a man said, "This makes it even more urgent. They need to get back to the salt water, where they can feed," I felt sheepish. I had had a chance to help them, and I hadn't done a thing.

"They can't eat here?" asked Quinn.

"We think the baby is still nursing," said the woman. "A little old for that, but it appears she hasn't weaned. We're worried the mom is getting depleted, though."

The water began to churn. A large black hump, the center spine jutting like a sharply folded napkin, rose out of the water, then slid back under. The people on the boat yelled and started to bang their pipes again. Quinn jumped off the deck onto the pier. Abcde was standing on the levee in a nightgown, no doubt composing a poem in her mind: A big clatter. A baleen congregation. A blistering cacophony. She and I both rushed toward Quinn on the pier. I was pleased that I got there before Abcde climbed down the metal stairs.

"Did I see what I thought I just saw?" Abcde asked, her dark nipples showing through the thin fabric. Her body odor was sharp and yeasty, like a garlic bagel.

"Whales," said Quinn, and I felt as if she had betrayed our secret even though it was no longer a secret at all.

AFTER THE SUN rose, a small inflatable boat puttered up to the pier; a woman with auburn hair jumped out and knocked on the door of the houseboat.

"Mind if I come in?" she asked. She must have used about a 700 SPF sunscreen—her skin was alabaster, her eyes a clear pale green, like sea glass. "You guys have the best seat in the house."

She introduced herself as Sam, a member of the animal care team from the Marine Mammal Institute.

"Is it okay for us to be here?" I asked. I was still in my pajamas, still groggy; she looked wide awake, jazzed, even at that early hour. Somehow she made her blue windbreaker, her khaki pants, her orange life vest, look fashionable, as if she was born to wear them. I wondered what it was like to have that kind of confidence, that kind of ownership of your life.

"I'll have to talk to my supervisor," she said. "But as long as you don't turn on your propeller or do anything to spook the whales, you should be fine. They've had some bad run-ins with propellers already."

She walked out to the deck, leaned over the railing, her hair lifting around her head like fire.

"What are the whales doing here?" I asked.

"No one knows for sure," she said. "Some of my colleagues think it's disorientation from Navy sonar, illness, maybe toxic algae. Others think they followed a school of sardines into the river, maybe tried to go someplace safe to heal their wounds . . ."

"What do you think?" I asked.

"Me?" She turned toward me and grinned. "I think they're on an adventure."

I liked to think of the whales coming here on purpose—exploration, not discombobulation. It meant they knew what they were doing; it meant they could leave whenever they were ready.

SAM CAME TO give us an update later in the day. When she showed up in her little boat, I felt giddy, like a Southern belle receiving a gentleman caller. The banging didn't work, she told us, so the Marine Mammal Institute had started to pipe recordings of whales underwater. I couldn't hear the real whales themselves, but I could hear the tapes, feel them buzzing through the floor of the boat, deep and eerie, like ghosts trapped under the water. The theory was that the sound would attract the whales and they'd follow the boat back to the ocean.

"I've gone diving with humpbacks before," Sam told me. "You can feel the vibration of their song all the way to your bones."

"That must be amazing," I said.

"Oh man," she said. "It's like your whole body turns into an electric toothbrush or something."

Quinn giggled.

"Only males sing, though," said Sam. "We're pretty sure these are females."

"That doesn't seem fair." I wished I could give our whales a voice, help them tell us who they were, what they wanted.

"But the females make pink milk!" she said. "I haven't tried it myself, of course, but I like to think it tastes like Strawberry Quick." She smiled and I remembered all the shirts I had stained yellow when I was nursing Quinn. Work shirts that were hard to wash thoroughly in a bathroom sink. Bras that never fully came clean. I wondered if it would have been better or worse to have pink stains instead of yellow. Then her smile brought me back to the moment, so inviting I wanted to climb inside it and take a nap.

THE RECORDINGS SEEMED to work a bit, at first—the whales trailed the Coast Guard cutter and we lost sight of them for a while, but they quickly circled back to Comice, this time followed by the boat. I was happy to see them return—both the whales and Sam, her hair waving like a flag.

Mrs. Vieira brought trays of snacks out to the rescue workers—dried pears, slices of pear tart, hunks of pear bread. All eagerly consumed. Sam especially seemed to love the tart—I saw

her polish off two and a half wedges of it. I found myself looking
for her almost the way I had looked for Ben—not that I wanted
to throw myself at her, at least not that I could tell; more that I
wanted her as a friend. Quinn had been the only person I had
needed for so long; I felt a bit disloyal that part of me longed to
connect with someone else.

"The recordings aren't going to work," I heard one of the
blue-windbreakered men say, his beard full of crumbs. "The tapes
are Alaskan whales. It's like a person talking in Russian to someone from Jamaica. They're both humans, but they're not going to
understand each other's language."

"Maybe they'll understand poetry," said Abcde. She convinced Sam to ferry her over to the Coast Guard boat, where she
read a motivational whale poem over a megaphone:

"A baleen can do everything faster," she said in an encouraging voice. "Go home. It's just kicking, little motions, nothing ob-
jectionable. Pretty quick results. See, take ur vacation westward.
X-it your zoo."

I hadn't thought of the river as a zoo, but it probably did feel
like a cage of sorts. The whales were so used to so much space
around them; they probably didn't realize how big they were
until they were hemmed in by the levees, large blood cells thud-
ding through a small vein.

Abcde got a polite smattering of applause on the cutter, a few
snickers. Sam clapped heartily, which sent a surprising pang of
jealousy through my chest. *You're my friend,* I wanted to say, *not
hers,* but I wasn't sure if Sam thought of me that way. Maybe she
was just friendly to everyone. Abcde gave a little curtsy and blew
a kiss to the whales before Sam ferried her back to the pier.

I watched them get out of the small inflatable boat. Abcde
walked up the metal steps like a queen, obviously pleased by her
performance. As Sam came toward the houseboat, my palms
went clammy.

"So," she said as she stepped onto the deck. "You asked about

the whales, but you never told me what brought you here."
Something a friend would say.

"Pears," I said.

"You run the orchard?" she asked.

"No." I blushed. "I just pick. I've only been here a couple of
weeks."

"Wow. You're a migrant worker?" Her face clouded, and I
thought, *Oh no, I've lost her.*

"I guess so," I said. I hadn't used that term to describe myself
before. "Migrant worker" made me think of that iconic Dust
Bowl photo by Dorothea Lange: the woman with tired eyes gazing off into the distance as two of her children rested their heads
on her shoulders, her face so consumed with worry, she almost
looked serene. Maybe I could relate to her, after all. "Quinn and
I follow what's ripe."

I could see Sam gather herself together. "That's cool," she
said, and a cautious trickle of relief slid down my back. "Actually,
that makes you like the whales."

"How?" I asked.

"'Migrant,' 'migrate,' same root," she said. "*Migrare,* to move
from one place to another. It's what 'immigrate' comes from,
too." The teacherly, slightly patronizing tone that crept into her
voice made me wince.

"To move toward," Quinn said without looking up from her
book.

Sam nodded, smiling. "And 'emigrate.'"

"To move away from," Quinn said, still reading.

I was never able to remember the difference between those
two words; I was suitably impressed. Sam seemed to be, too.

"So which are you doing?" Sam plunked into the chair next to
Quinn's, her voice more friendly again, although a hint of conde-
scension remained. "Moving from or moving toward?"

"Just moving." I leaned against the rail, hoping she wouldn't
press further.

Quinn asked, "Why do whales migrate?" and I wanted to kiss

her for changing the subject. We had both been wondering——the library books weren't clear about that.

"To feed and to breed," said Sam. "They breed near the equator in the winter, feed near the poles in the summer."

"So they're way off track," I said, and she nodded.

"We don't usually see them around here this time of year."

"And they need to eat," said Quinn, her book now on her lap.

"The baby is nursing, so she should be fine."

"Pink milk," said Quinn.

"Strawberry Quick," I said, and Sam gave me a thumbs-up.

"So why picking?" Sam asked; it sounded like she was asking why I ate garbage or something equally distasteful. I still couldn't tell if she wanted to be my friend, or we had become another research subject for her now. Migrant mother and child in their natural habitat.

"It keeps our heads above water," I said.

"I always wanted to keep my head below water, personally." She laughed. "I've known I wanted to work with whales since I was a little girl."

"You're lucky to be able to do what you want," I said.

"If you could have any job in the world . . ." She leaned forward in her chair, her eyes full of mischief, maybe a slight glint of superiority. "What would you want to do?"

Sure, lady, I thought. *Toy with the poor migrant mother when you have a chance. Fool her into thinking anything is possible.*

Before I could answer, the baby whale nosed up near Sam's inflatable boat, popping it briefly out of the water. Quinn gasped, delighted and a little wary as our houseboat rocked.

"Sam!" someone yelled on the megaphone from the Coast Guard boat. "Get your ass back here!"

"That's my cue," said Sam. "I better go."

We watched her head back to the cutter in her inflatable boat, using paddles instead of the small propeller, the baby whale following her like a puppy, the mother whale tagging behind, keeping a watchful eye. There was something magnetic about

Sam—even the whales felt it. I hope I hadn't repelled her completely; I hoped she'd see there was more to me than my migrant status and give me another chance.

ON OUR WAY to raid the Vieiras' pantry again, Quinn and I came upon Abcde sitting on the ground outside her tent, furiously scribbling in her notebook.

"Can I do one of your alphabet poems?" Quinn asked. She had gone through a short haiku phase—it made sense she'd want to try another form.

Abcde looked a bit disoriented, as if we had woken her up, but she ripped a piece of paper from her notebook and handed it to Quinn, along with a pencil wrapped in purple grosgrain ribbon.

"Go for it," she said.

"I want to write about the whales," said Quinn.

"We all do," said Abcde, and I wanted to say "I don't!" but then I realized part of me wanted to try my hand at it, even though I hadn't written more than a grocery list in years. If I could have any job in the world, would I want to give writing a try? It hadn't occurred to me before. The only thing I knew for sure I wanted to be was Quinn's mom.

"Twenty-six words or twenty-six lines?" Abcde leaned toward Quinn. I fought the urge to say "Back off."

"Twenty-six words," said Quinn. "Easier."

"It's actually harder," said Abcde. "With twenty-six lines, you have more leeway."

Quinn frowned at the page until her face lit and she lifted the pencil. She spoke the words aloud as she wrote, "A . . . big . . . creature . . . dives."

"Great beginning," said Abcde.

Quinn didn't even look up. "Everybody fears," she said.

"Some people do," I said. Quinn scowled at me and went back to her page.

"Giant heavy . . . ichthyosaurs . . . jump."

"I don't think whales are ichthyosaurs," I said.

"Close enough," said Abcde, and I wanted to slap her. "Plus, it's a great word."

"Killing . . . little . . . miniature . . . n . . . n . . . n . . . nematodes!" Quinn looked ecstatic at the word she had pulled out of thin air.

"Another great word." Abcde held out her hand for a high five. Quinn slapped it.

"I learned it in my biology book." She grinned. *I bought you that book,* I wanted to remind her. Another library sale find. All hail libraries!

"I don't know what to write about next," she said.

"Well, think of *O* words," said Abcde. "Ocean. Octopus. Ogre. Oricchiette."

"What's that?" asked Quinn.

"A kind of pasta," she said. "It looks like a little ear."

"Gross," said Quinn.

"Onion. Olives. Oil. Oranges."

"Someone's hungry," I said.

"Famished." Abcde rubbed her soft stomach. "I only had some muesli this morning. Dry."

"Only!" said Quinn. "Only . . . only . . . only . . . pears . . . No, only, p, p, p . . . *professional* . . . only professionally . . . qualified . . . researchers . . . swim . . ."

"Like Sam," I said.

"Yeah!" said Quinn.

"Keep going," said Abcde, and I wondered if she felt jealous that I knew Sam by name.

"Tucking . . ."

"Ooh, great word," said Abcde. Quinn shot her a look to get her to shut up and I felt a rush of satisfaction.

"Tucking . . . under . . . v . . . v . . . v . . . v . . ."

"Vibrant," said Abcde. "Vitamin. Vigorous. Velvet."

"I can write it myself," said Quinn.

"Please do." Abcde didn't look stung at all, much to my chagrin.

"Tucking under violet water."

"That's beautiful, Quinn," I said. I knew better than to say the water wasn't violet. Some hours of the day it was. Plus, Abcde would probably be surprised, but I *had* heard of a little thing called poetic license.

Quinn smiled down at her paper. "*X*," she said. "*X* is hard."

"I told you," said Abcde. "You have to be creative with *X*. It's okay to spell words wrong. X-tra. X-ample. X-traordinary."

Quinn bit the eraser. "I got it," she said. "X-citing. X-citing your zeal."

"Perfect!" Abcde snatched the paper from Quinn's hand and jumped to her feet. She read the whole thing out loud in a dramatic voice: "'A big creature dives. Everyone fears. Great heavy ichthyosaurs jump. Killing little miniature nematodes. Only professionally qualified researchers swim, tucking under violet water. X-citing your zeal.'"

I gave Quinn a squeeze. "I can't believe you wrote that so fast," I said.

"Congratulations, Mom." Abcde shook my hand. "You have yourself an abecedarian poet."

I flashed briefly upon Quinn's motel-room birth. I was the one who said "It's a girl"—in wonder, in shock—as she emerged face-up, inside the drained bathtub. The midwife, my diner boss's sister, said "Congratulations, Mom," then, too. The word, "Mom," was almost as shocking as the birth itself. How could that label apply to me? I was glad Quinn called me "Eema"—it felt less official, somehow. Easier to wear.

I looked out to the water. Sam was back on the cutter now, doing the work she wanted to do all her life. I thought I saw her look at me standing on top of the levee; I waved, but either she didn't see me or she ignored my ridiculously flapping hand.

KAREN

THE HALLS OF THE SQUAT BRICK PERKINS PERMANENT
Care Facility were decorated with gloppy handprint turkeys.
Karen felt sorry for the aide who had to dip gnarled, half-conscious
palms into paint and press them against construction paper, then
scrub the color out of all the dried-up life lines, love lines. So
many funky-looking turkeys everywhere she turned, their five
feathers crooked, thick-knuckled.

Nathan's father still had a touch of orange on the edge of his
right thumb. He was asleep, if not comatose, his face puffy, like a
drowned man's. Karen could detect a resemblance—the square-
ness of the forehead, perhaps. The set of the jaw. His skin was yellowish, but not from paint, his hair still mostly black, but sparse,
with swaths of silver fanning over his ears. Dark purple shadowed
his closed eyes.

"Hey, Pop." Nathan sat in the olive green molded chair next
to the bed. His father didn't stir.

Nathan gestured for Karen to sit on the edge of the bed, but
the thought of being so close to his dad's bloated abdomen, his

wide open mouth, made her queasy. She slipped into the chair beneath the TV, tuned to a football game, the sound off.

"I brought Karen with me," he said. "The girl I've been telling you so much about."

His voice sounded strange, strained, as he spoke, but it was thrilling to know he had talked about her. For a moment, she didn't smell the urine in the air, the smell of boiled green beans, the unmistakable scent of bodily decay. For a moment, "Help me" wasn't ringing in her ears, echoes from the woman in the wheelchair who had clutched Karen's jacket so fiercely, Karen had ended up pulling her halfway down the hallway.

"Nice to meet you, Mr. Main." She gave a little wave, as if Nathan's dad could see her.

"Look," chuckled Nathan. "You gave him a woody."

She grimaced and closed her eyes, not wanting to know if he was telling the truth.

"I told you she was hot, Pop, didn't I?" His voice had a weird edge to it again.

She found herself flashing on *Hop on Pop*, two little monsters jumping on the belly of a bigger monster, her mom leaning over her, reading in a deep, soothing voice. She loved how her mom used to read to her, before she could read to herself. *Hop hop, we like to hop* . . . Before daily skating practice, before competition. When she could hop just because she wanted to, just because it was a fun thing to do. Her mother smiling as she hopped around the coffee table . . .

"And you know a thing or two about hot women, don't you, you bastard."

When Karen opened her eyes, she was startled to see Nathan's eyes were as wet as hers.

"Fucking bastard," Nathan said, quietly at first, then louder. "Fucking drunkass bastard." He smacked the bed with his fist. His dad's eyes opened a slit; they looked like turtle eyes, slow and prehistoric. The irises slid to the side before his swollen eyelids clamped shut again.

Karen held her breath, heart pounding in her ears.

"Fucking piece of fucking shit." Nathan smacked the bed again, this time closer to his dad's head. His dad startled, let out a garbled moan. His monitors began to beep madly.

"We gotta get out of here." Nathan grabbed the sleeve of Karen's coat, much like the woman had from her wheelchair. She had to run to keep up with him down the hallway. *Help me, miss. Help me. Help me. Help me.*

NATHAN COULDN'T STOP muttering as he drove—Karen couldn't make all of it out, but at least every other word was some sort of curse. He banged the steering wheel, the car fish-tailing over the wet road.

"Maybe I should drive." Karen tried to keep her voice calm. She had gotten her license but hadn't had much of a chance to use it. And she had never driven in a car without her mom, who was always ready to critique her use of brakes and turn signals.

"I'm fine," he said, but then a deer bounded across the street a good block ahead of them and he swerved, narrowly missing an elm tree.

"I don't think so," she said. He grudgingly put the car into park and let her take the wheel. She sat in the driver's seat and breathed deeply until she felt ready to tackle the rainy drive. The streetlamps flickered on, making the street look slicker, even more treacherous.

She flicked the windshield wipers on faster as he slumped lower in the seat. He hadn't put on his seat belt. She leaned forward to try to get a better glimpse of the road.

"Does that happen every time you visit him?" Even twenty miles per hour felt too fast. She was grateful there was no other traffic.

He shook his head again. "It's been building up," he said. "I thought if you were there, it wouldn't . . ." He karate-chopped the dashboard. "Fuck!"

Karen nearly jumped out of her skin. "You're going to make us crash." Her mom would kill her if they got in a crash just before Nationals.

He blew on his hand, shaking it. "Fucking asshole."

"And you're going to need that hand, too," she said. "Get it together."

"Fuck." Tears streamed down Nathan's cheeks. "I don't want to be like him." She had never seen his face like this, in such agony. It looked sort of like when he was dying as Tristan, but more horrible, more real. His head dropped down to his chest. "Please. Oh my fucking God, please. I. Don't. Want. To. Be. Like. Him."

IZZY

I SUPPOSE IT WAS INEVITABLE. AS SOON AS THE NEWS hit the wires, people began to arrive, wanting to see the whales. People in wheelchairs, young families with strollers, older couples, college kids. People wanting to invade our space.

The Vieiras didn't let anyone onto the property unless they paid twenty dollars and picked a bag of pears for the orchard, and then they only let them in for a couple of hours each afternoon, so we didn't have too big a crowd on the island, but Roberts only charged five dollars a day and, for ten dollars more, let people set up camp in the dead part of the orchard. They could easily look across the slough and see us in our houseboat. I warned Quinn to keep the blinds down, especially when our lights were on at night.

"I think we need to think about taking off," I told Quinn. "Too many people." And not any time with Sam. She had stopped giving us updates, stopped hanging out on our deck. Every once in a while, she lifted her chin and smiled in my direction, but it seemed a formality, an empty gesture. How ridiculous of me to think she might want me for a friend. I could feel my heart shrink quickly back down to hold just me and Quinn, our tight little circle.

"We can't leave now," said Quinn. "We need to make sure the whales are okay."

"The whales don't need us," I said. "We better pack before this becomes even more of a circus."

Quinn threw herself on the bed and glared at me. "I'm not going," she said. "You can leave, but I'm staying right here."

"I know you don't want to go, sweetheart," I said, "but we have to."

"Why?" Her face was a red mask of grief. It pained me to see the creases between her eyebrows, the violent downward crank of her mouth.

"There's too many people."

"So?" Her voice was strangled.

"So . . ." I searched for an explanation. "Something could happen."

"Something could happen even if no one's there," she said.

"It's different," I told her.

"How?"

"People are unpredictable."

"So are whales." She spit out the words. "So are pears."

"Pears are pretty predictable," I said.

"So are bees," she said, and I instinctively reached for the EpiPen.

"Just start packing." I grabbed her blue suitcase from the closet, set it on the bed. She turned away from me, so I opened the drawers and started to pull out the shirts and shorts she had folded herself—she was better at folding than me. She curled herself into a ball next to the suitcase and sobbed. I took her books off the shelves, set them on top of her clothes. I got her toothbrush, her bathing suit, from the bathroom. Our life felt so spacious when we were sitting on our deck, looking out at the

Delta sky, but it could be easily compressed into a few small containers.

I packed my own suitcase, packed our food, our toiletries, into paper grocery bags.

"We better head out," I said, walking to the door. Quinn didn't move.

"I'm not going," she said. "I'm a Delta girl now."

I felt a little chill. "They won't let you stay here without me," I said. "You'll end up in foster care." Just saying the words made my stomach clench.

She unfolded herself, glared at me again, and followed me, head down, to the car.

"Can we at least say good-bye?" she asked after she strapped herself into her seat belt.

"Bye, Abcde's tent," I said as we drove past. Quinn looked out the window, arms crossed over her chest. "Bye, pear trees. Bye, more pear trees. Bye, sheep. Bye, stable." My voice felt too cheery, like a picture book narrator, like I was talking to a two-year-old, but I couldn't seem to stop myself. "Bye, Vieiras' house. Bye, Mrs. Vieira. Bye, Ben."

Ben?

I stepped on the brakes. The car bounced, kicking up dust. Ben was with his mother in the garden, picking tomatoes. His UC Davis T-shirt had a few holes at the collar. He was barefoot, dusty. Beautiful. I felt something loosen in my chest.

"I thought we were leaving," Quinn said through her teeth as the car settled into the dirt.

"We are," I said. "But you're right. We should take the time to say a real good-bye."

BEN'S FACE BROKE into a grin as Quinn and I got out of the car. He had shaved off his soul patch; it made his face look younger, even more touchable.

"Hey, you," he said.

"Hey, you." I could feel the smile on my own face. Such a silly girl.

"Why didn't you tell me about the whales before I left?" He set down the basket of tomatoes and walked toward us.

"Why didn't you tell me about the girlfriend?" I tried to keep my voice light, joking, but my throat closed in on itself and I had to cough.

He flinched a bit, but the smile didn't leave his face. "It's not the same thing."

"They're both big," I said.

"She's quite petite, actually," he said.

"You know what I mean." I rolled my eyes and tried not to picture him lifting someone petite and perfect into the air, her wrapping her beautiful legs around him, but I couldn't help myself.

"You sound jealous." He playfully cocked an eyebrow.

"Maybe I am." Again, I attempted to sound like I was kidding around. Again, it didn't work so well.

"I'm jealous, too." Thankfully, he didn't seem to take me too seriously. "You got the whales all to yourself. I have to share them with everyone now."

"If you hadn't run off so fast, I would have shared them with you," I said.

"Too bad I ran off so fast, then." He took a step closer to me.

"Yeah, too bad." When I breathed him in, he smelled like tomato leaves and sunshine.

AFTER WE GOT back in the car, I found myself driving into the island, toward the houseboat, instead of away from it. Muscle memory, I suppose. Or some other part of my anatomy asserting itself.

"Are we staying?" I could tell Quinn wasn't daring to let hope into her voice.

"I guess we are," I said, even though it hadn't been my plan. My whole body felt oozy from seeing Ben, the same loose floppy feeling I would get when I climbed out of a pool after swimming for a long time. "We just have to be extra careful with these extra people, okay? Just don't talk to anyone you don't know. And make sure you stay close to me; I want to be able to see you at all times."

Quinn started to cry again, but this time her eyes were bright and happy. I knew how she felt; I couldn't keep the smile from bubbling up inside of me, either. If Sam never spoke to me again, it wouldn't matter. Ben was back.

KAREN

AFTER THEIR VISIT WITH HIS FATHER, NATHAN STOPPED disappearing at night. He stopped flirting with women at the rink. He didn't slip innuendos into every other sentence. He held doors open for Karen and Deena, helped with the vacuuming, didn't argue with the new choreography or complain about the new short-program costumes—unitard tuxes—even though the slick black outfits looked more like wetsuits than skating gear. Karen found the sea change sweet, if a little spooky. Definitely preferable to swearing and striking out at inanimate objects. Sometimes, though, she found herself missing the sassy comments, the probing eyes, found herself waiting for them like an expected cymbal crash that never comes in a song, leaving some part of her unsatisfied.

"You're doing good," she told him when she could feel how hard he was trying, how hard he was holding himself back, and he would look at her with such gratitude, it made her want to weep. And she got those looks often. She was with Nathan just about every second of the day. Breakfast. Driving the now snowy roads to the rink. An hour of figures to work on their edges. An hour of freestyle before the rink opened to the public. High-protein snacks. Another two hours with the rest of the skating club, where they were given preferential treatment. If Deena wanted the sound guy to play their program twice in a row, no one complained, at least not to their faces; they were the only club members to be going on to Nationals, after all. Then there was Pilates. Ballet. Weight training. Lunch. Another hour or two on the ice. More high-protein snacks. Visualization exercises. Cardio. Dinner. Physical therapy, as needed. The occasional water-training session. Homework, when Karen could fit it in. An early bedtime, both of them falling asleep to their Walkmans, their short and free-skate program music set on an endless loop.

Karen loved knowing they were listening to the same thing as they lay in bed across the hall from each other; she liked to think they even dreamed in sync. They felt more like a team than ever. She knew each groove of his hands. His hands knew just where to hold on to her body for maximum lift, maximum speed. Their eyes would lock and they would know things they didn't have to say out loud. It was like having a twin. A twin you just happened to want to kiss.

FOR CHRISTMAS, NATHAN designed a necklace for her, had it made by a local jeweler—a flat, oval opal set in silver, with little silver circles and stripes to represent all the markings on an ice rink, a small silver heart at the center of the iridescent stone. It was the most beautiful thing she had ever seen. She felt silly handing over the Old Spice cologne and shaving mug she had begged her mother to pick up at Woolworth's—it was the only "male" present she could think of, and he ended up getting matching sets from three other people at the rink, but he seemed touched. At least she had made her own card:

Without you, I am single, not jolly like Kris Kringle.
Together we're a pair and you throw me in the air!
I wish I could lift you, but instead I will gift you.
So thanks for the spins——now on to the wins!
I hope that Nationals won't be too irrational!
Love from Karen, your rarin' pairin'

"Sorry it's so cheesy," she said, sure he was going to make fun of her and her silly rhymes, rhymes she had slaved over much longer than she'd ever admit.

"It's perfect." He wrapped her in a big hug and whispered a breathy "I'm rarin', too," in her ear. A warm shiver traveled down her body.

"Sorry." He sprang away from her. "That's the old Nathan."

Bring the old Nathan back, she wanted to say, but she let him maintain his decorum. "You're doing good," she said, and his smile sent more warmth through her limbs.

ON NEW YEAR'S Eve, Deena brought a portable TV into the garage dance/Pilates studio, along with a space heater, so they could watch the countdown to 1997. They didn't normally work out that late into the night——Karen was usually sound asleep for a few hours by midnight——but the rink was closed on the first, and Deena thought they should ring in the New Year training.

"It will set our intention for the year," she said. "Let the skating gods know we mean business."

Karen could barely keep her eyes open as she did her exercises on the Reformer, slipping her feet into the straps and moving her legs in big circles as her body slid back and forth on the castered table. She knew Nathan tried not to look over at her when her legs were at their widest open. She watched him steal glimpses of her in the studio mirrors and wondered what the old Nathan would have said when he saw her in that spread-eagled position.

Deena had a bottle of champagne and a bottle of sparkling cider ready in an ice bucket, a glittery paper hat on her head.

"One minute to go," she said. "Better grab your glasses." She had been sipping from hers all evening as she led them through their workout.

She handed them each a glass and a noisemaker as seriously as if she were handing them a parking ticket.

"May 1997 be the year you hit the big time." Deena took a swig even though the countdown hadn't started.

Karen hadn't been too excited about New Year's, but when Dick Clark said "Ten" and the ball started its descent in Times Square and Nathan grabbed her hand, she started to feel giddy. The three of them counted down together, Karen and Nathan smiling into each other's eyes. After "One," they all cried out "Happy New Year!" Just as Nathan leaned toward Karen, Deena swooped in and kissed him right on the mouth. Karen knew she should be upset, but Nathan kept his eyes locked on hers the whole time, and she felt as if he were kissing her, too, as if he were kissing only her, as if her mom's lips just happened to get in the way.

IZZY

WE USUALLY FINISHED PICKING BY THE TIME THE SUN
was at its most punishing, but some days the heat was fairly intense. The shadows cast by the pear trees offered a measure of relief, and the Vieiras would put up a couple of portable shades so
we'd have a place to rest out of the sun, plus they'd always set out
a couple of plastic jugs full of ice water. Sometimes, though, one
of us would get a little woozy, a little dehydrated. The other pickers knew the drill; if there were any signs of heat illness, they'd
make sure their fellow worker lay down in the shade; they'd tear
strips of cloth from their shirts, drench them in ice water, lay
them on foreheads and backs of necks and across inner wrists.
They had seen too many co-workers fall in the more exposed
fields—grapes and melons and peppers; they even knew of fore-
men who had succumbed to heatstroke after driving tractors all
day in the sun.

It was worse with the new people, the spectators. First of all,
they didn't know how to pick. Even though Mr. Vieira gave them
a tutorial, showed them how to lift the fruit from the tree, they

thought they knew better. They looked for shortcuts. Yanking pears, causing the stem to separate, leaving the top of the fruit an open wound. Throwing the ladders into the trees to knock fruit down, scarring the bark. Climbing up into the trees, scratching themselves from head to toe, letting the fruit fall with a splat. They often tripped on the shaggy, uneven grass between the rows of trees. They weren't used to this kind of work. Their faces turned beet red; their clothes clung to their bodies, soaked with sweat.

"You need to be careful, Dad," Ben said to Mr. Vieira. "These people aren't covered by workmen's comp. You could get your ass sued so easy." I felt embarrassed that hearing Ben say the word "ass" made my heart skip, especially given the context. He and I had both been so busy since I decided to stay; we hadn't had much time to talk. But I was always happy to see him in the orchard, always happy when our eyes briefly met.

"We need the pickers." Mr. Vieira's mouth was set; a shimmer of fear crossed his face.

"You could lose a lot more than the crop if one of them gets hurt," said Ben before he drove off in the tractor.

I watched an elderly woman lose her balance as she reached for a pear. Her husband caught her by the elbow. His face was flushed and wet beneath his fisherman's cap.

"You might want to take a rest," I told them. They looked both startled and grateful as I led them to the shade and got them each a cold cup of water.

"Do we know you?" the woman asked. "You look so familiar."

"I doubt it." I tried to keep my voice from shaking. "I don't know too many people."

"You're not Carol's granddaughter?" the man said. "From Des Moines?"

I let myself breathe again. "Sorry." I smiled, adrenaline still prickling my nerve endings. "I'm afraid you have the wrong girl."

THE HOUSEBOAT FELT exposed, even with all the blinds closed, even with all the campers across the slough set back from the edge of the levee. The Coast Guard cutter often hovered not too far outside, depending upon the location of the whales. And the whales kept circling back to our little island, to the nice big turn-around spot by the pier.

Sam showed up in her boat just as Quinn and I were finishing our dinner on the deck—it had been a long time since we had spoken. She had become a stranger.

"Hey," she said as she tied up her boat. "I have to talk to Ben—is he around?"

My cheese sandwich got stuck in my throat. "He's working on the tractors," I said, coughing. Why did she need to talk to him? I felt a surge of panic. She would pull him right into her orbit, if she hadn't already; they were obviously on a first-name basis. I wanted to grill her, to tell her to stay away from him, but instead I just asked, "What's going on? Is it safe for us to be here?"

"As long as you don't turn on your propellers, the whales should be fine," she said; I guess she had forgotten she had told me this before. Probably the only thing she remembered about me was that I was a lowly picker.

The mother whale made a brief appearance; when her back arced up, I could see the festering cut on her side. Other boats weren't allowed to come within five hundred yards of the whales now.

"What about us?" I asked. "Are we safe here?"

"The whales won't do anything to you," she said, giving me a smile that felt like pity. "But I can't speak for anybody else."

A NEWS HELICOPTER buzzed overhead, crimping the water into fine pleats. I ducked into the buffeted houseboat before the camera could find me. More and more reporters had been showing up lately to cover the story; they wanted to talk to me, to Quinn, since we were the first in Comice to see the whales, but

I begged them off with a "No comment" and the harshest, most unphotogenic glare I could muster. Quinn was furious with me—she wanted to be on TV, to have her picture taken for the paper—but I didn't back down. We watched Abcde get interviewed again and again, watched Mr. Vieira, Ben, Sam, others on the rescue team, some of the spectators, wax rhapsodic about the whales into one microphone after another. Reporters came from as far as Hong Kong, but Mr. Vieira thankfully only let a couple of them in at a time. They usually weren't too keen about picking a bag of pears to get their story.

"I want to be famous, like Abcde," Quinn said, pouting.

"No you don't," I said. "Fame screws with your life."

"*You* screw with my life," said Quinn.

"You wouldn't have a life if it weren't for me," I reminded her, a bit more sternly than I had intended. She let out the loudest sigh in the world and turned back to her book, but not before fixing me with a withering stare.

I slit the blinds with my fingers and looked outside. The whales must have moved on for the time being; the Coast Guard boat was gone, leaving just the shadow of a wake. Sam would have to catch up with them somehow when she was done talking with Ben. I tried not to think about how long she had been up there with him. The helicopter had thankfully left, too; only the barest of its reverberations still shivered across the water, rocking the boat gently. Everything left a trace in a slough; the water showed when something had been there. At dusk, the setting sun caught every wake, made the trails behind the Coast Guard boat, behind the whales, shimmer like quicksilver. I wondered what markings Quinn and I would leave behind here. Hopefully ones that would briefly glimmer, then disappear, impossible to trace. Unless Ben wanted to find me.

KAREN

IN NASHVILLE, DEENA HANDED KAREN A KEY TO HER own room in their giant atriumed hotel.

"You're turning eighteen this weekend," Deena said. "Consider it your birthday present, sweetheart."

Karen raced up the glass elevator as her mom and Nathan were still checking in. Her very own hotel room! She stripped off everything but the necklace Nathan had given her and jumped on the bed naked—something she had never let herself do at home—the necklace thwacking against her chest. She threw the comforter aside and rolled around on the velvety blanket. She felt like Marilyn Monroe as she smiled for an imaginary camera above the bed, posed with her legs in the stag position, her head arched back.

Then her mom knocked on the door. "Everything okay in there?" she called, and Karen immediately crawled under the covers, embarrassed.

"Fine!" she called back, grabbing her tracksuit out of her luggage, quickly wiggling into it.

"Get some rest," her mom called. "We'll head to the rink in a couple of hours."

Karen lay on the bed, catching her breath. She was tempted to slip the tracksuit back off—it felt scratchy against her skin— but didn't want to risk having her mom show up again.

THINGS HAD BEEN tense with Deena since New Year's. They hadn't talked about that midnight kiss, but every once in a while, Deena sidled over to Nathan as if it had made him hers, and Karen's stomach would press in on itself.

She thumbed through the heavy binder full of hotel information, lingering on the room service menus. When she dialed downstairs and tried to order a hamburger and crème brûlée, though, she found out Deena had put a block on her account. The minibar was locked, too, with no key in sight. She wandered over to the small bowl of fruit that sat on the table overlooking the pool; a card stuck inside read *Congratulations, Skaters!* Karen found herself getting excited again. They were really here! She took a bite of the waxy green apple and jumped around a little bit more.

NATIONALS WERE THE first major event held at the new Nashville Arena. Karen could hear other coaches and skaters grumble over the fact that the place was so big and impersonal, that it didn't have any skating history, any lore, any old gossip ringing in the rafters. Karen was glad it was someplace new. It meant they could forge their own fresh history.

Gossip did make it into the stadium, though. Tonya Harding was briefly kidnapped—or so she said—in Portland, Oregon, but everyone seemed to agree it was a ploy to stay in the skating news during Nationals. People were still buzzing, too, over Oksana Baiul's drunk-driving accident in Connecticut in January, a few towns away from where Karen and Nathan trained. She had insisted she wasn't drunk after four or five Long Island iced teas—"I'm a Russian," she told Oprah—but her car was still totaled.

"You want news," said Deena. "But not news like that."

She handed them a tube of toothpaste as they headed in for their first practice session. "I saw Eisler and Brasseur do this," she said. "It's supposed to keep your mouth from drying out during your program."

"I don't know if it's such a good idea to try it for the first time here," said Karen, but Nathan grabbed the tube from the center and squeezed a thick worm of the paste, striped white and blue-green, onto his finger. He must have been nervous. She had never seen him follow her mother's orders so readily. Plus, he had always bristled against any associations with Lloyd Eisler and Isabelle Brasseur before—he didn't want to be seen as the American version of the bad-boy/good-girl Canadian pair, even though they had been world champions a few years before. He wanted them to be seen as their own team, unlike any other to step onto the ice.

"Just rub it on your teeth," said Deena, licking her own like someone in a commercial. When Karen scowled at her, she said, "It's better than the beauty pageants. They use Vaseline to keep their lips from sticking to their teeth."

Nathan was rubbing away. Karen could smell the mint wafting out of his mouth. He smiled at her, a glob of the paste stuck to his lip, and she couldn't help but smile back. She squeezed a small dab onto her finger, then swiped it over her teeth, staring into Nathan's blue eyes. This was it. Nationals. Here they were, together, minty fresh, ready to take on the best the country had to offer.

BEFORE THE SHORT program, some of the skaters—skaters Karen didn't really know, skaters she had only seen on TV, but who somehow knew about her—came out holding a birthday cake covered with sparklers, big white *1* and *8* candles rimmed with green stuck in the center. The sparklers sizzled with orange light, like cigarettes skittering along the highway, tossed from a moving car. She could feel their hot pinpricks on her skin. The whole rink—the crowd, the announcers, maybe even the judges—started to sing "Happy Birthday." Their voices roared off the walls.

She didn't have to think hard about a wish, but she squeezed her eyes shut anyway and blew with all her might. A mighty cheer rang through the arena. She opened her eyes and waved to the bleachers. Gray smoke spiraled up from the wicks, two thin ghosts braiding and dissolving.

One of the coaches cut the cake and started to hand her a slice, but Deena intercepted the plate. "You're not eating that," she said. "All that sugar before a competition?" She glared at the coach as if he were deliberately trying to sabotage their performance.

It was chocolate cake, moist and dark, with a darker frosting, topped with pink frosting roses. The smell of buttercream made her light-headed.

"Couldn't I have just one bite?" Karen asked. "It's my birthday."

"And now you're losing your focus." Deena lobbed the plate into the trash.

A few fans tossed stuffed animals and flowers down from the stands; they fell around Karen like soft shrapnel.

"They couldn't have waited until after the program?" Deena was exasperated, as she often was at competitions, but Karen bent to pick up the gifts, then blew a few kisses into the stands. Nathan usually got the bulk of the fan presents, but these were for her alone.

"Happy birthday, sweetness," Nathan said as Karen dumped the stuffed bears and cats and giraffes, the roses and carnations

and irises, into her mother's Macy's bag. They'd have to make another trip to the children's hospital soon to drop off the toys she
didn't want to keep. "You ready to do this thing?" He held out his
hand. The tuxedo unitard had looked seal-like and rubbery to her
before, but now it looked dapper, like he was going to escort her
to a ball. Deena had decided to sew a little skirt onto Karen's
matching unitard a couple of days earlier—she realized she
didn't want them to be *too* unconventional at their first Nationals.

"As ready as I'm going to be." She put her hand in his.

THE STADIUM WAS the biggest Karen had ever skated, the
crowd the biggest she had skated for; her mother had estimated
at least eight thousand people—they filled only about half the
stands, but it still felt intimidating. The lighting was harsh, bright;
it made the ice seem extra shiny, extra slick. The bank of television cameras didn't make the place feel any warmer, either.

Nathan put one knee down in the center of the ice. She sat on
his other leg, splayed one hand over her face, waited for the first
notes of the music so she could sweep it aside and smile at the audience. Her heart felt bigger and faster than usual in her chest;
she wondered if Nathan could see it beat through her clothes. He
took a deep breath behind her; she could feel a little tremor of
fear in his leg. She squeezed his side with her other hand, and the
music began.

It felt good but scary to try a new routine in public, especially on so important a stage. The short program felt shorter
than usual, somehow—it went by in a blur, but she could tell it
was a clean blur; they hit every jump, every spin, every bit of
footwork. At the end of "If My Friends Could See Me Now," she
knew that not only had they seen her; they had liked what they
saw.

BECAUSE IT WAS her birthday, and because they were, amazingly, thrillingly, third after the short program—the top contenders, Jenni Meno and Todd Sand, had ended their program on their backs after botching a death spiral—Deena said they could have a night on the town, as long as it was a relatively early night. Karen wanted to go to Opryland, especially since it was rumored to be closing soon—she had never been to an amusement park before—but Deena was worried that the rides would make Karen sick, and she'd be too tempted by all the fried food. They went to the Grand Ole Opry instead, after having large salads for dinner—not Karen's idea of a birthday bash, but the show was historic, and lively enough, even if some of the music made her nerves stand on edge.

"Maybe we should do a country number next," said Deena, sitting between them in the cab on the way back to the hotel. "The judges eat that patriotic shit up."

"I don't think so," said Karen. "Too twangy for my taste."

"She turns eighteen and she suddenly thinks she has taste!" Deena rolled her eyes, then kissed Karen on the cheek.

"I think she has excellent taste," Nathan said, and Karen wanted to climb across her mom, climb onto his lap. "I'm not a country boy, either, Deena."

"Fine." Deena pouted theatrically. "Gang up on me."

Nathan leaned forward to look at Karen and said, "I'm glad to be part of your gang." She couldn't have asked for a better birthday present.

BACK AT THE hotel, Karen wondered if she should invite Nathan over to her room. She tried calling him on the hotel phone to say good night, to say thank you, to talk about the coming free skate, maybe slip in "Why don't you come over here so we could run through the choreography one last time," but there was no answer. *Maybe he's on his way over here,* she told herself. She waited for a knock, but nothing came; he must have taken the phone off the hook to get a good night's sleep. She slipped off all her clothes so she could sleep naked for the first time, her birthday gift to herself. The sheets felt smooth and cool against her skin.

I'm eighteen now, she thought, running her hands over her body. *I can do whatever I want.*

IZZY

THE SACRAMENTO BEE COINED NAMES FOR THE whales—they named the mother Bartlett, to honor the mother pear of the region, the baby Seckel, a small, sweet variety. The names caught on, and soon all the reporters, all the spectators, were calling the whales by their given pears.

"Pears and whales go together," said Mr. Vieira as we walked back into the orchard after lunch. "My grandfather used to spray whale oil on the trees; whale oil and tobacco to kill the pear thrips."

"From real whales?" Quinn was aghast.

"Their blubber. Blubber all over the trees. Killed the thrips."

Quinn pressed her face against my ribs.

"Don't worry, Miss Quinn," he said. "They don't make whale oil no more."

I wondered if any whale molecules were left in the tree trunks, if whales had braided their way into the branches, blossomed out from the buds, if when you bit into a pear you were tasting some ghost sliver of a long-dead whale.

"We use fish oil now," he said.

A breeze sent the leaves shimmering on all the trees, and for a second, out of the corner of my eye, I saw them as schools of fish, sardines corralled by humpbacks, flashing and beautiful and about to be devoured.

"My people came to this country on whaling boats," said Mr. Vieira. "Wouldn't be here if it weren't for whales."

"I thought they came here for gold," I said.

"Gold was what they wanted. Whaling was how they got here."

"And pears kept them around," I said. Even though I was pretty sure Ben was a lost cause, I liked knowing more about where he came from. I hadn't seen him, hadn't seen Sam, since she had gone looking for him, plus there was the small matter of the fiancée in Oregon, but learning about his family somehow made him feel close by.

Mr. Vieira nodded, looking out at the orchard.

"What will you do if you can't get enough pears picked this year?" I asked. "Will you be okay?"

"We have the eau-de-vie," he said.

"Will that be enough?"

He didn't answer me. Just kept walking through the trees.

SEVERAL OTHER AGENCIES got involved in the whale rescue effort—the California Department of Fish and Game, the Governor's Office of Emergency Services, U.S. Fish and Wildlife, different oceanographic schools and county officials wanting in on the action. A lot of people to keep Sam busy, keep her away from the orchard. There was a "stranding manager," a team of veterinarians, a "herding team," biologists, ethicists, animal rights activists, trying to figure out how to get the whales back to sea. Thankfully, we got a bit of a reprieve when the whales took off and decided to hang around the Rio Vista bridge for a while. It was nice to have the place more quiet, even though a few spectators and media people hung around just in case the whales came back. The rescue team was trying to give the whales a bit of a rest, too. After the recordings didn't work, they had tried fire hoses to get them to head south, but that only stressed the whales out. The team was hanging back, giving Bartlett and Seckel the weekend off to see if they'd decide to swim under the bridge on their own. I hoped Sam would take some time off, too, preferably somewhere far from Comice.

EVEN WITH SMALLER crowds, it was going to be a busy weekend for us. Every year, the Friday before the Sunday of the Pear Fair, the Vieiras made a big feast for all the workers to celebrate the harvest. There was still much picking to do, not a whole lot to celebrate, but, as Mr. Vieira said, tradition is tradition, and Mrs. Vieira lived up to her reputation. She and some of her women cousins set up a mini *festa* on several picnic tables pushed together in a line—huge vats of *sopa* and that wonderful dense, sweet Portuguese bread, plus salt cod, rice, fava beans, fried potatoes, sausages, and a sort of bread salad made with garlic, coriander, and shrimp, next to a simple salad of tomatoes and onions dressed with vinegar and olive oil. Plus pears in all shapes and forms—tucked into preserves, chutneys, sweet breads, stews, even a few fresh ones that had ripened in paper bags and in bowls on the Vieiras' kitchen counter. Not to mention bottles of Madeira wine.

True to the spirit of *festa,* the Vieiras gave all this away for free—even to the whale spectators. Even to the reporters. There were probably at least fifty people crowded around the tables, digging into Mrs. Vieira's food. I made a point of sitting as far as possible from the journalists. As close as possible to Ben.

"So you're engaged, huh?" I tried to sound casual as I scooped some more potatoes for Quinn, her favorite dish of the evening. She was deep in conversation with Abcde, who was teaching her a bit of Spanish.

"I just said that to my dad to get him off my back." He sounded sheepish. "He's in a hurry for me to settle down."

I tried not to get too excited, especially since he had been spending time with Sam. "Does your girlfriend know you're not engaged?" I didn't want to talk so loudly, but everyone else was talking loudly, a din of English and Spanish and Portuguese. Most of the workers were still sweaty and dirty from the fields, but some had cleaned up as if they were going to a fancy restaurant. I wondered where they had been hiding their clean button-down shirts; maybe they were saving them just for this occasion. I myself had put on a clean but wrinkly sundress, and the mosquitoes were making their own feast of my bare arms.

"It's more of a friends-with-benefits kind of deal," he said. "Neither of us gets out much. If one of us is lonely, horny, whatever, we have someone to turn to."

A couple of people looked over at the word "horny." Thankfully not Quinn, but Abcde gave me a wink.

"Must make fieldwork more interesting." I tried hard to keep any jealousy out of my voice.

"On occasion." He grinned and spooned more fava beans onto his plate.

A ROUND OF toasting started. "To pears!" said someone, and everyone lifted their glasses.

"To whales!" said someone else.

"To Bartlett and Seckel, in specific," shouted Quinn, to laughter.

"To the Vieiras, for this amazing spread!" said a meaty-faced reporter with grease on his chin.

"Here, here," everyone called out; a couple of the sorter women gave ululating whoops.

"To fieldwork." Ben raised an eyebrow and clinked my glass, and I almost choked on a sardine. Before I could say anything in return, he smiled and headed off to talk to his father.

MRS. VIEIRA AND her cousins set out a table of desserts just as the sun was going down——rice pudding spiked with cinnamon and lemon, custard pastries, pear tarts, and some pungent sheep's milk cheese, along with more ripe pears, more bottles of Madeira wine. They also uncorked a bottle of Eau de Vieira and gave people samples in Dixie cups. I was tempted to try it again, but I wanted to keep my wits sharp with so many people around. A couple of workers had brought their children, and Quinn wanted to run around with some kids her age, maybe a little younger; as always, I told her she could if she stayed where I could see her, especially since it was getting dark. She practically growled at me.

"I'll keep an eye on her," said Abcde. "I don't mind hanging out with kidlets. I'm a big child myself."

"A Big Child." Quinn did a little dance, moving her ribs back and forth with each alphabetic syllable.

"You haven't been getting into the wine, now, have you?" I joked.

Quinn rolled her eyes. "It's not like I'm going to die if you can't see me for a second, Eema!"

"I would certainly hope not!" The word "die" made my ribs contract.

I suddenly flashed on my own childhood. How I never was able to get away from my mother, either. How I told myself that if I had a little girl, I'd let her do whatever she wanted. I'd let her have all sorts of freedom to play, to explore. And here I had gone and put my daughter on an even tighter leash than the one I had grown up with. She hadn't been more than a few yards away from me since the day she was born. The realization hit me like a frying pan. I had to blink a couple times to make sure the stars popping into the sky were not figments of my dizzy brain.

"Fine," I said, a bit short of breath. "Stay where Abcde can see you."

"Thank you, very wonderfully!" Quinn jumped up and down. "And that's 'u' like the letter *u,* not 'you' like Y-O-U."

Abcde gave her a high five.

I had to force myself not to chase after them as they ran off into the orchard in search of cottontail bunnies. Ben was still deep in conversation with his father, so I helped Mrs. Vieira and her cousins carry all the plates and bowls back into the kitchen. As they chattered away in Portuguese, I tried not to look back over my shoulder, hoping to catch a glimpse of Quinn.

And then Sam showed up and made a beeline straight for Ben. My stomach clenched as he gave her a quick hug and she smiled at him with that sparkly smile of hers, that stupid smile that makes you want her to smile at you forever. She wasn't in her usual uniform; her sapphire-colored V-neck sweater made her hair look extra lustrous; she had put on makeup, and wore heels beneath her tailored jeans. I could see both Ben and his dad light up as they talked to her. I didn't bring that out in people. I made people anxious. Or maybe I made myself anxious around people. Either way, I didn't have her glow. I wanted to run over and tackle her to the ground.

SOMEONE HAD MOVED the picnic tables into a circle and started a bonfire in a fire pit at the center. At least four of the pickers, including Jorge, and one of the sorters, had guitars; they were sitting on top of the tables, strumming away together, playing what sounded like a heartbroken ballad in Spanish at the top of their lungs. All of them were either drunk or pretending to be, weaving their heads around and opening and closing their eyes comically. The crickets in the orchard provided a bass note to the music, chirpy staccato strings.

"'*El Borracho.*'" Mr. Vieira sidled up next to me with his glass of Madeira. "'The Drunk.'"

"That's the song?"

He nodded and lifted his glass. "And me, if I finish this." He took a big swig. I was tempted to grab the wine from his hand and glug it down myself.

"It's a sad song," I said; the singers looked like big goofballs with their drunken mugging, but their voices sounded shattered, forlorn.

"You think that's sad?" He downed the rest of the glass. "Wait till you hear the fado."

The nightly breeze started to pick up; I wrapped my arms around myself and wondered if I should go back to the boat to get a sweater, or maybe just turn in for the night, when Ben walked down his front steps, tuning what looked like a lute.

"I didn't know you played," I said, suddenly feeling a bit warmer. Sam was chatting someone else up now, one of the windbreaker guys who obviously had a crush on her.

"I haven't for a while." Some guys, you can tell they pick up guitars to try to look sexy. Ben looked a little awkward with his teardrop-shaped instrument, and somehow that made him all the more appealing. And not just to me. I caught Sam throwing glances his way even as she was talking to her besotted colleague. She hadn't acknowledged me at all.

"What's this fado your father is talking about?" I asked, trying to will some of Sam's radiance into my face.

He shook his head; he and Sam shared a brief smile before he looked at me again. "It'll rip your heart right out of your chest." *Too late,* I thought.

The *"Borracho"* song ended, to uproarious applause, raised glasses.

Mr. Vieira called Jorge and his guitar over.

"The fado needs two guitars," Ben told me. "The Portuguese," he held his up, "and the classic."

Jorge and Ben sat on one picnic bench, and began to pick out a few simple but moving notes; it was as if they had reached into my body and plucked at my innards. I had to wrap my arms around myself even tighter, Ben's guitar resonating inside me like a bell. I tried not to look at Sam, who looked equally rapt. A hush fell over everyone who had been so raucous just a moment ago; it was as if we were in the presence of something important, maybe even holy. Mr. Vieira sat in silence on another bench, looking down at his lap. Then he took a deep breath, unfurled his spine, closed his eyes, and began to sing.

Even though he and Ben had both warned me, even though I had ample time to prepare myself, even though I had no idea what any of the lyrics meant, I found myself choking back a sob. The mournful tone of Mr. Vieira's voice somehow uncorked all the sadness that had been hiding in the corners of my bones for the last ten years. The sadness I had been hiding from myself.

My throat burned. I hadn't given myself the chance to cry, really flat-out, full-body cry, since Quinn had been born; I'd had to hold it together for her, to not scare her, to keep at least one thing steady in her life. Now, with Quinn off with Abcde, with only myself to look after, with Sam making eyes at Ben, I fell apart.

I ran from the music, ran, nearly blind with tears, into the orchard, where I could hear only the faintest cry of the guitar. I collapsed on the uneven grass and let myself weep until my throat was raw, until my bones released their cache of grief. I wept and wept until I came back into myself enough to notice ants were crawling up my legs, enough to see the white owl swooping above me on its nightly rounds. Sadness still coursed through me, but I felt calmer, lighter. I wondered if other animals felt sadness. I thought I had seen it in the eye of the whale, at least the mother whale, who had led her baby so far off course. When I heard coyotes at night, they sounded like they were keening. I stood, trying to shake the bugs off my skin. I had been living like an animal for so many years—seeking food and shelter, avoiding predators. What had I done to myself in the process? What had I done to Quinn?

I touched a pear tree to steady myself, felt the groove of a scar on its trunk, sliced against the grain. Mr. Vieira once told me about how he and Ben "anguish" each pear tree during the winter. They carve gashes into the trunk to make it think it's threatened, that it has only one more season to live. The tree ends up producing loads of fruit the next spring, much more than it would have if it had never been hurt. The Vieiras trick it into a premature swan song, and the next year, they trick it again. You'd think it would learn, the pear tree. You'd think it would know it was being tortured into abundance.

KAREN

KAREN AND NATHAN STEPPED ONTO THE FRESHLY
resurfaced ice for the practice session before the free skate.
Karen loved that moment, when the ice was still pure. She found
that first dig of her outside edge, the crackle and crunch beneath
her blade, the resonance of it throbbing up her leg, deeply satisfying. When the ice was well used, the snow that fell from
skaters' blades clumped into small white drifts, but on clean ice,
the shavings sparkled like diamonds. Everything turned to glitter.

Karen and Nathan held hands and stroked around the rink,
blades searching for uneven patches to avoid, raised swaths left
like scar tissue by the Zamboni. Sometimes another skater's toe
pick carved a divot that could snag your blade during a spiral or
landing. Good places to dial into your body and avoid. This ice
felt good, though, smooth. No swampy sheen of water, no noticeable dips or imperfections. It was fast ice; they stroked harder
and harder, gaining speed. He put his left arm behind her back
and grabbed her left hand, held her right hand against her rib

cage. They stroked around the rink some more as other pairs
swept by, doing lifts and jumps.

"What are you waiting for?" Deena called out from the side
of the ice. "You need to practice your combination!"

Karen and Nathan just kept stroking. Neither of them said a
word. They didn't need to—Karen could tell they both somehow knew they had to save up their energy, let the jumps and
spins build inside of them so they'd be ready to explode during
the actual program. They'd keep the audience in suspense, let the
anticipation grow to a fevered peak. No sneak previews. Karen
felt her mind meld with Nathan's. She had never felt so fully in
tune with anyone in her life.

"You blew it," Deena said when they stepped off the ice. "You
just threw the medal away."

They were besieged by reporters. "Are you injured?" they
asked. "Why didn't you practice?" Nathan just winked at the camera while Karen beamed only at him.

KAREN THOUGHT SHE had felt the free skate as deeply as possible at Sectionals, but that was nothing compared to this. After
their nonpractice practice, their free skate at Nationals felt truly
free, truly alive. She became Isolde in every cell of her body. Her
nerve endings registered every emotion, every swell of music,
every twitch of Nathan's muscles. She knew he had become Tristan, too. Their bodies were absolutely in sync, absolutely connected. The choreography didn't feel like choreography—it felt
like it was born out of their bodies, organic and whole.

At the end of the program, they lay dead in each other's
arms, their faces touching in masks of grief and bliss. Even after
the music ended, they remained there, breathing against each
other. The crowd grew silent, waiting for them to get up and
bow. Instead, they stayed on the ice and kissed.

So many times, Karen had wanted to kiss him during that

final moment of the program, had thought she felt him wanting to kiss her, their bellies and chests rising and falling together, lips yearning. Now, cameras rolling, the crowd rising, roaring, all of it fed that first kiss, its urgency, its inevitability. It was as if Karen's body was split in half—the back of her frozen numb against the ice, the front of her warmed by Nathan's lips, his arms, the taste of mint still on his tongue. So much sweeter than chocolate cake. The front of her felt it could lift away, fly to the rafters with him, leaving the back of her stuck to the rink like a discarded jacket. Her life was split in half, too. Life before the kiss, life after the kiss—two entirely different equations.

IZZY

I STUMBLED BACK OUT OF THE ORCHARD, SPENT. THE crowd was much smaller now. A couple of the pickers were playing guitar softly, the Rolling Stones. Empty wine bottles littered the tables. The fire was dwindling in its pit. Quinn and Abcde were waiting for me, eating leftover pear tarts they had begged from Mrs. Vieira.

"Where were you?" asked Quinn. It was kind of nice to know she was worrying about me for a change.

"Just went for a walk," I said, grateful for the cover of night—hopefully my eyes didn't look too swollen, too red. Hopefully my weeping hadn't carried like the coyotes'.

"Did you see the wild turkey?" she asked.

"I saw an owl." My whole head was congested, dizzy.

"We saw two owls and a fox and a wild turkey and seven bunnies," she said. "And bats."

"Very wild," said Abcde, and Quinn held up fingers—two in a V on one hand, three in a W on the other—before running over to the porch to get a drink of water.

"Thanks for watching her," I said, trying to keep the tremor out of my voice.

"Any time, Izzy, I'm serious. She's a joy. A beautiful child."

Ben stepped onto the porch, next to Quinn. He waved at me, then bounded down the steps, Quinn trailing him. I caught my breath, wishing I could splash cold water on my puffy face.

"Where'd you run off to?" he asked.

"I needed to get a sweater," I said, then felt like an idiot, since of course I hadn't grabbed one. "Where's Sam?"

"Sam?" he asked, as if he wasn't sure who I was talking about. "Oh yeah, the whale girl—I've been helping her with some environmental data—pesticide use in the area, mostly. I think she took off with one of the reporters."

I wanted to cry all over again, this time from relief.

"Hey," he said. "Would you mind if I came down to the house-boat for a little bit tonight? I love to be on the water when the moon is full."

Longing filled my body near to bursting. I looked back at the orchard. Did the trees suffer when we couldn't pick their bounty fast enough? Were they like a mother whose milk comes in and her baby doesn't want to nurse and she thinks her breasts will ex-plode?

"We're heading there now," I said.

"IT'S SO PEACEFUL here." Ben sat on a deck chair, his feet up on the railing. The houseboat rose and fell gently. A few campers across the way had lit bonfires. I could see some of them in sil-houette, standing by the levee, watching for spray, for spines, even though the whales hadn't made an appearance for a while. The full moon cast its glow all over the water, like a slick of cream.

"I love it," I said, bundled in a sweater for real now. My body felt relaxed and sleepy after my big cry. I lay my head against the back of the chair and looked up at the stars, felt them prickle somewhere inside of me, lighting up the sadness that still lingered there.

"You should see it in the winter," he said. "It's cold, but I love when the tule fog starts to roll in."

"What's that?" asked Quinn.

"It's the fog that settles into the valley after the first big rain," he said, "really low and dense. Sometimes stays for months."

"What do you like about it?" I asked.

"I don't like it when I'm driving," he said. "You can't see the road. But when you're in the houseboat, it's awesome. It's like you're in some sort of misty magical place." He sounded a little bit drunk, but in a loose and pleasant way. I could smell Madeira on his breath.

"Like Niflheim," said Quinn excitedly.

"Just like that," said Ben. "Where the world began."

"Will we be here this winter?" asked Quinn.

"No, sweetheart." I felt a pang of loss. "All the work will be done here by then."

"Oh, there's stuff to do all year long," he said. "Pruning, spraying, you name it. I'm sure my parents could find something for you to do if you want to hang around."

I wanted to hang my arms around his neck, hang myself all over him. I was tempted to inch my foot a little closer to his on the railing, but stopped myself. "I'll look into it," I said, trying not to get my hopes, Quinn's hopes, up too much.

We sat in silence, looking out at the water. I must have drifted off to sleep in my chair; when I woke, Quinn had put herself to bed and Ben was gone. Someone had draped a blanket over me. My legs were stiff as I took them off the railing and limped into the boat. Quinn's body gave off warmth under the sheets; I pulled the cold blanket from outside to my chest and ached for a different kind of heat.

KAREN

For the first time, the kiss-and-cry held real meaning for Karen. Tears of relief, of joy, of complete overwhelm, streamed down her cheeks as she and Nathan kissed again. Deep, slow kisses that made the arena disappear, that created a warm, sweet bubble around their bodies. They kept kissing as the judges revealed their scores, as those scores moved them into first place, as Deena screamed in triumph, waving flowers over their heads, showering their flushed faces with petals.

"National champions!" Deena kept saying in the cab after the medal ceremony. "National fucking champions, baby!"

Karen snuggled against Nathan, his hand on her leg. They pressed their medals together, made them kiss, too. Karen felt the metal clang inside her, as if her whole body were a tuning fork, open to a new vibration. She kept stealing glances at her mom to see how she was reacting to all the cuddling, nervous that she would try to break them apart, but Deena barely looked at them; she was too busy talking about all of the upcoming events. Karen hadn't let herself think beyond Nashville. Deena had put such a focus on Nationals, on getting noticed this year so there would be a better chance of getting on the Olympic team in 1998. They hadn't talked about what would happen if they actually placed—the Champions Series Finals in Canada in two weeks; the World Championships—the Worlds!—in Geneva, Switzerland, in March. The invitations to appear on *The Today Show, The Tonight Show,* the calls from potential sponsors. Deena was in her glory, already scheduling interviews, setting up photo shoots.

"Now that you're a couple," said Deena, finally looking at them directly, as if sizing them up, scrutinizing them as a unit, "you're even more of a hot commodity." Nathan winked at Deena and lifted both thumbs. Karen nuzzled her head deeper into Nathan's neck, breathed in the spice of his sweat and hair gel and cologne, avoided her mom's appraising eyes. All she needed for glory was this.

AFTER WORK THE NEXT DAY, THE VIEIRAS ASKED ME TO go to Rio Vista, a few towns south, to pick up bags for our booth at the Pear Fair before the store closed. I hoped Ben would be able to join me, but he was busy helping his dad gussy up the old tractors for the parade. Abcde came along, instead. After so many years of just me and Quinn in the car, it felt weird to have her with us, almost like having a live tiger in the back seat; the car didn't feel big enough to contain her energy. I half expected her to pounce as I drove. I rolled down my window so the scent of her dreadlocks—sweaty, herbal—wouldn't suffocate me. Rio Vista wasn't too far away, but it felt like we were in the car for hours, what with her alphabetical exclamations—"ferry greets humble itinerants," "river seems terribly undulatory." I wondered if her use of the alphabet was related to her hormonal cycle in some way—it seemed to be peaking.

Rio Vista was a small town, but compared to Comice, it felt huge, with its fast-food restaurants, its large drawbridge that the whales had been milling around of late. I had looked forward to seeing them again, but they had moved on by the time we got there. Hopefully on their way back to sea.

We stepped into Foster's Bighorn, a legendary local restaurant; the walls were covered with taxidermied animal heads— bear, deer, lion, rhino, some animals I couldn't even identify.

"Antelope, boar, cougar, deer . . ." Quinn pointed to the different heads, cringing.

"Creepy dead elephant," said Abcde. "Fuck."

"Language," I warned, tilting my head at Quinn.

"Yes, it is." Abcde sounded defiant. "Yes, it is language. And I intend to use all of it."

"Abcde," I started.

"No word is off-limits for a poet." Her eyes blazed in the dim room. "Quinn should know that. 'Fuck,' 'shit,' 'cunt' . . . all of it's fair game!"

Quinn clapped her hand over her mouth, scandalized and giddy.

"Nice," I said. "Real nice, Abcde," but she just shrugged.

"This, however"—she swept an arm out to take in all the animal trophies—"this is truly unfair game."

A couple of people in the restaurant threw us dirty looks, and we slunk back outside. At least I slunk; Abcde and Quinn held their heads high. We walked to the end of the street, which overlooked the water, and found a monument to Humphrey, the humpback that had visited the Delta in 1985. Donated by "Silva's Memorial's" ("Why can't people learn to use apostrophes correctly?" Abcde huffed), it looked like a large gray tombstone, a large picture of a whale engraved onto its smooth marble front, these words underneath:

TO REMEMBER THE VISIT OF
HUMPHREY
THE HUMPBACK WHALE
OCT. 10, 1985   NOV. 4, 1985

A poem by a twelve-year-old boy was carved below in smaller letters, the boy's signature also engraved in the stone:

HUMPHREY THE HUMPBACK WHALE, A MIGHTY WHALE WAS HE.
HE SWAM INTO THE DELTA, TO SEE WHAT HE COULD SEE.
THE PEOPLE STOOD AND STARED, THE FISH WERE SCARED.
HE WAS FAMOUS ACROSS THE NATION, UNTIL THEY ENDED
HIS VACATION.

"You call that a poem?" Abcde was livid.

"It's cute," said Quinn.

"Cute doesn't cut it." Abcde smacked her purse against the monument. "Cute isn't worthy of being immortalized in stone! All bewail cute!"

"He was only twelve when he wrote it," I said. "Give the kid a break."

"I give no one a break for sloppy writing," said Abcde. "I've seen twelve-year-olds write very sophisticated work. 'Until they ended his vacation.' Who is this mysterious 'they,' and what did they do to the whale?"

I suddenly felt sorry for the students in her workshop at Squaw Valley.

"They saved him," said Quinn. "The rescue people." She had heard the story many times about the humpback's visit over twenty years ago. The fact that he found his way back to the ocean after almost a month in the Delta seemed to give her hope for Bartlett and Seckel, but I knew she was still worried.

"He saved himself, honey," said Abcde. "That's what all of us have to do."

A little tingle ran across my ribs.

"Anyway," she said. "Quinn could write a much better poem, and she's nine."

"I don't know . . ." Quinn looked down at her blue flip-flops.

"We'll work on it," she said. "We'll work on it so we'll be ready when they make the monument for our whales."

"If our whales die," said Quinn, "do you think they'll put their heads on the wall of that restaurant?"

"I doubt it," I said. "Their heads would take up the whole place."

Quinn looked bereft.

"They're not going to die on our watch," said Abcde, and I wanted to tell her not to say such a thing to Quinn. Even if they were on their way to the ocean, they weren't out of the woods. Sometimes death can sneak up on a person. You can't always keep someone alive, no matter how hard you will their heart to keep beating.

WHEN WE RETURNED with cartons of bags for our sellable pears that evening, there was a big commotion in the slough. The whales were back. This time, the Marine Mammal people were piping sounds of killer whales, the humpbacks' natural predators, into the water. Bartlett, the mother whale, was thrashing around, trying to protect Seckel, her baby. She was smacking her tail against the water in a way I had never seen before, sending huge plumes into the air that crashed onto the deck of the houseboat, which was already bucking from her movements. I had left some windows open—the houseboat was going to be drenched inside. I looked out at the Coast Guard boat but couldn't tell which life-jacketed person was Sam—all of them had their windbreaker hoods on, ducking against the assault of water.

"Maybe you should stay in the house tonight." Ben stepped up next to me as I watched from the levee. "We have a guest room." His breath was warm on my neck. My heart flopped fishlike in my chest.

The mother whale thwapped her tail against the slough again, shooting more water through my window. I was glad to see she still had such strength in her—she had seemed a bit listless lately, her color growing dull, her sores looking worse—but I hoped the beautiful bedspread wouldn't be ruined.

"Thanks," I said, avoiding eye contact, biting down a smile. "That sounds like a good idea."

KAREN

SHE DIDN'T HAVE TO INVITE NATHAN INTO HER ROOM that night. It just made sense for him to follow her through the door, for him to kiss her against the hall of the entryway, for them to walk, kissing, into the room, drop, kissing, onto the bed.

She held her breath as he unzipped the jacket of her tracksuit, as he slipped all her clothes off before she even really knew what was happening—he did it easily, swiftly, like a magician pulling a tablecloth out from under plates and knives. She held her breath as he took off his own clothes and stood above her, naked, just staring at her body. She hoped she looked sexy enough on top of the bedspread. She hoped he wasn't disappointed in the sparseness of her curves. She could barely bring herself to look between his legs; when she stole a quick glance, his penis looked like a small arm raising a fist—a gesture of victory, or maybe threat.

"Look at you," he said, wonder in his voice. "You're like ice before anyone's ever skated on it."

She thought about fresh, new ice, that pure white gleam. Did it long for a blade to dig into its surface or did it cringe against the metal? Was that first slice a relief or a wound? She closed her eyes and tried to be like the ice, welcoming the blade, letting it tear her surface to shreds.

IZZY

AFTER THE WHALES TOOK OFF, I WENT DOWN TO THE houseboat to gather our belongings. The place was drenched; so were all our clothes that weren't safely tucked away in the closet. I tossed our wet things into the washing machine; the bedspread, sadly, was soaked through, and too big to fit in the small stacked washer. I wondered if the Vieiras would let me wash it in their house.

I had only been in their kitchen before, with glimpses of the living and dining rooms; most of the furniture looked like it had been there for generations—well used, well maintained, just a touch of formality in some of the armchairs, some of the carved dining-set legs. I had never been up the staircase with its thick wooden banister. Mrs. Vieira showed me where to put my things in the guest room that was also her sewing room, neat piles of fabric next to the sewing machine, colorful spools of thread mounted on dowels on the wall. I tried to catch a glimpse of Ben's room on the way back down the hall, but all the other doors were closed. Everyone was busy preparing for the fair the next morning.

Abcde, Mrs. Vieira, and I stayed up until 2 a.m. bagging pears to sell from our booth, about ten pears per bag, while Mr. Vieira and Ben worked on the tractor. The paper bags were adorable—like little pale blue gift bags with a single white paper handle arching across the top; they were the same color as a box from Tiffany's, and nicely set off the pale green of the pears. The packages looked like they should be on the cover of Martha Stewart's magazine. We stuck a flyer for Eau de Vieira in each bag, plus a pamphlet about why organic was better.

Quinn helped for the first few hours, but eventually passed out on the padded swing on the front porch. I had to carry her upstairs to the guest room.

"You're strong." Ben stepped out of the bathroom; it smelled as if he had just brushed his teeth. He was wearing pajama pants and a T-shirt so old, you could see through it. His chest hair looked like some sort of plant pressed under wax paper.

"Lifting all those pears." I could hear the strain in my voice. Quinn was a bit heavier than a bag of fruit—especially when she was asleep.

"Well, good night, I guess," he said. He must have showered recently, too. I could smell the spicy tang of his shampoo, feel some residual steam rising from his skin.

"Yeah, tomorrow's a busy day," I said. If Quinn hadn't been in my arms, I would have taken a step closer. Part of me was tempted to just set her on the floor, take a step closer anyway.

"Sweet dreams, then." He smiled and disappeared into his darkened room.

After I put Quinn on the bed, I stood in the doorway for a while, shifted to make the floorboards creak beneath me, but Ben's door stayed closed.

I FELT DISORIENTED when I woke up on a stiff tall mattress with a wrought-iron headboard, a bumpy chenille spread. The light coming through the windows looked different from the light in the houseboat, thinner, brighter. Quinn was still sound asleep as I got up to brush my teeth, use the bathroom. I could smell coffee wafting, so I threw a sweatshirt on over my pajamas and padded downstairs to finagle a cup.

Ben was in the kitchen, still in his pajamas, too, leaning over a bowl of pears. The thin cotton pants rode low on his hips; as he bent forward, his shirt rode up, exposing a strip of his lower back. His skin looked so smooth; I clenched my hands to keep myself from reaching out to touch it.

Ben turned around, cupping a pear in his palm.

"You know," he said, as if we were already in the middle of a conversation, "Emerson said, 'There are only ten minutes in the life of a pear when it is perfect to eat.'"

"Nice quote," I said.

"This pear I have here?" He held it out in front of him. "This pear is perfect."

I walked across the room, leaned toward the fruit. Its scent was sweet as rain.

"Take a bite." He grinned mischievously.

"Really?" I asked.

"We only have a ten-minute window." He held the pear closer.

I touched my lips to the skin, warm from the sun through the window, and could feel it give slightly, like a sigh. I pressed harder until juice flooded into my mouth. The skin of the pear curled against my nose as my teeth went deeper. Ben took a bite from the other side. My eyes met his. He pulled back slightly.

"Melting flesh," he said, his lips wet.

"Yes," I said, my whole body turned to liquid.

"That's what you look for in a pear," he said. "Melting flesh."

The pear's flesh *was* perfect, ambrosial, melting like butter on my tongue. He took another bite. I took another bite, bigger, my mouth open a bit wider. Our lips moving toward the slender, thready spine, our cheeks covered with juice, chins dripping.

"Eema." Quinn walked into the kitchen. "There are enough pears. You don't have to share one."

I jumped back and laughed nervously, wiping my face with the collar of my sweatshirt.

"I was just teaching your mom the proper way to eat a ripe pear," said Ben. He lifted another from the bowl. "You should try."

"I know how to eat a pear," said Quinn, and took it from his hand.

KAREN

KAREN CURLED ON THE BED AS NATHAN SLEPT NEXT to her. She hoped the ice didn't burn like this. She hoped her blade didn't send pain all the way up the center of the rink. How could this be what everyone raved about? How could this be the subject of songs and poems, the cause of sly whispers and winks? How could this be what she had wanted?

"YOU LIKE THIS? You like this?" Nathan had grunted as he pounded into her.

She had nodded, eyes clamped shut, tears streaming down her face.

Afterward, he had kissed her so sweetly, cleaned the blood off her thighs with a wet washcloth, promised it would get easier over time, but she wasn't sure she believed him.

SHE COULDN'T FALL asleep with him beside her. She tried to match her breathing to his, but it made her feel claustrophobic, as if she had forgotten how to breathe on her own. She closed her eyes and willed herself, uselessly, to get some rest. She didn't want to be bleary-eyed and groggy for the full day of interviews ahead. She finally drifted off for an hour or so before she woke to Nathan nuzzling her breast. She could feel him hard against her side, and it filled her with a cottony panic.

"I don't think I can . . . ," she started, her head ringing with exhaustion.

"You don't need to do anything," he said. "Just relax."

He took one nipple in his mouth, then the other, sending delicious shivers through her body. The raw place between her legs began to throb. His mouth trailed down her belly, to that broken, aching place, and he soothed it with his tongue, he lavished it with his tongue, he lapped until the pleasure crested over the discomfort, and her whole body filled with liquid light.

AS THEY SAT for press conferences and interviews in the morning, Karen felt spaced out—between lack of sleep and her body still reverberating from Nathan's ministrations, she couldn't answer reporters' questions with much more than a knowing smile.

"It's a year of upsets," said a tall woman in a bright red suit from one of the networks. "Tara Lipinski unseated Michelle Kwan for the ladies' title; you, a new team, unseat Meno and Sand. Karen, do you consider yourself part of the teen queen phenomenon at Nationals this year?"

Karen swallowed hard. Up until the day before, Karen had looked at Tara and Michelle as her peers. Not her friends, but her peers, all of them serious teen skaters on the national stage—not that Nathan thought Tara was serious; he called her a "naughty little monkey," which made Karen more jealous than she knew she should be. Today, those fourteen- and sixteen-year-olds looked like little girls to her. Their bodies hard, untouched. They thought jumping was the closest they could get to heaven. Just wait until they found out what they were missing. Just wait until they found out what their bodies could really do.

"No," said Karen. "I just consider myself Nathan's queen." She turned to kiss him; even with her eyes closed, the flash of the cameras was blinding.

IZZY

THE PEAR FAIR WAS HELD IN A LARGE PARK IN
Courtland, about twenty minutes northwest of Comice. The
Vieiras hoisted their shiny red vintage tractor onto the trailer;
the back of the pickup truck was already filled with our freshly
bagged pears. I felt giddy driving behind them, pear still lingering in my mouth, the scent of Ben still filling my senses.

A church across the street from the park had "Praise Pears
with Prayer" on its marquee, and I said "Hallelujah" out loud as
we drove by. A group of people in tank tops on the five- and ten-
mile Pear Fair fun run disappeared around the corner a few
blocks ahead.

People were setting up their booths around the trees when
we arrived—some under E-Z Up tents, others inside big
wooden boxes, like Lucy's psychology stand in *Peanuts;* Ben and
Mr. Vieira quickly hammered together theirs, pale green with
yellow pears painted all around the top. Our booth was situated
in the food area—mostly pear-related goods, but people set up
grills for big lunches full of sausages and gyros and fajitas, too.

There was also an area for local artists to display and sell their work, a beer garden where the Vieiras planned to give out some samples of Eau de Vieira, a general vending area where people sold things like fuzzy marionettes and smelly skin care products and fleece ponchos printed with wolves and football team logos. A kids' area full of carnival games and inflatable structures for jumping. A large tent arching over picnic tables and a small stage set up for a roster of entertainers. Several booths for community organizations. A small local history museum set up inside the old stucco gym/auditorium on the grounds. A giant papier-mâché pear to house the Big Pear Contest.

"Can I look around, Eema?" Quinn asked.

"Only if Abcde goes with you." I was slated to work the booth; the Vieiras were going to pay me for my time. That wasn't a concern for Abcde; she had been volunteering in the orchard. I was surprised a poet didn't have to worry about money.

"She'll be in good hands, Izzy." Abcde winked.

I gave Quinn a hug and a few dollars. I had put her in a bright red and orange striped T-shirt so she'd be easy to spot in the crowd. I myself was dressed as a farmer, even though I never dressed that way on the orchard—overalls, checkered shirt, big floppy straw hat, a bandanna around my neck, all supplied by the Vieiras. Plus my sunglasses. They were expecting thousands of people.

I started to lug bags of pears over to the stand. Roberts walked up just as I was setting the first batch on the little wooden counter.

"You can't put that there." He pointed to our sign proclaiming ORGANIC.

"We're organic," I said.

"You haven't been certified yet. You need to put 'transitioning.'"

"We're close enough." I looked over at Mrs. Vieira for backup, but she was taking money from the customers who had already lined up. Plus she couldn't—or at least wouldn't—speak

English. I glanced around for Mr. Vieira or Ben, but they had disappeared.

"Then I can put it, too," he said. "I didn't spray today."

"It's not the same thing," I said. The Vieiras hadn't sprayed for almost three years.

"You bet your sweet patootie it is." He stalked off to his booth.

A COUPLE OF hours into the day, I took a short break to use the restroom inside the auditorium, and decided to take a moment to wander through the historical display inside—old crates and scales and sorting tables, plus easels full of posterboards covered with photos of the region, black-and-white pictures of old floods, old houses and orchards when they were new, old schools, Chinese and Portuguese children mugging for the camera in their stiff white collared shirts. Big clamshell dredgers scooping up dirt for the levees. Pickers looking serious and noble on their spindly wooden ladders. I found a couple of pictures of the Vieiras standing in front of their farmhouse in the late 1800s, working their fields in the early 1900s, holding serious-looking babies in the 1930s—including Mr. Vieira—and was happy to see a whole display of Ben's grandmother's crate labels, her name and portrait prominently featured at the top. All around me, fairgoers pointed at old pictures of their grandparents, their aunts and uncles, their houses, and I felt a wave of nostalgia for something I never had.

A cooking demonstration had been set up near the stage; the large fans in the corners wafted the scent of pears sautéed with butter and cinnamon across the room, along with a welcome—if loud—blast of cool air.

As I walked through the building, a prickle traveled up the back of my neck as if someone was watching me. I turned, hoping it was Ben, hoping our eyes would meet in some meaningful way, but there was no trace of him. No one else's eyes seemed pointed in my direction, either. I told myself it must have been just the fan ruffling against my skin, but I couldn't shake the feeling of being watched. I slipped my sunglasses on as a shield.

On my way back to the booth, I walked through the tent where people were eating their roasted corn and barbecue sandwiches and pear fritters and giant sausages. A band at one end of the shelter—a bunch of white guys at the far end of middle age—played loud boppy classic rock, everything from the Rolling Stones to Bob Marley, full of synthesized cheer. At the other end, a mechanical bull was set up inside an inflatable ring. A drunk woman with overtreated hair was trying to look sexy as she rode on it, but it looked more like she was having some sort of seizure. The bull tossed her off, her limbs splayed awkwardly in her tight clothes.

"You should try." Ben sidled up behind me.

"Nah, I'm too good," I joked, enjoying the feel of his breath on my neck. "No one would want to get on after me; they'd be too embarrassed."

"I'd like to see that," he said.

"I bet you would."

I wanted to keep flirting, but I was suddenly gripped with another sensation of being watched—not by Ben, whose presence felt warm and lovely against my back; this was a colder tingle.

"I better go find Quinn." I turned around and looked Ben in the eye. He seemed a bit confused, a bit disappointed, but he shrugged and said, "Okay."

"Maybe we can hang out later," he shouted after me. I gave him a thumbs-up and kept walking, my heart in my throat until I found Quinn inside the bouncy castle in the children's area.

"She's doing okay?" I asked Abcde.

"Doing especially fine." She made her dreadlocks bounce.

"Don't let anyone weird talk to her, okay?" I asked.

"I hope that doesn't include me," Abcde said.

"Bad weird, not good weird." I was starting to feel less paranoid. The sensation of being watched had left my body. Maybe

Sam had been there, shooting daggers when she saw me talking to Ben. Her eyes seemed capable of causing goosebumps. Quinn waved at me, her face gleaming. "I better get back to work," I said, waving back. I looked for Ben on my way to the booth, but he had disappeared into the crowd.

ROBERTS HAD SET up a hand-lettered sign, "Transitioning to Organic," and was selling his pears inside reusable cloth bags. Our bags were cute, but paper, and the eco crowd was swarming to Roberts's booth.

"That sonofabitch," said Mr. Vieira. "I knew he'd steal my thunder."

"He can't do that, can he?" I asked. "Is there somewhere we could call to complain?"

"The organic police don't work weekends." Mr. Vieira rubbed his face with his bandanna. "I should sock him in the nose."

"I don't think that's going to help matters," I said.

"We gotta get ready for the parade," he said with a sigh. "We'll deal with that numbskull later."

JORGE STAYED BEHIND at the booth to make sure no one would steal any pears, and the rest of us took off to either be in the parade or watch it go by. Mr. Vieira had asked if Quinn and I wanted to sit on the back of their vintage tractor and wave to the crowd. I had decided against it—there was the potential to end up in too many photos—but Quinn jumped at the chance.

The parade was a small one—a woman dressed like a pear, a bagpipe band, a few hot-rod convertibles carting the teen Pear Queen and Pear Princesses, a trailer full of little girls wearing "Pear Blossom" sashes, a couple of people dressed up as whales, "Bartlett" and "Seckel" on signs hanging from their necks, some people in uniform on horses, a fire truck covered with waving kids, and the procession of tractors—but the community was out in force, cheering everyone on.

Abcde sat with Quinn on the back of the Vieiras' vintage tractor, and they tossed handfuls of wrapped hard candy—pear flavored, of course—into the crowd. It felt weird to stand on the curb, surrounded by strangers, and watch my daughter drive by, elated, throwing candy to the masses. She was usually too close for me to see her clearly, to see her the way a stranger might, to notice the slightly lumbering, unself-conscious way she moved her limbs, the way the sunlight shone on her dark hair from a distance. She seemed to love having that extra space, that time away from me, her whole face beaming.

Roberts's tractor was right behind, his robot hoisted on the lift in front of it, a big crepe-paper pear coming out of the cone on top. I wanted to boo him or toss something to knock over the robot, but restrained myself.

Then Ben appeared, playing his Portuguese guitar as part of a roving band of musicians that closed the parade—some of them workers from the orchard, others I hadn't seen before. Thankfully they weren't playing the fado—it was lively music, contagious. He looked over at me and winked as he passed. The taste of pear flooded my mouth.

AFTER THE PARADE, some of the workers set up their own booth in the front yard of a bungalow across from the fair. Signs were taped all over it, saying things like "We pick your pears so you don't have to," "Don't let your harvest go to waste," "Meet Needs Of Pickers" (that one was Abcde's idea). The booth had flyers and petitions people could sign to make it easier and safer for people to cross the border to work the fields. The workers knew Bush wouldn't pass any decent immigration laws his last year in office, but they wanted to set the groundwork for future change.

From the Vieiras' booth, I could see a steady stream of people, including Roberts, yell in the workers' faces, but my colleagues didn't back down. Carlos and Oscar, who also spoke fluent English, shared information calmly. Every once in a while, someone shouted, *"Sí, se puede!"* and others would join in. I wanted to go over to lend my support, but was too busy working.

"Do we have some posterboard and a marker?" I asked Mrs. Vieira. "Or a big piece of paper?"

She tore a large square of cardboard from the bottom of an empty box, handed me a Sharpie.

I wrote DON'T BE FOOLED—THESE ARE THE ONLY ORGANIC PEARS IN THE DELTA.

"Is it okay if I put this up?" I asked.

She squinted at the sign and shrugged.

I wanted to write something more inflammatory—ROBERTS LIES! or ROBERTS CARES MORE ABOUT ROBOTS THAN WORKERS—but didn't want to turn a family event into a brawl.

I propped the sign up on the counter, pulled my hat down lower on my head, and waited for the fallout.

KAREN

KAREN FOUND HERSELF COUNTING, NARRATING THEIR time together in her mind. "This is the third time we've done it." "This is the seventh time." "The twelfth time."

The fourteenth time was on the plane on their way to the Championship Series Finals in Canada. Nathan hustled Karen into the tiny bathroom as Deena slept off her Bloody Marys in the darkened cabin.

"Have you joined the Mile-High Club before?" Karen asked, nervous about the germs that must be crawling on every inch of the lavatory.

"I'm a card-carrying member, baby." He shut the door behind him. "But never with anyone like you."

He had said this when he brought out the video camera for the first time, too—he had filmed himself with other lovers, but never anyone like her. Other women had acted like porn stars, contorting their faces and arching their backs for some future imaginary audience; he said he liked how she was shy about the camera, how she was focused more on him, how the sounds that came out of her mouth were more like whimpers than moans.

The scent of air freshener and toilet cleaner was overpowering—not sexy in the least. Karen's body was still sore from their last encounter, which had lasted a lot longer than usual—she felt raw between her legs, felt like she had to pee all the time, but when she sat on the toilet, only a few burning drops came out.

She wanted to say no, but she let him unzip her pants, push her up against the door, lift one of her legs up over his shoulder. The surface was bumpy and cold against her bare bottom; she tried to focus on that sensation, and not him ripping into her, banging her against the door, making it rattle so hard, she was worried it would fly open.

"They're going to hear us," she said, but that only seemed to excite him more. He moaned and pulled out of her, spurting into the air. His semen glopped against her shirt, warm and wet, like a bird dropping.

"I need to use the bathroom," she said. She set the waxy cover on the seat, but when she tried to pee, nothing happened. Just fire. Nathan crouched before her and kissed her, dabbing at her shirt with a paper towel.

"You're amazing," he said, and kissed her again.

THE BURNING GOT worse, and she started to cramp low in her abdomen. By the time they got off the plane, she could barely stand up straight; she had no idea how she'd be able to carry her luggage, much less skate. She was too embarrassed to tell her mother about the symptoms, especially since she was worried about STDs; after they checked in to their hotel, Nathan drove her to an urgent care center on the outskirts of Hamilton.

The doctor called it "honeymoon cystitis" and Karen felt a flush of excitement, as if it meant she and Nathan were practically married. She was given a shot of antibiotics, plus prescribed more to take during the week, and a vial of purple pills that would turn her pee bright orange. The doctor also told them to take a break from intercourse for at least five days. Karen was relieved; intercourse wasn't her favorite part of their intimacy— it was the part she tolerated, not the part she enjoyed. When he was inside her, she never experienced the same stunning rush he could give with his tongue.

"And good luck out on the ice," the doctor said, winking as he handed them the prescription slip. Karen blushed and hoped her urinary condition wouldn't wind up in the news.

THEY RECEIVED SIXTH place in the competition. "Not bad for your first international event," Deena had said. "Not bad at all."

That didn't feel like her biggest accomplishment, though. Over their "break," Nathan taught her how to use her mouth, her hands. She gagged at first, but slowly got used to his taste, his movements, his release. It made her feel proud to know she was capable of such a grown-up skill, that she was capable of giving Nathan so much pleasure.

After the twinging lessened when she peed, they started up again, slowly, to avoid reaggravating her system. By the twenty-sixth time, she stopped counting. By the twenty-sixth time, she started to realize what all the fuss was about. She learned to not cringe, to not hold her breath when he pushed into her. To not care that the video camera was rolling. To not let her mind take her someplace else.

It was like skating, she realized, like skating without choreography, the exhilaration and the flow and the contortion of it. The heart-pounding, cheek-reddening splendor. It was like skating without her mom watching.

"I THINK WE should fire Deena," Nathan said as they jogged along the shore of Lake Geneva the day before the World Championships. The Alps rose in the distance, snowcapped, majestic.

Karen felt a blast of excitement and fear.

"We got us to Worlds, she didn't," he said.

"True," said Karen, even though Deena had choreographed all their programs, sewn all their costumes, supervised all their workouts, gotten them to all their events. She felt a sudden rush of gratitude for her mother, for all that she had done for them.

"We know how we move best," he said. "We know what works for our bodies. We don't need a coach to tell us what to do."

Maybe this would be better for Deena, thought Karen. Maybe it would release her to find a different life. Maybe it would stop her mom from looking at her the way she did sometimes when she thought Karen wasn't looking, that gut-clutching mix of jealousy and pride.

Karen took a deep breath, her lungs sore from the jog. The air smelled different by the lake. Sweet, like sugared rose petals. It was almost overwhelming, the scent. It drowned out thoughts of her mother as Karen and Nathan kept running, stopping every once in a while to kiss and grope on benches, in parks, but when they got back to the hotel and found Deena waiting in the lobby, Karen could barely look at her.

"You smell good." Deena leaned toward Nathan, took a big sniff from his neck. "Like the trees. It's the trees that smell so good, you know. The pittosporum." She held up a guidebook to show she had done her homework.

"It smells like love," said Nathan, and Karen melted into his arms, making sure her mother saw it, making sure she knew, over and over again, that Nathan was hers.

WHEN THEY BROKE the news to Deena over dinner that they no longer needed her coaching services, she looked as if someone had shocked her with a cattle prod, but she quickly straightened her spine, regained her composure.

"I suppose I should have seen this coming," she said, looking into Nathan's eyes, her own eyes wet, hurt, tears hovering but not falling. Karen held her breath.

"I suppose it will give me more time to be your manager." Deena started to rearrange the salt and pepper shakers. "I have tons of calls to make. Disney wants to do a special, and I think I have a Got Milk campaign lined up . . ."

Nathan squeezed Karen's knee under the table. Karen held back the urge to tell her mother they were just kidding, that she could still be their coach, that she had been a wonderful coach, that they were silly to ever think otherwise.

"It's just you and me, babe," Nathan whispered into her ear, and a chill ran through her whole body. "You and me against the world."

IZZY

I HAD BEEN LOOKING FOR BEN SINCE THE PARADE, SO I was thrilled to see him walking toward the booth. At least until I realized he was holding hands with a small Indian American woman. She wore khaki shorts, a bike race T-shirt, Tevas, a big smile. My heart sank.

"Izzy, this is Shanti," he said, his face apologetic.

"Your research partner." My voice sounded flat in my ears.

"You've been talking about me, Benjamim? How sweet!" She wrapped her arms around his waist and I wanted to slug her. "I've heard so much about . . ." I thought she was going to say "you," but then she said "the Pear Fair. I had to come check it out for myself."

"She surprised me." Ben gave a half-smile, half-grimace. "I didn't know she was coming."

Shanti was not much taller than five feet, but she was formidable. She looked like someone who could run a marathon and barely break a sweat. Or stand in front of a room full of students and make them fear her and fall in love with her all at once. Her body was wiry and compact, her eyes large and dark, like a deer's, her shiny black hair pulled back into a neat ponytail. I took some comfort in the fact that her cheeks were a little ashy, her lovely eyes rimmed with dark circles.

"Plus I have to see the whales, of course." She smiled as if she were running for office.

"Of course you do." I could feel a sneer on my face, but didn't do anything to wipe it away. "If you two will excuse me," I said, avoiding Ben's eyes, "I have more pears to sell."

"Izzy . . . ," Ben started, but I turned away before he had a chance to say more.

I could hear Shanti ask him about my handwritten sign. So far, Roberts hadn't shown up to protest it; maybe his eyesight wasn't good enough to see it from his booth. I hoped he'd come over to complain so I'd have an excuse to punch someone in the face. When I turned back around, I could see Ben and Shanti walking arm in arm toward the auditorium.

"Are you okay?" Abcde asked. She and Quinn were both drinking pear smoothies.

"Hmmm?" I asked, watching the happy couple disappear into the building.

"You look like you've seen a ghost." Abcde took a big, rattling slurp.

I had seen just the opposite, in fact; the abstract girlfriend made flesh. When she was just an idea, just a floating thought, she didn't seem so bad. Not nearly as threatening as the shining sun of Sam. Now that I saw her real self glommed onto Ben, I wanted to throw up.

"Just a little tired," I said.

"Can I have some more money?" asked Quinn. "I want to try to win a goldfish."

"Where are we going to keep a goldfish?" My voice turned shrill. "We can't bring a goldfish with us on the road!"

"I thought we were going to stay . . ." Tears sprang into Quinn's eyes.

"Not for long." I slammed a bag of pears on the wooden counter so hard, the paper sack ripped open. Pears flew out, one hitting Roberts, who was storming toward the booth, in the chest.

"And now you try to kill me!" he shouted.

"Take your sign down!" The words roared out of me like a hurricane. They surprised me as much as they did Roberts. Quinn and Abcde took a step back, too.

"Jeez, woman," he said. "Get ahold of yourself."

"Take it down!" I could feel my whole face turn red, the veins in my neck bulge.

"If you take your sign down"—he nodded to my cardboard—"I might be persuaded to get rid of mine."

"If I take mine down," I said, "and you don't get rid of yours, I'm reporting you." To who, I wasn't sure, but it seemed sufficient enough of a threat.

He glared at me, grabbed my sign, and stomped back to his booth. For a moment, he put my sign up on his counter, mocking me with my own words. I held up a pear, ready to lob it at his throat, when he wagged his finger at me and ferried both signs away.

THE VICTORY OVER Roberts was short-lived. My little outburst had attracted more attention than I would have liked. A reporter came up to me and asked what the ruckus was all about. Thankfully, Abcde took over. "Organic politics," she said. "Quite real shit." She let him lead her over to a quiet place to talk about the situation. I told Quinn to come into the booth with me and help me sell pears.

My limbs were so full of adrenaline, I could barely stand still inside the little booth. Luckily, a new crowd had formed—people who had spilled out of the auditorium after the latest cooking demonstration—so I was able to keep my hands busy. Quinn was happy to take money and make change, too—her math lesson for the day. I tried not to pay attention as Ben and Shanti emerged from the auditorium—Shanti talking animatedly, waving a bunch of pamphlets around. I tried not to notice when Ben briefly looked over at me before turning his attention back to his girl-friend. I was glad when they disappeared around the corner, most likely for Shanti to expound in some profuse and intelligent way upon all the offerings at the art fair. She was undoubtedly a better conversationalist than me. How did I stand a chance against someone so educated, so confident in her opinions? How could I ever dare to think I could compete with the Shantis and Sams of the world?

AFTER HER IMPROMPTU interview, Abcde managed to steal the microphone from the stage before the last band of the day performed. I was glad I had a good view from the booth.

"I have a little pear poem," she said. "A list, really. Did you know there is a pear for almost every letter of the alphabet?"

Not many people were paying attention, but a few in the crowd whooped.

"Here is a sampling," she said, and read, in very dramatic intonation:

"Anjou." A slight smattering of applause.

"Bartlett." A huge cheer.

"Comice." A cacophony from the Vieira contingent.

The next pear names didn't receive as much of a response: "Dana's Hovey, Easter Beurre, February Butter, Giffard, Hardy, Idaho, Joan of Arc, Kieffer, Lucrative."

One person shouted out, "Lucrative, baby!"

"Marguerite Marillat," she continued. "No *N*," she said with a wink. "Onondaga, Philopena, Rossney, Seckel." More cheering. "Touraine, Urbaniste, Vicar of Wakefield, White Doyenne."

I wondered what every pear on the list tasted like, if each of them was capable of melting flesh.

She did a little spin on the stage, her dreadlocks and skirt fanning out. "X out *X*," she said mischievously. "Y no *Y*?"

Then she took a deep breath, and sang, in a surprisingly pure tone, "Zoe." She gave a little curtsy, said, "Thank you," and left the stage to a wide round of applause.

A MAN STEPPED onto the stage and announced that the Big Pear Contest winners were going to be revealed.

"Can we go over there?" Quinn asked excitedly.

I looked across to Mrs. Vieira, who nodded, even though the line was fairly long at the booth. I let Quinn pull me over to the tent.

Someone walked out of the giant papier-mâché pear, holding a basket full of large fruit.

The third-place winner was the Silveira family.

"They're Portuguese, too," Mr. Vieira said proudly as he stepped up next to me.

Roberts won second place. He accepted his ribbon with a nod and a wave. I snarled when he looked in my direction.

Quinn shrieked and jumped up and down when Vieira Pears was named the first-place winner.

"You wanna go up there and get the prize?" Mr. Vieira asked. Quinn looked at me for confirmation. I nodded and she ran to the podium.

"I want to thank Jorge for picking the best pear," she said breathlessly, her mouth a little too close to the microphone. "And the Vieiras for growing the best pear. And my mom for taking us to Vieira Pears, the best place, in the first place."

She looked so confident up there, so at home. I wondered what other prizes she could have won if I had let her go to school, if I had let her take some sort of classes—dance or piano or acting or science fairs. What talents had I not encouraged? What unknown gifts had I carelessly let wither away by keeping her tucked so firmly beneath my wing?

She hoisted the giant blue-ribbon-bedecked pear high in the air, looked at Abcde, and said, exultant, "A Bartlett can do everything!"

KAREN

THE YEAR WAS A BLUR OF CITIES, OF COUNTRIES, OF airplanes, tour buses, hotel rooms luxe and dingy, a year of interviews, exhibitions, competitions, public appearances at county fairs and store openings and kids' sporting events. They had placed fifth in Worlds, the top U.S. team in the rankings, plus fourth in Skate America, again the top U.S. team. They had become a favorite at exhibitions—shows where they could do moves that they weren't allowed to use in competition: back flips, more daring lifts, sexier clinches. People began to look at them as the great hope for the U.S. Olympic pairs team; the U.S. had never won an Olympic gold in pairs and only two in Worlds, and those were 1950 and 1979. Article after article talked about the "Coronation of Karenathan." The country was ready for them, their love story, their fairy-tale success.

WHEN DEENA DIDN'T join their travels, Nathan took over as the food police. He kept a careful eye on Karen's caloric intake, making sure she stayed away from carbs and refined sugar, anything with too much oil. She had been hoping for a reprieve on the road, a respite from their grueling training schedule, but Nathan made sure they worked out throughout the day—Pilates and choreographic work in their hotel room, cardio in hotel gyms and pools, and jogs around each new city. Interspersed with their favorite form of exercise.

"We're burning three hundred calories an hour," he would say, sweating onto her back, the video camera whirring next to the bed. "We should sell this as a workout tape."

She preferred when it didn't go on for hours, but he lived for those epic encounters, marathons where he twisted her into as many positions as they used during their routines, where she had to take an antibiotic afterward to stave off the urinary tract infection that was sure to follow. Plus a Diflucan to avoid a resulting yeast infection. The medicines made her stomach churn, but made it possible for them to keep going, for her to not worry about Nathan looking elsewhere, despite the constant showers of panties, phone numbers, the constant reaching hands.

DEENA SET UP one photo shoot after another, one meeting after another—meetings with soup companies, sports drink companies, cereal companies, skating boot manufacturers, condom companies, in search of the most lucrative endorsement. Nathan was the only constant; Karen held on to him like a life preserver. He held on to her, too; he didn't let her out of his sight, started to accuse her of flirting with other skaters on the circuit.

"I saw the way you looked at Todd on the bus," he said in their hotel room.

"Todd's married. Jenni's a sweetheart." Karen would have loved to have Jenni Meno as a friend, but Nathan didn't like when she spoke with anyone but him, even the guys who were openly gay.

"They fell in love on one of these tours," he reminded her. "They were both with other partners at the time."

She knew the other skaters thought she was stuck-up, aloof, but it made things easier to keep to Nathan alone, to not do anything to make him jealous. The closest thing she had to a friendship was the tentative email relationship she had established with Isabelle, but even then, Nathan asked to read every message before she sent it off, and didn't let her reply when Isabelle asked her what she would do with her life if she couldn't skate anymore. She didn't know how she'd answer, anyway. If she tried to think about life without skating now, her mind went snow-blind.

Karen tried not to worry when she heard whispers behind her back, when other skaters accused Nathan of stealing laces, dulling blades, ripping costumes to make them look bad. She tried not to worry when she found blade marks all over a strop that he had used to tie her wrists to a bedpost—strops could be used for sharpening, she told herself, not just dulling. She tried not to worry when the Russian pair who usually closed the show came down with horrible diarrhea after Nathan had passed them some chocolates on the bus. Karen had wanted one herself, but Nathan waved her off, saying, "Too much sugar."

"Did you give them Ex-Lax?" she whispered in their hotel while the Russians were whisked off to an urgent care center just hours before the show was set to open at Madison Square Garden.

"Now, why ever would you think that?" His voice had a mock tone of shock.

"Nathan, that's so stupid. We could get kicked out of the tour. We could get kicked out of the ISU."

"I saw how worried you looked about Dmitriev," he said. "You wanted to nurse him back to health, didn't you? You wanted to be his little nursemaid."

"Nathan—" she started.

"I'm a one-woman man now," he said. "I expect you to be the same."

"You expect me to be a man?" She wanted to laugh, but his expression made her swallow it down. *It's grief,* she told herself. *He's acting this way out of grief.*

Nathan's father had died while they were in Switzerland; he got the voice mail after they finished their long program. They flew back just in time to see him lowered into the grave. Nathan had fallen to his knees on the damp ground; he tossed a stone so hard against the coffin, it left a nick in the shiny wood.

"I don't need anyone but you, baby," she said, and he looked at her as if to say *You better believe you don't.*

Quinn skipped circles around me and Abcde as we walked back to the booth to help pack everything up; she held the prize-winning pear over her head, chanting all the names of pears that she could remember.

"How'd you get into this whole alphabet thing, anyway?" I asked Abcde as I tried not to bump into Quinn, who had now latched onto three names in particular, repeating *Hardy, Joan of Arc, Luc-ra-tive* in a singsong rhythm.

"My parents fought a lot when I was a girl," she said. "I would sing the alphabet to myself to drown them out."

Hardy, Joan of Arc, Luc-ra-tive. Hardy, Joan of Arc, Luc-ra-tive.

I wasn't expecting an answer like that. I tried to picture Abcde as a girl; it was hard to imagine her without the dreadlocks.

"It was my constant," she said. "My mantra. It was a known quantity, always there."

Hardy, Joan of Arc, Luc-ra-tive. Hardy, Joan of Arc, Luc-ra-tive.

"So you started writing poems around it?"

"I started writing poems around it," she said. "Twenty-six line, twenty-six word, eventually doubles."

"What's that?" Quinn fell into step with us, cradling the giant pear like a baby. Her chant kept running through my head as if she were still saying it. *Hardy, Joan of Arc, Luc-ra-tive.*

"Double abcedarians are the hardest," said Abcde. "You go at the alphabet from both directions—the first line starts with *A* and ends with *Z*, the next line starts with *B* and ends with *Y*, and so on. I don't do too many of them."

"I want to hear one," said Quinn.

Somehow, amazingly, Abcde knew one of these double poems by heart. She stood still by the bucking-bronco machine and recited it with a faraway look on her face, a softness in her voice:

"A creak in the door's hinge—that god-damn razzamatazz
blasting across this neat sleep-tight nighty-night sky
clear as a wide white waxy moon until that paradox
dong-dinging my stars awake, that low-below sullen saw
ever-so-slowly screeching as you, cat, wedge in your fat luv,
foisting insidious noise toward my sleep-sloppy boys, you,
gluttonous in your lust for heat, prowling for feet.

"Heave-ho we're thrown—one, two, three, onto awake's bus
in our going-nowhere-beds, a groaning-growling child-roar
jaggedly pointed at my dreaming head—strolling sultry Sadiq,
kneeling, fingering garments massed in a basket . . . POP!
Leave me alone, go back to sleep, but they won't go.
Mama, up, Up, UP! Lights, Mama, on, On, ON!
No, I say, stinging the surly dark, the darkling room."

She continued on until she ended with "Zounds how you sleep—I, almost as far from Zzzz's as A."

"You have sons?" I asked. It was a poem only a mother could write. I could feel the truth of it all the way to my bones. Quinn's rhythm had left my ears; now all I could hear was my heart pounding.

"I haven't seen them in a while." She took a deep breath. "I lost custody a couple of years ago. The flighty poet, you know."

"Oh, Abcde," I said, heart aching. "Is there anything you can do?"

"I want to take my ex back to court," she said, "but he's threatening to dig up all the major dirt. As you can imagine, there's plenty."

"I'm so sorry." I didn't know what else to say.

"People, they screw you over." She ran her hand over Quinn's head; Quinn looked on the verge of tears. "Sometimes the alphabet's the only thing you can count on."

WHEN WE GOT back to the orchard, we learned the whales had returned to Comice Island looking listless, their skin dulled to a chalky gray. The Coast Guard boat hovered, despite their plans to leave the whales alone all weekend. While we were at the Pear Fair, more people had snuck onto the Vieiras' property to get a better look. More cameras, more reporters. More potential for mayhem.

After the Vieiras chased most of the nonpaying people away, I went down to the dock to check out the houseboat. I had hoped to move back in that night—I didn't want to be anywhere near Ben and Shanti—but it was still drenched and dank inside; I still hadn't cleaned the comforter, plus I had to rewash the laundry that had grown sour sitting in the washer all day. There was no way Quinn and I could stay there.

After I put everything in the drier, and sent good night wishes to the whales, I lugged the wet bedspread up to the larger washing machine at the main house and tucked Quinn, still holding the prize-winning pear, into bed in the guest room, then crawled under the sheets next to her. I tried not to listen to the giggles and hushed conversation coming from across the hall, the occasional thumps and squeaks of furniture.

I had barely been able to look at Ben earlier as we broke down the booth at the fair and loaded everything back into the Vieiras' truck; Shanti was going on and on about the research she and Ben were doing, the difference between California and Oregon pears and pests. Everyone—except me—was nodding and interjecting a word here and there, but she was obviously the queen of the conversation. I declined a post-fair dinner with the Vieiras, picking up some dry last-minute turkey legs for myself and Quinn before the food vendors closed.

Shanti's laugh rang out like a bell from Ben's room, as if she wanted me to hear it. I put my pillow over my head; it was hard to believe it was the same day that Ben and I had been in the kitchen together, our lips so full of juice. I was tempted to bang on Ben's door, tell him to keep his girlfriend quiet, tell him to keep his pears to himself.

THERE WAS NO time to recover from the fair; the next day was a normal picking day. I made sure to get up early, before Ben's door opened again, to get out into the orchard without having to see Ben and Shanti at the breakfast table together. Quinn was still asleep; I left a note to tell her to stay in the house until I came back for lunch. It was the first time I had left her alone asleep like that. I tried to tell myself I was not a horrible mother for doing such a thing, that she would be safe, even if there were things she shouldn't know about happening across the hall.

Shortly before noon, Ben came up to my ladder holding a yellow pear, one that had ripened in his family's kitchen.

"You're not getting me with that trick again," I said, glad to be standing above him, to be able to look down at his sorry head; he winced as if I had struck him.

"Pears are in the rose family," he said, offering up the fruit. "A yellow rose is a sign of friendship."

"Did you give Shanti a red pear?" I didn't take the pear from his hand. I picked some more green pears instead, pears that were starting to get more of a yellowish tinge, starting to get grainy inside from too much waiting.

"Shanti left this morning," he said.

"Are you going to follow her?" I lifted more pears, put them in my bag.

"She's going to India, Izzy."

"Visiting family?" My shoulders and lower back were starting to ache from the weight of the fruit hanging off my body.

"She's getting married."

I stopped picking for a moment.

"It's why she really came here," he said. "To let me know." His hand holding the pear dropped down to his side.

"Are you okay?" I arched my back to compensate.

"She's only met the guy a couple of times," he said. "Her parents arranged it."

"And she didn't tell you until now?" Shanti seemed too modern, somehow, too headstrong, to agree to an arranged marriage. I thought about pairs skaters, how they were often thrust into arranged marriages of sorts themselves, coaches creating teams based on various compatibilities, hoping they'd have a lasting and fruitful run. I wondered if her future husband knew what he was getting himself into.

Ben shook his head. "She wanted a last hurrah."

"Hurrah," I said flatly, and started to pick again.

"I always knew it was just temporary," he said, and I didn't answer because I wasn't sure if he meant Shanti or me. Or both. I just kept picking one pear after another, making sure each one was big enough, firm enough, pretty enough for sale.

Ben stood there for a while before he said, "I guess I'll see you later," his head hanging down.

He looked so forlorn as he was walking away, something in me softened.

"I might as well take that pear," I called after him. "But only because I'm starting to get hungry."

It broke my heart to see the hope in his face when he turned around.

"That was nice yesterday," he said as he handed me the pear. "That moment in the kitchen." It felt funny to hear him acknowledge it—putting the experience into words made it seem both more real and more small all at the same time.

The pear was warm in my palm, and smelled wonderful, but I didn't want to eat it in front of him. I didn't want him to think it would be so easy to get back to that moment. Not with Shanti still lingering on his skin.

"Yellow's for friendship, remember," I said, but when I turned the pear around to show him, I noticed a small blush had bloomed on its hip.

KAREN

WHEN THEY WERE HOME FOR THE HOLIDAYS, DEENA sat them down in the family room and said, "We have to think about the Finkels."

Lance and Cindy Finkel were a brother and sister out of Omaha. They looked like twins, but Lance was seventeen, Cindy fifteen. Curly auburn hair framed their freckled and open pixie faces. They had done well as Junior competitors—national Juniors silver medalists, fifth in Junior Worlds—but their first year competing at the Senior level, they were on fire. They had won every competition since—local, regional, sectional—and were considered strong competitors for the National title. The advance buzz was deafening; there was even talk about a quadruple toe loop in the works.

"How could they improve so much in one year?" Nathan fretted as he and Karen watched a DVD of the Finkels' latest program, Karen's mom wedged between them on the den couch. The Finkels were skating to a medley of songs from the cartoon

Anastasia, which Deena thought was pandering to any future Russian judges. Plus riding on Tara Lipinski's coattails. "Steroids?"

"They're so tiny," Deena said. "It's not likely."

"Plus they're total Jesus freaks," said Karen. They actually seemed like nice, decent kids, who prayed before every competition, whose parents were kind and supportive, but she knew she had to say something that sounded edgier.

"See." Her mom pointed to the screen. "See how Cindy doesn't flex her wrist back during their camel? It's like you're directing traffic when you spin, Karen. It's like you're telling the judges 'Stop. Stop considering me for the gold.'"

Karen rolled her eyes behind her mother's back. Nathan beckoned her with his hand, the opposite of stop. Watching his fingers curl in slowly, one by one, she felt a tingle imagining them on her skin. She stepped in front of her mom and sat down between Nathan's legs. Her mom stiffened, but Karen didn't care. She leaned back and let Nathan breathe for the both of them. The Finkels were good, yes, they were adorable, yes, but they were siblings. They didn't have that quality that makes you wonder if they're going to tear each other's costumes off once they leave the ice, sequins and feathers flying. That's what the audience wanted, she thought—chemistry, not love.

IZZY

THE MOTHER WHALE WAS NOSING UP AGAINST Roberts's levee when I went down to the houseboat to grab some more underwear. I hoped she wouldn't beach herself on the slope of gravel, hoped the fresh water of the Delta wouldn't keep eroding her skin, that the erosion wouldn't go deeper, into her veins, her liver, her giant muscled heart.

Big knobs protruded all over her head; it made her look like those body mod people who have ball bearings implanted under their skin. I had read in the library that these were actually hair follicles; I wondered if the bumps itched or ached like razor burn, if she even noticed they were there.

She listed slightly on her side, showing more of the corrugated-looking folds of her lower half, and I remembered a goldfish I had as a child, a goldfish that started to tip over as it swam, that drifted through the bowl on its side for two days, fins barely flapping, before it went belly-up for good. I could barely look at the goldfish, knowing the end was near. I couldn't stop looking at the whale, though. Neither could the crowds on both sides of the slough. Her pocked graying skin, the white beneath her flippers, the large rheumy eye warily taking us all in.

The Coast Guard boat, full of people from the Marine Mammal Institute, idled several yards away. Sam had taken off her blue windbreaker; the tank top she wore beneath her life vest showed off her slender, muscled arms. Her auburn hair was pulled back into a ponytail. She and her colleagues were all wearing headphones—some sort of listening device, I imagined. It took me a moment to notice the gun in her hand. She talked to one of her colleagues, the guy she had been chatting with at the party, who nodded, and then she lifted the gun, steadying her wrist with her other hand, and pointed the barrel toward Bartlett's side. My stomach lurched. I was so glad Quinn was up in the house so she wouldn't have to see this. I wondered if Sam would shoot the baby, too, if both whales needed to be put out of their misery. I wanted to shout out *No! Don't do it!* but my voice was stuck in my throat.

I turned my head before the gun fired. The pop was so loud, it made my head seize with pain. I dropped down to the deck to catch my bearings. When I heard cheering, I thought it was just my ears ringing. But no, I turned to see everyone on the boat celebrating, giving each other high fives, jumping up and down. Sam looked triumphant. How could she whoop after killing such a majestic creature? I couldn't bring myself to look at Bartlett. I didn't want to see the life bleeding from her enormous body.

My legs wobbled as I made my way up the metal steps. The spectators on top of the levee looked surprisingly happy and excited, and I wondered what sort of alternative universe I had entered—a place where people celebrated the shooting of a whale. Maybe they were just buzzing from the drama of it, the adrenaline kick of gunfire.

Abcde came over to me, concerned. "Are you okay?" she asked. "You look miserable."

"They shot Bartlett." My eyes stung.

"Isn't it wonderful?" Her face lit up, and my sense of being on some strange other planet returned. Abcde, too?

"Why is everyone so thrilled about this?" The tears were falling freely now.

"Oh, honey." She wrapped an arm around me, pulled me close to her warm, patchouli-scented body. "You must not have gotten the memo."

She explained to me that the gun was rigged to shoot a blank cartridge, which in turn propelled a syringe full of antibiotics. I felt weak with relief. The Marine Mammal people had passed around a flyer so no one would be alarmed by the gun, but somehow they had missed me.

"It's the first time they've used antibiotics on a whale in the wild," said Abcde. "A little place called Grandpa's Compound Pharmacy over in Placerville mixed up the meds. Can you imagine Grandpa getting that call? 'I need enough penicillin for a whale—stat!'"

I laughed, grateful for her thick arm around me. All the time I spent pining for Sam as a friend, I hadn't let myself realize what a good friend this weirdo poet woman had become. Sam would be in even greater demand now that she was potentially a whale savior; I was glad I didn't feel compelled to wait in line anymore.

Bartlett was thrashing gently in the water. I closed my eyes and imagined the medicine entering her blood and turning it briefly silver, like mercury, sending the gleam of health through her enormous body.

WITHIN A DAY, the whales gained back some strength, some color; they started to swim again, too, although they didn't go far. Just circle upon circle around Comice Island. It was like we were being orbited by two breathing satellites, stretched-out moons with beating hearts.

"Makes me think of whirling disease," Ben said. We had been

careful around each other since the yellow pear, polite as we crossed paths in the hallway, the orchard.

"What's that?" asked Quinn before she started whirling herself. I grabbed her arm before she spun too close to the edge of the levee.

"A parasite," he said.

"Like mistletoe," I said, glad to show off my recent knowledge.

"You don't want to kiss under this one." His eyes briefly caught mine at the word "kiss" before he looked away again. "The trout sometimes get it around here."

"Does it actually make them whirl?" I couldn't help but imagine kissing Ben underwater, under a bunch of pirouetting fish, but I tried to chase the daydream away.

"Yep," he said. I wondered if he was having similar images in his mind. "It makes them spin and spin until they die."

It must be beautiful, I thought. All those iridescent fish scales twirling, glinting in the sun. Beautiful and horrible all at once. I knew what it was like to spin until I thought I would die. To spin past the point of dizziness; to spin until the rest of the world was a blurred cylinder around me, one I was never quite sure I'd be able to reenter again. Just thinking about it gave me a wave of vertigo.

"But the whales don't have that, right?" said Quinn.

"Not unless it makes them go round and round the island," said Ben.

I MOVED OUR things back to the houseboat that afternoon, after some Marine Mammal Institute people assured me they wouldn't do anything else to agitate the whales into more tail slapping. The cabin had aired out quite well. I did a thorough mopping and scrubbing and vacuuming to get out any lingering mildew, dragged the now-clean comforter down from the Vieiras' house. It was nice to be back in our floating bed that night, to hear the gentle lapping of the water, the soft whine of the Delta breeze. Every once in a while, I could sense the whales moving past us during their laps around the island, deep and slow, like a thought that keeps returning, a song you can't get out of your head. I missed having Ben right across the hall, though. As awkward as our dance had become, it was nice to walk past his room and be able to hear him breathe.

KAREN

Karen and nathan met up with the finkels for
the first time in Paris, when they were invited to skate an exhibi-
tion together a few weeks before Nationals.

Karen caught Lance gazing at her from across the lobby of
their glitzy hotel as Nathan and Deena waited to check in. She
met Lance's eyes and he blushed. He took a deep breath, as if to
compose himself, and walked up to her, biting down a giddy
smile.

"It's so wonderful to meet you," he said. "I can't believe we'll
be skating on the same ice!"

His hand was startlingly soft and warm when she shook it.

"Looks like you're the ones to beat this year," said Karen, and
he blushed even more deeply under his freckles.

"I don't know." He looked down, grinning. "Cindy and me—
we didn't expect to get this far this fast. I mean, we've been skating all our lives, so it's not overnight or anything, but still . . ."

Nathan strode over pulling his large suitcase, hitting them
with a blast of cold, hair-gel-scented air.

"Sorry to break up the play date, kids," he sneered, "but we have work to do."

"It was nice to meet you," Karen said.

"No, no, the pleasure was all mine." Lance flushed again. Karen found herself wanting to press her cool cheek against his warm one.

Nathan grabbed Karen's elbow and led her away. "If I hear him mention you and pleasure in the same breath again . . . ," he hissed under his breath.

Karen turned her head and Lance waved.

THAT NIGHT, NATHAN straddled Karen on the grand, ornately carved bed, video camera in hand. She was still naked, but he had put his boxers back on; she loved seeing the line of hair that rose from his waistband, went up to his navel. She reached out to pet it.

"So what are we going to do about the Bobbsey Twins?" He leaned his belly toward her fingers. She could feel his pulse there, strong.

She looked right into the lens. "Let's poison them," she said, keeping her face as serious as possible before she cracked up, waving the camera away. He set it on the end table and pounced, muffling her laughter with his neck.

IZZY

THE AIR WAS MUGGY IN THE ORCHARD THE NEXT morning, as if water had been siphoned from the Delta and hung suspended, invisible, in the space between the trees. I imagined the molecules of water glomming together, coalescing, turning back into a river over our heads; it would crash down to the ground under its own weight, drowning all of us in its warm rank depths, a river that would smell more of sweat than river, the flop sweat of the earth tinged with the sweet rot of overripe pears.

The pears had started to ripen on the tree. Our crews couldn't pick them fast enough. Mr. Vieira had a constant crease in his forehead; I watched it deepen as the skin of the pears lightened, turning from a deep green to a pale green to a pale yellow, the brown freckles coming into sharper relief, liver spots on aging beauty queens. The air filled with their scent.

"It turns my stomach," said Mr. Vieira. "All that sugar in the air."

We picked them as fast as we could, one bag after another, one crate, one trailer after another, but by the time the pears made it to the packinghouse, many of them were too far gone. "Broken," as they're called when they turn ripe. Mr. Vieira had to weed those out before the trucks came to take them away to baby food companies and grocery distributors; he began to pile the rejects up outside, a mass grave, flies buzzing around the sweet rot, the pears browning, melting, the pile shifting as it sank its way into the earth.

A BUNCH OF the workers left for Oregon, their next stop on the picking circuit. It made me surprisingly sad to watch them go; I hoped the farmers in Oregon would treat them well, give them decent places to live, decent wages. I wished I had learned more Spanish; at least Quinn was able to say "Good-bye" and "Thank you for the big pear," in Spanish, to Jorge, who gave her a huge smile and ruffled her hair before he looked over at me, worried he had crossed a line. I smiled and nodded and he shook Quinn's hand, both of them beaming.

The Vieiras said I could stick around—there was more work to be done in the distillery and still a few decent pears to pick if you looked carefully. A few of the local pickers and sorters stayed, too, as did Abcde, who had a couple of weeks before she had to be in Squaw Valley.

More spectators showed up at the orchard after news spread of the whales' dwindling health, their hopeful recovery, their constant island circling. The Vieiras raised the price of admission to twenty-five dollars for just two hours of access, but people were willing to pay anything to catch a glimpse of the whales. I steered away from the new folks as much as possible, but sometimes Abcde dragged me over to meet someone with a particularly interesting story—the guy who had recently started walking across the country and had vowed to not buy food for a year, only eating fallen fruit and foraged plants and food people gave him for free; the woman who flew in from Hawaii to play her pan flute for the whales; the "whale whisperer" who was sure he could say a few magic words and the whales would find their way back to the sea. When anyone asked about my story, I would say "I'm just a mom," or "I just work here."

The fallen-fruit guy, Danny, seemed to take an interest in me, though. He was only nineteen, about to take a leave of absence from UC Berkeley as he went on his quest. He had big bushy hair, a springy beard—he seemed to have willed himself to go feral just a month into living off the land. He certainly smelled feral.

"I appreciate a woman who works with her hands." He gave me a knowing look as he scooped some pears up and put them in his canvas satchel, already stained from overripe fruit.

I wasn't attracted to him in the least, but I let him hover around me just to watch Ben sneak glances at us, clearly trying not to look jealous. I even let Danny kiss me once before he left for other pastures, while Quinn was off making an alphabet bead necklace in Abcde's tent. His lips were chapped and his beard scratched my face and his breath was awful, but Ben was watching, so I pretended I enjoyed it.

"I see you have a new boyfriend," Ben said later as we boxed up more bottles of eau-de-vie.

"Just a friend with benefits," I said, and watched Ben's face fall.

KAREN

BY THE TIME THEY GOT TO PHILADELPHIA FOR
Nationals, Karen's period was a couple of weeks late. It didn't
concern her too much—she thought maybe she was lucky
enough to get amenorrhea, like so many of the other girls. She
was training extra hard, dialing the new choreography into her
muscles. Plus, this was the most important competition of their
career so far—their stepping-stone to the Olympics. It was not
surprising her body would close up shop under the stress. But
then she started throwing up every morning. And noticed how
dark her nipples were getting. And the fact that her center of balance was just a little bit off.

The throwing up didn't concern Deena. "It's just nerves," she
said, "and it's helping keep your weight down." Karen knew it
could be more than that, though. Nathan hated condoms but didn't
always pull out in time. The morning before the short program, she
told her mom she had to go to the pharmacy down the street.

"I'll go with you," said Deena. "I need some Dulcolax."

"I'll pick it up," said Karen. "I need some time to clear my head." It was disconcerting to have Deena around after spending most of the year away from her.

After making sure no one with a camera had followed, she ducked into the alley behind the Walgreens and asked a grizzled man with a "Homeless, God Bless" cardboard sign under his arm if he would go in and buy the Dulcolax and a pregnancy test for her. She showed him a fifty and said he could keep the change if he didn't tell anyone about the transaction.

He was hesitant at first. "They gonna think I knocked someone up," he said, his breath filling the cold air with white puffs.

"I wouldn't worry about that," said Karen.

"I'm a gentleman," he said. "And I can take a shit without no pills."

"If you don't do it, I won't pay you," she said, jiggling her legs to keep warm.

"Fine. Don't let nobody touch my sign." He propped the cardboard against the wall, plucked the bill from her hand with his gloved fingers, and trudged around the corner.

Snow was starting to flurry again. She tightened the hood of her long down coat and stood with her back to the street, turning when someone came out onto the loading dock behind the store to throw trash in the Dumpster. If she, one of America's sweethearts, was seen doing back-alley dealings with a bum, it would cause a stir, especially the morning before her big performance, the one bound to seal her Olympic berth. Maybe she should have waited to get the test, she told herself. At least until after the program. But she wanted to know for sure. She didn't want to be distracted by uncertainty. Even if she was going to freeze her butt off in the process.

The guy shuffled back with a green plastic bag. After she thanked him and started to walk away, she looked inside the bag and saw that there was a pack of chocolate calcium chews along with the two boxes.

"Hey, you forgot these." She held out the foil-wrapped packet. Her face was so cold, it hurt to talk.

"No, ma'am," he said, hoisting his sign under his arm. "Little bitty thing like you, baby'll pull the calcium right out of your bones."

SHE FOUND A coffeehouse restroom where she could take the test. It was a one-person bathroom, the only one there, and people pounded on the door or jiggled the knob every minute or so. She got used to saying "Sorry, I'm still in here," trying to disguise her voice as much as she could. The small room was painted a deep burgundy, with ornate, gold-framed mirrors on every wall and a little vanity stool covered with matted gold velvet near the black pedestal sink. The white plastic wand in her hand looked so flimsy in the middle of the baroque trappings. She sat on the black toilet and stared at the front and back of her head all at once, a never-ending row of Karens stretching out in all directions. Soon her face would be covered in makeup, soon her hair would be yanked into a tight bun, lacquered smooth with hair spray, but for now she was pale and freckled, her bleached hair riddled with split ends. She looked in the mirrors and watched the pink line on the wand get darker and darker, endless pink lines surrounding her like a kaleidoscope.

Mr. Vieira came into the distillery the next morning, waving the *Sacramento Bee*. "You made the paper!" he said, looking amused. "Miss Keep-me-away-from-the-cameras."

I snatched the paper from his hands. My profile was in the foreground of the photo, the right corner, as I gazed out at the whales. The wind was blowing my hair against my cheek, but it didn't obscure my face. Danny's beard and hair poofed out behind me. The top of Quinn's head floated in front of me like an island at the bottom of the photo, split ends lifting. The caption read: *A spectator enjoys watching the humpbacks at Vieira Pears on Comice Island.*

"You're famous!" said Quinn excitedly.

"It's an AP photo, too," said Mr. Vieira. "Gonna be picked up by other papers."

"Oh my God." I hadn't signed a release for my photo to be used. At least they hadn't printed my name.

"I wouldn't let it get to your head none," Mr. Vieira joked.

I was stunned. How could this happen? How could I have let

this happen? Why didn't I just run away when people with cameras showed up?

"It's yesterday's paper, too," said Mr. Vieira. "Didn't read it till today."

"You look beautiful," Ben said softly, and for the moment, all my worries dissolved.

THAT AFTERNOON, BEN asked if Quinn and I wanted to go for a walk. I was excited until he started talking about smelt, which is probably the most unromantic word in the English language. Mr. Vieira had mentioned smelt before; the governor had decided to cut off much of California's water supply from the Delta that summer because opening dams would negatively impact the dwindling smelt population.

"I don't get what the big deal is over such a little fish," I said as we walked into the orchard.

"The smelt aren't healthy, the Delta's not healthy," said Ben. "They're like the canary in the coal mine."

"Whoever smelta delta." Quinn giggled, then ran off into the trees.

"But tons of people aren't getting water." I watched her red shirt flash between trunks, then disappear. "Tons of farmland won't be irrigated."

The Vieiras were lucky, not having to irrigate, water rising up through the peat soil on Comice Island, making it rich and moist, like chocolate cake. Most farmers weren't so fortunate.

"We need all the little critters. Like the bees," Ben said. "They're disappearing all over the country."

"Fine by me," I said.

"You'd miss them more than you realize."

"Quinn's allergic." The less bees, the better, as far as I was concerned. It would be wonderful to not have to worry about stings, to not have to carry an EpiPen, to not have to picture Quinn lying on the ground with her throat closing up whenever she got out of my sight. I whipped my head around until I could see her playing with one of the barn kittens.

"Every third bite you put in your mouth comes from a bee," he said. "Pear trees don't need them, but cherries do. Almonds. Avocados. Tons of crops."

"Why don't pears need them?"

"They pollinate themselves," he said.

"No fun in that." I immediately blushed.

Ben smiled without looking at me. "Have you ever smelled a pear blossom?"

I shook my head.

"They stink," he said. "Like rotten meat."

"Really?" I thought of the perfume of a Gravenstein apple blossom, the thick, dense sweetness of an orange grove in bloom.

"I imagine it tells the bees they're not needed," said Ben.

"I want to smell one," I said.

"Trust me," said Ben, "you don't."

He wrinkled his nose, but I liked knowing something stinky could lead to something delicious.

"What do you think happened to the bees?" I asked.

"No one knows," he said. "Could be cellphones. Mites. Some sort of apian AIDS."

"They should start using condoms." I felt my face go red again. I wasn't used to flirting, especially sexy flirting, but somehow Ben brought it out in me. I was glad to feel I could flirt with him again.

Ben grinned. "But we need bee babies."

We walked for a while longer. Mosquitoes whined by. Some of the leaves on the pear trees had partly folded up, creased in the center like a book perched on someone's lap. I wondered what it would take for them to open back all the way.

"Everything's out of balance." His face was serious again. "Bees disappearing, whales where they're not supposed to be."

"Do you think they're connected?" I asked.

"Everything's connected." He twined his fingers in mine. He

did it so simply, so easily, I wasn't sure it was a conscious decision. He didn't look at me, but his palm was warm and felt sweet and solid against my own. We were still holding hands when we met up with Quinn, a kitten perched on her shoulder. She hadn't seen me hold hands with anyone her entire life, but she didn't seem fazed by it. She took my other hand and we walked back to the distillery.

KAREN

KAREN WAS SURPRISED NATHAN WASN'T WAITING FOR her in their hotel room, but he burst in shortly after she got back, the pregnancy test wrapped in toilet paper inside her purse.

"I did it." Nathan swooped Karen up in his arms.

"You did what?"

He trembled against her. Her own heart started to pound with anticipation. He knelt before her on the wildly patterned carpet and pressed his head against her belly, wobbling as he rummaged around in his pocket.

Was he about to propose? Karen's blood flashed through her veins. She would say yes. How could she not? This was just like Nathan—spontaneous, romantic, given to grand gesture. They knew they belonged together—why not make it official? Especially with the baby. Now she could tell him about the baby. Now she could think about keeping the baby. She wouldn't be showing by the time the Olympics started. They would win, go pro, take the baby with them on the road—it would be perfect.

He pulled his hand out of his pocket, but there was no plush velvet box there; no diamond studded with lint. Just a tiny zip-lock bag, the kind she used to hold spare beads, the microscopic seed ones, for her competition dresses. At the bottom lay a thin layer of white powder.

"It's what you wanted." He laughed wetly into her shirt.

"Drugs?" She jumped back and he folded to the ground. "I never said I wanted drugs! Are you crazy? They do random test-ing, Nathan!"

"Not drugs," he said, but when he lifted his face, his eyes looked glassy and bloodshot, stoned.

"What the hell?!"

"It's what you wanted." He crawled over to the end table and grabbed the remote. The TV hummed to life. Karen recognized the front of the hotel. An ambulance was parked on the U-shaped driveway by the revolving doors. SKATER COLLAPSES read the cap-tion at the bottom of the screen.

"What skater?" Karen felt a wave of vertigo. She had the strange sensation that she was the skater, that she was the one who collapsed, that she was having an out-of-body experience, her mind floating in the hotel room while her body was strapped to a gurney downstairs. She watched the ambulance pull away from the curb on TV. She watched a picture of Lance appear in its place. She ran to the window. The ambulance was racing down the street, followed by news vans.

"Your wish is my command." Nathan knelt before her again, then put his face in his hands.

IZZY

THE BUILDINGS WERE EMPTY WHEN WE GOT BACK, BUT we could hear a clamor on the other side of the island, so we piled into Ben's truck to check it out. A big crowd was gathered at the levee. Ben waved to his father and went to talk to him, and Quinn and I walked toward the crowd. Maybe it was because my hand was still vibrating from Ben's, but my edges felt porous, open. I didn't feel separate from the group of spectators, scared of the group of spectators, as Quinn and I entered it.

The whales had responded so well to treatment—or, who knows, maybe to the pan flute and the whale whispering, as skeptical as I was of both—they were breaching, jumping out of the water, showing us their beautiful ridged bellies, landing with such a splash that some of us got wet, even twenty feet above the slough. I was grateful that I had closed all the windows in the houseboat that morning. I was grateful to bear witness to the most beautiful twisting duet I had ever seen, the two whales leaping in tandem, their bodies full of joy.

We stood at the edge of the berm, a breathing mass of people, an orchard of us, a singular organism. Our identifying characteristics melted away—we were pears before the sorting, a unified field. We stood and waited, all our hearts knocking. The whales' hearts booming beneath ours, a slow bass note to our clattering snares.

We wanted to see them leap again, to see something monumental. That's what we do, we humans. We slow down at accidents. We buy outrageously priced tickets to watch athletes, singers, dancers in their prime. We fly to exotic locales. We squint at museum paintings. We move toward majesty, toward anything that makes us feel big. Anything that makes us feel small. Anything that reminds us we're alive. We humans flock toward awe.

THE WHALES FINISHED their show and swam off, and the crowd dispersed, each of us still ringing with amazement but ourselves again now, aware of the places where our skin met the air, aware of the spaces between us. I kept holding Quinn's hand as I looked across the slough, trying to hold on to that sense of wider connection.

I had come to recognize certain people who camped on Roberts's land. They were too far away for me to see their faces clearly, but close enough that through body language and shape, I could tell that the woman who wore the Mickey Mouse shirt had been the one wearing the Pokemon shirt the day before, could tell the shirtless paunchy guy in Hawaiian print shorts had been the one with the large video camera all week. So when I saw a wiry guy in a tight black T-shirt and jeans, at first I thought he looked familiar because he had been there every day, rooting for the whales. But there was a different quality to his movements— while everyone else had looked excited, concerned, hopeful, he looked frantic. Desperate. Bobbing his head around, bouncing on the balls of his feet like some sort of addict. His energy made me nervous. Then he turned his face and the sun caught his jawline and my heart stopped. All my blood seemed to pool in my neck, ready to explode. I looked down to catch my breath; when I looked up again, he was gone.

KAREN

KAREN STAYED GLUED TO THE TV SCREEN. A SOMBER-looking anchor appeared. "Terrible news to report," he said. "We just received word that rising sixteen-year-old figure skater Lance Finkel died en route to the Children's Hospital of Philadelphia. We will keep you updated as we receive more information about this tragic situation."

Karen was dizzy. There had to be some mistake. Lance wasn't dead. Reporters were wrong all the time. It had to be some other boy. Some other Lance.

"I bought him a Shirley Temple, down at the open bar," Nathan said. "Stirred some powder in before I brought it over. Told him it was a peace offering."

Karen's mouth filled with something sickly sweet. She swallowed hard so she wouldn't be sick. "What kind of powder?" she asked.

"Just some pills ground up. Downers. Just to knock him out awhile." Nathan looked dead himself, all the color drained from his face. "Make him too sleepy to skate."

"Nathan!"

"You told me to poison him," he said, and she could feel the wheels turning in his head, foisting the blame in her direction.

"I was kidding when I said that." Her whole body was suddenly numb. "I would never . . ."

"You told me to do it, Karen." His voice filled with steel. So did his eyes. "You told me, and I have it on tape."

Ben walked up to me.

"That was incredible, wasn't it?" I asked, still looking across the slough. There was no sign of the wiry guy. He must have been an illusion, just a figment of my imagination. I tried to quiet my racing heart.

"I only saw a little," he said. "My dad had to show me something."

"What?" I couldn't imagine anything else worth seeing when a whale was leaping in your backyard.

Ben grabbed my hand—this time with intention, with a firm, sure grip—and I grabbed Quinn's. He ferried us into his truck and drove us to the cold-storage house. When he rolled the door open, the smell of ice hit me like tear gas.

"The pipes burst," he said. "Lucky we already shipped out most of the pears. Only lost a few boxes."

The concrete floor of the wooden building was covered with a rime of ice. It glittered in the shaft of sunlight that came through the open door, wet and slick.

"We keep this room at thirty degrees," he said. "The pears don't freeze because of all the sugar. But water sure does."

I felt light-headed as I stepped through the doorway. The ice gently sucked the tread of my work boot, but with my next step, I slid a few inches and felt a giddy zing up my spine. The air was cool and sweet; I inhaled deeply as I took another sliding step, then another, until I was slipping all over the small warehouse, the wood beams bent over me protectively, like a rib cage. Ten years. How could I have been off the ice for ten years?

"Come here, Quinn." My eyes stung; I told myself it was from the cold, from the wind I created by rushing around.

Quinn tentatively stepped onto the ice. She had never seen snow, had seen ice only in glasses.

"Don't worry." I held out my hand, and Quinn walked toward me in tentative steps. "Just let yourself move with the ice." Maybe we could go up to the mountains that winter, rent a cabin somewhere near a good sledding hill. Maybe an outdoor rink, one that wouldn't be too crowded. Maybe I could pick up a pair of skates—not rentals with their floppy ankles and dull blades. Something with a spongy tongue, sharp edges. My work boots felt way too clumsy with their thick rubber soles.

Quinn and I stumbled and slid across the surface, Quinn shrieking, face lit up, whenever she lost her balance. Ben grinned, leaning against the doorway.

"Why don't you join us?" I called to him.

"Maybe in a little," he said.

"Hold both my hands," I told Quinn. "Keep your arms nice and tight."

I bent my knees, then hoisted her all the way up over my head, her legs stretched out behind her in the air.

Quinn shouted, "Mom! Put me down!" but I started to spin—nothing too fast, just a slow rotation, step by step, until Quinn started to wobble, legs flailing, and I set her back onto the ground.

"Jesus, you're strong," said Ben.

"I told you—it's picking pears." I shook out my aching wrists. Quinn was a lot heavier than a bag of pears; I hadn't lifted her that high since she was a toddler.

Quinn lost her footing and crashed onto the melting ice, reddening her palms. Ben ventured out to help her and fell, too, drenching his entire side, sending his khaki baseball cap flying.

"Cold, huh?" Quinn laughed.

"Soaked to the bone." He crossed his arms in front of his chest to keep warm. "We better go change before we catch pneumonia or something."

"I think I still have some stuff at the house," said Quinn.

"You start on ahead," I said. "I'll close everything up."

Ben and Quinn slipped a couple of times as they struggled to get upright, then helped each other over to the door with stiff, careful steps, their clothes splotched dark from the cold water.

I waved as they walked away. So lovely to see Quinn comfortable with Ben. So lovely to be able to look at Ben from behind. So lovely to have the ice all to myself as they walked toward the farmhouse.

The ice was not great. It was slushy in places. But it was ice and I was on it, and I wanted to see what I could do in my clunky boots. I tried a simple scratch spin, not too fast, my free leg crossing, sliding down the front of the other, my hands pulled together in front of my heart. It felt good and not good all at once; my body was happy to be spinning again, but I found myself distressingly dizzy. I put my hands on my knees until I caught my bearings again. I thought of all the pears that had been in that cold-storage building over the years, "sleeping" as Mr. Vieira called them, holding still inside their green skins before they were allowed to come out and ripen. Maybe the spins were sleeping inside my muscles all these years, shoved into cold storage, waiting to be unpacked. Maybe the jumps were there, too. I stood and inhaled deeply.

There wasn't much stroking room, wasn't much decent ice, but I took a few sliding steps and tried the easiest jump—a waltz jump, just half a rotation. The landing wasn't the same as on skates—I landed planted rather than sliding backwards, but it felt wonderful to be up in the air. I tried a single jump—a loop: back outside edge, full rotation in the air, back outside edge again, not that my boots had edges. But that felt good, as well. Then an axel, one and a half rotations, taking off forward, landing backwards, a waltz jump and a loop combined in the air. A little wobbly on landing, but the form felt right as I corkscrewed through the room, the wooden slats of the walls spinning with me. A double was the next obvious move—a double lutz, like a double loop, but starting with a toe pick. I slipped a bit on take-off and the landing was a little squirrelly, but not bad. I was contemplating whether I should attempt a double axel, when I saw someone out of the corner of my eye. Ben, standing in the doorway.

"You sure know what you're doing," he said.

"I used to," I said, heart pounding.

"Left my hat." He bent to pick it up; the bill was partly melded to the ice and took some tugging.

His eyes suddenly seemed closed off. Quinn appeared behind him, eating a green pear she had swiped from one of the remaining boxes.

"You shouldn't eat too many of those," I said, "you'll get a stomachache."

I held my breath and waited for Ben to say something to Quinn like "Did you know your mom could do tricks like that?" or "Do you know who your mom is?" but he just said, "I've eaten hundreds of green pears. I'm still alive."

KAREN

WHEN NATHAN WENT INTO THE BATHROOM, KAREN RAN downstairs to the lobby. It was full of skaters, coaches, all looking stricken, looking for answers. Reporters were busy corralling the most famous skaters they could find; Karen walked sideways, head down, trying to avoid the cameras. She needed to get outside, get some fresh air.

Isabelle was standing by the doorway. She and her cousin had made it to Nationals for the first time; Karen was happy for her, but kind of sad, too—Isabelle seemed more serious this year. Her emails had focused on her diet and training regimen lately, her body mass index, her costume design. Karen hoped Isabelle would still take time to visit the Liberty Bell and whatever other fun touristy things she could find in Philadelphia. Things Karen knew she herself would never see, unless she was driving or jogging past them.

"Karen!" Isabelle yelled. Karen had been excited to see Isabelle, but not like this.

"I need to get out of here." Karen felt sick. Isabelle ushered her outside, and Karen threw up on the sidewalk.

"Your trademark move!" Isabelle laughed nervously before she said, "Isn't it awful what's happened? Poor Lance—poor Cindy!"

"I need to get out of here," Karen said again.

"You need to see a doctor?" Isabelle asked.

Karen nodded, looking back to make sure Nathan hadn't followed her.

"Do you need a ride?" Isabelle asked.

"You have a car?" Karen perked up.

"My mom's . . ."

"Can I borrow it?" asked Karen.

"Are you sure you're up to driving?" Isabelle asked. "God, I hope you don't have the same thing as Lance." She took a step back from Karen.

"I'll be fine," Karen said, but thought, *No I won't. Nothing will ever be fine again. Ever.*

"It's the blue Pontiac with the polar bears in the back window." Isabelle tossed over a set of keys with an Epcot Center key chain. Karen ran off to the parking lot without saying thanks, without saying good-bye, without thinking anything but *Get out, get out, get out.*

IZZY

WHEN ABCDE ASKED IF I WANTED TO GO OUT TO DINNER
with her in Isleton, I jumped at the chance. It would be a relief to
get away from the orchard for a while, to get away from Ben's un-
spoken questions, to get in the car and drive. Maybe we should
have followed Jorge and the other guys up to Oregon. Maybe it
still wasn't too late to join them.

Abcde had heard about a restaurant and hotel called Rogelio's that featured American, Chinese, Italian, and Mexican food
all on one menu. It looked like a Wild West saloon on the outside—I was worried it might not be a good place for kids when
we pulled up to it—but the inside was full of cozy tables and fake
flowers and big families sitting down to plates of chile relleno and
fettuccine Alfredo and sweet and sour pork. We couldn't even
tell people were playing blackjack and poker on the other side of
the back wall.

Quinn slid into the aqua-colored booth next to Abcde. They
were wearing the necklaces they had made—Abcde's had her
name spelled out in alphabet beads; Quinn's spelled INNQU, her

name in alphabetical order. She told me she was going to use it as her pen name when she herself became a famous abecedarian poet.

Our server, an older Asian woman, set down bowls of chips and salsa and handed us large menus.

"At least they don't serve whale," said Abcde, thumbing through the pages. "They serve just about everything else here." She ordered the spinach and mushroom enchiladas—so did Quinn, who wanted to become a vegetarian, just like her new idol. I was going to order the veal scaloppine, but Abcde and Quinn gave me such withering looks, I changed my order to pasta primavera al pesto.

"Nice alliteration," said Abcde. "We approve." Quinn nodded. Since when had they become "we"? I felt continents away even though I was just across the table. I wanted to say something, but then I thought about how Abcde's boys truly were continents away, out of her reach even when they were close by, and I held my tongue.

"You plan on keeping in touch with Danny?" Abcde said after we got our meals. I was kind of glad to see spinach stuck in her teeth. I hoped my own teeth weren't slathered with green from the pesto.

"Fallen-fruit guy?" I shook my head.

"He's cute," she said.

"If you like them hairy and smelly."

"Oh, I do." Abcde grinned wickedly. "I do."

"My mom's in love with Ben," Quinn said, digging into her little cup of pinto beans.

"Quinn!"

"You were holding his hand," she said matter-of-factly.

"You were, were you?" Abcde's eyes sparkled as she leaned forward. "Tell me. Everything."

"That's all there is to tell," I said, blushing.

"Your mom," Abcde said to Quinn. "She's full of secrets, isn't she?"

I swallowed my sip of water the wrong way.

"She's going to marry him," Quinn said with her mouth full.

"Quinn, I held his hand once," I said, coughing. "That doesn't mean I'm going to marry him."

"And then we can stay at the orchard for ever and ever." Quinn held up her hand for a high five, but Abcde wrapped her arms around her instead, and Quinn, to my surprise, started to cry.

She was still crying when the woman brought us our fortune cookies. Mine said, *Now is the time to try something new.* I didn't show it to Quinn—she had been on the "try something new" tour all her life. I knew she was ready to stay put.

KAREN

K AREN HAD NEVER DRIVEN ALONE BEFORE. EITHER HER
mom was teaching her or Nathan was teaching her, or one of
them was coming along for the ride. More often than not, she
was in the passenger seat—sometimes the back seat, with her
mom and Nathan up front. The driver's seat felt like a throne, the
unfamiliar car cavernous as she drove. At first, her heart was
pounding so hard, she could barely see where she was going, but
once she found the highway, everything turned cool and silent.
Every once in a while, she turned a corner and one of the plush
polar bears in the back shifted, startling her, but otherwise, a
strange calm descended upon her. She was no longer a competitive figure skater, a girl whose boyfriend had just killed someone.
She was just a body moving forward through space, stopping only
to drain money from her savings account or use the bathroom or
get something at a drive-through, the grease a serious shock to
her system.

She drove and drove well into the night. She wasn't sure what
state she was in, what state she was heading toward. All she could

see were her headlights scraping the road, bits of snow gleaming softly from the surrounding pine trees. The whole world blanketed by silence.

She fished around in her purse for her cellphone; she had turned off the ringer. There were eleven missed calls. She listened to her messages, deleting most as soon as she heard her mother's voice. One from Nathan, from jail, said, "You need to turn yourself in, sweetheart. It's the right thing to do." A second, logged in a few minutes later, said, "Karen! You can't do this to me! I love you!" She didn't know prisoners were allowed more than one call, but there was a third, too, his voice sharper now, harder: "If I'm going down, Karen," he said, "you're going down, too." A fourth said, simply, "Bitch." Karen swallowed the acid rising in her throat, tears warm on her cheeks. There was one more message, from Isabelle: "You better ditch the car soon." She sounded frantic. "My mom just noticed it's gone."

WHEN WE GOT BACK TO THE VIEIRAS', THE LIGHTS WERE
on in the distillery and Mr. Vieira was standing outside, screaming his head off.

I stopped the car and got out.

"What's going on?" I asked.

"That asshole Roberts!" I had never seen Mr. Vieira so upset.
"That fucking asshole Roberts!"

"We don't know it's him, Dad," Ben said. Mrs. Vieira paced in
tight circles behind him, talking to herself in rapid Portuguese.

"What happened?" Quinn looked terrified.

"Fucking Roberts smashed all our eau-de-vie," Mr. Vieira
said, before shouting something in Portuguese to his wife. She
stopped pacing and scurried into the distillery, her large body
moving faster than I had ever seen.

All that work we had put into those bottles. All that income
they were expecting . . .

"Not all of it," said Ben. He couldn't seem to look at me.

"More than half!" his father shouted. "I'm going to beat the life out of that sonofabitch."

"We need to let the police deal with it," said Ben. "No need to take matters into your own hands."

"He took matters into his hands," said Mr. Vieira. "Now I'll take matters into mine."

KAREN

KAREN PULLED INTO A FOREST PRESERVE, STOPPED the car in front of a small frozen lake. The headlights illuminated the icy surface, bumpy, almost grainy-looking. How could she go back to smooth, slick ice now? There was nothing she could do to make things better. Nothing she could do but disappear.

Hot air blasted from the vents; she turned the heat off so she could feel the coldness of the night against her face. She found a thin gas-station pen in the glove compartment, a page with directions on one side. She turned it over and wrote:

> Dear Mr. and Mrs. Finkel (and Cindy),
> I'm so sorry. I didn't mean what I said to Nathan. I never meant to hurt anyone. I was just joking around—I never thought he would really do it. You have to believe me. I am sorry. I am so sorry. I know I can't bring Lance back, but at least you won't have to worry about me anymore.
> Karen

CIRCLES OF LIGHT continued to float in front of Karen's eyes after she turned off the headlights. She blinked until they faded away, until she saw nothing but the dull glow of the winter night. She got out of the car and took a few steps forward, her boots crunching through the crust of snow, then inching onto ice. She took careful steps farther out onto the frozen lake, until she started to hear the ice creak, feel it crackle and shift beneath her. She was tempted to turn back to the safety of the car, tempted to think about the baby growing inside her, but she forced herself to stay where she was. She forced herself to stand still and let the ice split all around her, filling the air with its broken song.

IZZY

GLASS WAS EVERYWHERE. IF IT HADN'T BEEN SO AWFUL, it would have been beautiful—the shards reflecting the light, sending their shimmer all over the distillery walls. The room smelled amazing, too, all that pear essence released into the air, perfect green fruit lounging all over the floor.

Mr. Vieira had stormed toward the bridge, Ben following him.

Mrs. Vieira grabbed a broom and started to sweep up some of the glass. Most of the alcohol had already evaporated, but the floor was still wet.

"Can we help you?" I asked, and she just shrugged. I went to the main house and found another broom and a mop in the pantry. I tried not to look at the bowl of Bartletts as I walked through the kitchen, the fruit full of dark splotches now, well past its prime.

"Isn't this typical?" said Abcde as I handed her a broom. "The men go off to fight and the women are left to clean up the mess."

BEN AND MR. Vieira eventually stumbled back, Mr. Vieira cradling one fist.

"Well, he bloodied Roberts's nose," said Ben.

"Fucking asshole said he didn't know anything about the bottles," Mr. Vieira grumbled.

"He honestly didn't seem to know what we were talking about," said Ben.

"Bullshit!" Mr. Vieira opened and closed his fingers a few times, wincing.

"There was a big crowd here today," said Abcde. "Maybe someone came back . . ."

I had a sudden flash of the man I thought I saw across the slough. A shudder ran through me.

"I know it was that sonofabitch," said Mr. Vieira. "Probably broke the pipe in the icehouse, too."

Quinn continued to help clean, carefully lifting one pear after another from the ground and putting them in a trash bin, but I could tell she was shaken.

WHEN THE POLICE finally arrived, I busied myself with the broom, making sure to avoid eye contact.

"Thank God you're here," said Mr. Vieira.

Before he could continue, an officer said, "Demetrio Vieira, you have the right to remain silent," and pulled out his handcuffs. He looked as if he knew Mr. Vieira personally, as if he hated to have to arrest him.

"You have the wrong man!" Mr. Vieira yelled as the officer gently pulled his arms behind his back and cuffed his hands.

"I'll call your lawyer," said Ben. Out of the corner of my eye, I saw him flash me a look before he followed his father to the police car. Mrs. Vieira trailed behind, wailing as if someone had died.

"We better get back to the boat," I said, and Quinn nodded, a serious expression on her face. "We can drop off Abcde on the way."

EVEN THOUGH I had closed all the windows, the houseboat was still a little wet inside, the whales' stunning acrobatics powerful enough to send water through the tiny gaps in the frames. When I went to turn down the thankfully dry bedspread, my nerve endings lit up like a switchboard. There was a perfect, whole Comice sitting on the pillow, still smelling of eau-de-vie, a couple of chips of glass glinting from its sides like dew. Or ice.

"Eema!" Quinn whimpered. I gestured for her to be quiet so I could try to tell if anyone was still inside the houseboat. I grabbed a heavy-duty flashlight as a potential weapon of self-defense, and slid open the closet, the bathroom door, all the cabinets. When those turned up clear, I told Quinn to stay inside and I went onto the deck to check inside the life preserver box. No sign of anyone. Just the whales, whose sudden blowhole puffs almost made me jump out of my skin.

"Eema!" Quinn clung to me when I came back inside. "I don't want to sleep here."

"I don't either," I said. "Pack your bags."

WE CONVINCED ABCDE to come with us to the hotel.

"It's not quite a horse head in the bed," said Abcde when we told her about the pear, "but it's still a bit close for comfort."

Ben's truck was pulling into the driveway as we were pulling out. Mrs. Vieira was in the passenger seat; there was no sign of Mr. Vieira.

"They're keeping him overnight," Ben said after we both rolled down our windows. He looked more exhausted than I had ever seen him. He still seemed to have trouble looking at me.

"We're spending the night at Rogelio's," Abcde said, leaning

over my lap. "Someone left a pear on Izzy's pillow. From the eau-
de-vie."

"Maybe I'll head over there later," he said. This time he
looked into my eyes so directly, my heart knocked against my
ribs. "Izzy, we need to talk."

"OOOH," ABCDE SAID as we drove down the dark levee roads.
"He wants to 'talk,' eh?"

Quinn giggled a bit, although she still looked nervous.

"In a hotel, no less?" Abcde teased.

I just kept driving toward Isleton and tried to remember how
to breathe.

THE CHECK-IN DESK at Rogelio's was the bar, and it was
packed. As cozy as the restaurant had felt, I wondered whether I
had brought my child to a safe place for the night. A bunch of
heads swiveled toward us—I would guess dreadlocked poets and
nine-year-olds were not their typical bar clientele. I was tempted
to scoot onto a barstool, ask for whatever was strongest, whatever would knock me out for a few days; instead, I just asked for
a room.

"You guys were here earlier, huh?" said the tall blond bar-
tender/innkeeper. She was probably in her mid-forties, but wore
a tight shirt and low jeans that exposed a swath of her overly
tanned belly.

"For dinner." I nodded.

"I'll knock twenty off your rate since you already ate," she
said as she took a key down from its hook.

"Thanks," I said, grateful for any opportunity to save some
money.

"That woman's a poet," Quinn whispered loudly to Abcde.

"But she don't know it." Abcde winked, then said, "If you
consider rhymes poetry, that is. Which I don't."

WE HAD TO walk through the dark restaurant and the bustling but friendly poker room to get to the stairway that led up to the hotel area. I was happily surprised by our room, at the end of the long hallway. It was huge, with high ceilings, antique furniture, two queen-size beds.

Quinn threw open the doors of the large wardrobe and found the TV inside. "Can we watch it, Eema?" she asked. She hadn't watched TV for ages.

"Television rots your brain," said Abcde and Quinn immediately closed the doors, as if just looking at the blank screen would zap her intelligence. She continued to explore the rest of the room, picking up the miniature bottles of shampoo and lotion, the paper caps covering the water glasses.

"This looks like a table where you could have tea." Quinn sat in one of the pink Queen Anne–style chairs by the small table under the window, a window that, behind the wooden blinds, looked out to the brick wall of the old building next door. It comforted me to know it wouldn't be easy for anyone to look in.

"We could make some tea." Abcde thumbed through the tea bags next to the coffeemaker by the bathroom sink.

"It's too late," I said. "We should get ready for bed."

Abcde flung off her shirt, pulled down her gauzy skirt, stood naked in the middle of the room. Her body was substantial, like the Venus of Willendorf's, her breasts with their large nipples drooping downward, her belly lapping gently onto her pubic hair, but there was a dignity to it, a sort of animal grace. Her body was fully her own.

"What?" she asked when she caught me gaping. "You said get ready for bed. I prefer to sleep in the nude."

This was one instance where Quinn didn't follow her lead. She quickly looked away and took her pajamas into the bathroom to change.

THERE WAS A knock on the door after all of us had gotten into bed, Quinn and me in one, Abcde in the other. If Abcde had been wearing a nightgown, I'm sure Quinn would have chosen to sleep with her. The knocking continued, and my whole body stiffened until Ben said, "Hello? Izzy? Are you in there?"

"Hold on," I called out. I kissed Quinn, grabbed the key, slipped on some flip-flops, and said, "I'll see you later."

"We won't wait up." Abcde's voice was sleepy but sly.

BEN LOOKED TIRED. "We took a couple of rooms here, too," he said, leading me down the hall. "My mom didn't want to be at the house without my dad."

"He'll be out tomorrow?" I asked.

"If all goes well." He opened the door to his room. It was on the other side of the hall, so it felt a bit like stepping through the looking glass; everything was the exact opposite of our room. I tried not to look at his open duffel bag, the boxers folded neatly on top. I tried not to get too happy when I saw the toothbrush wet inside one of the room glasses. Had he brushed his teeth just for me? I wished I had taken more time to make myself presentable—I already had bed-head from lying down, and was wearing ratty sweats and a "Hawaii" T-shirt I had picked up at a thrift store in Idaho. My teeth were feeling furry even though I had brushed them less than an hour ago.

"So." He sat down on one of the Queen Anne chairs.

"So." I sat down on the other, dizzy with anxiety.

"So," he said, leaning forward, eyes serious. "Did you poison that kid?"

The floor may as well have dropped out from under me. No *Are you that girl?* No *Is your real name Karen?* Those were already givens for him, apparently.

"I didn't know he was going to do that." The words fell out of my mouth before I had a chance to come up with a suitable response, even the standard *I don't know what you're talking about.*

"They have you on video." He sucked his cheeks in. It made him look older, gaunt. Like his dad.

"I was kidding." My mouth was too dry to swallow. "I didn't think he'd really do it."

In a way, it was a relief to be able to admit the truth, to not have to keep making up stories.

"You looked hot, at least." He sounded weary.

I didn't. I looked tired in that video. Dark circles under my eyes, smudged mascara, blotchy skin. Hair a mess. But my shoulders were naked, the shape of my breasts evident beneath the pixelation. Maybe that was enough for a guy to consider me hot. You could probably find the entire unblurred, uncensored tape online. You could probably find more of the videos that Nathan had taped of us together. I hadn't had the stomach to search for them. I avoided anything that had to do with that story.

"Anyway," he said, "I thought you were supposed to be dead."

"That was the plan," I told him.

KAREN

KAREN FLUNG HER SCARF INTO THE MAW OF FRIGID water and nearly fell in herself as she ran across the rapidly breaking ice back to shore, chunks tumbling inches behind her feet. She was trembling, her throat raw with cold, when she got back to the car; she pulled out her money and left her wallet in the glove compartment with the note, left the passenger door open. Looking back, she could see her scarf floating in the hole in the ice, a streamer that said she was there, that said she was gone.

She walked for an hour in the snow, toes numb, tears freezing on her face, before a truck driver gave her a lift to a grocery store. She bought a cup of hot chocolate at the deli counter to try to warm up, then picked up some hair dye and a scissors. The grocery store didn't have a bathroom, so she walked some more, feet burning and stony inside her boots, until she found a quiet gas station with a restroom in the back.

————

KAREN DRIBBLED DYE onto the top of her head with her cold-stiffened hands, then realized she should have cut her hair first. No sense in coloring all ten inches when she was going to hack most of them off. The dye burned the strip of scalp down her part, began to drizzle onto her forehead, sting the inside of her nose with its vinegar tang, but the scissors made a satisfying scritch as they sliced through one thick hank after another, blond hair drifting to the floor like corn silk during a shucking.

Karen caught sight of the anxious concentration on her face in the mirror as she poured dye onto her chopped hair, and couldn't help but laugh. How many times had she seen this expression, this scene in a movie before—the woman running from the law, from her life, lobbing off her hair, getting dye all over her hands? She wondered if that's where she got the idea, or if there was some genetic impulse that led women to escape to a gas-station bathroom and change the color of their hair. It gave her comfort to think of all those other women with their boxes of Miss Clairol stepping out of tiled rooms into the next phase of their lives. It made her feel like a character, an archetype, something both bigger and smaller than herself.

She worked the burnt chestnut in with gloved numb hands, some of the color slipping inside, making the thin plastic glom to her skin. The dye probably wasn't the best thing for the baby, but it was better than what would have happened had she stayed. No way would her mother let her keep the baby, especially if she had to go to jail. Deena would have a conniption fit over her hair, too—the length, the rough edges, the color that brought out the Semitic features of her face—her dark eyes, her full lips. Deena always wanted her to look as WASPy as possible—no judge, she thought, would let a Jewish skater win. The Marilyn-blond hair, the nose job, the new last name, all of it to make her the perfect ice princess, as platinum and blank as the ice itself.

Karen bent her head and rinsed the excess dye into the sink. She scrubbed at the runnels of brown on her forehead with wet paper towels, but they left shadows behind, like scratches, stretch marks, proof that she had clawed her way into this new version of herself.

ON THE ROAD, when Karen stopped the Pilates, the ballet, the hours of skating, and let herself eat the carbohydrates she craved, the chips, the full-fat cheeses, the hamburgers, the vegetables dripping with real melted butter instead of a shake of the Butter Buds canister, her mother's worst fears came true. Her limbs and hips plumped out, softened. Her breasts, barely hills on her chest, grew heavier, more prominent. Karen was horrified at first, but over time, she found she was relieved. Relieved to not have to deal with all the training, the maintenance, the stress of trying—but never quite managing—to be perfect. Relieved to just sit around and do nothing, be no one. Her face looked better on a larger body, more at home. Her flesh felt more comfortable on her bones. She was building a good cozy place for her baby to grow. And people didn't recognize her as easily. Some would say, "You look a little like that skater girl," and she would say, "I don't know who you're talking about."

"That girl," they sometimes pressed on. "That girl who poisoned that skater." And she would say, "I'm sorry—I guess I don't follow sports."

KAREN WOULD RENT the cheapest motel rooms she could find to save money, and let herself sleep as late as she wanted. She couldn't remember ever waking up past six before. Even on weekends, her mother woke her up for an early morning jog, an extra figures session at the rink. Karen stretched under the scratchy sheets. The motel curtains were heavy, rubberized, dense, but cracked open just enough to let a band of sunlight, buttery and warm, across the bed, across her arm. Her limbs felt heavy, filled with wet sand. She didn't have to get up, she re-

minded herself; she didn't have to do anything at all. She luxuri-
ated on the awful sheets, soaked in the strip of sun as if her skin
were blotter paper, closed her eyes and drifted back to sleep.

When she woke, sometimes she let herself imagine she was
carrying Lance's baby. Lance wasn't really gone—part of him
was still alive, tumbling around inside her. They had shaken hands
with such purity, she told herself, it had sparked new life. The
baby would be born with red hair and freckles and a propensity
to blush. Cindy and their parents would be so happy. Lance
would get to start all over again. The thought filled Karen with
joy. Then the reality came crashing down again: Lance was gone,
forever; Nathan was in jail; she was on the run, alone. When the
baby kicked, it felt like a rebuke.

THE MONEY EVENTUALLY started to dwindle, and Karen realized she'd need to find work, and to find work, she'd need to find
papers. Papers with a name other than Karen. After a couple of
discreet inquiries, she made her way to an apartment in Biloxi
that smelled of beer and fried onions. She couldn't believe it
when the guy handed her the Social Security card: Isolde Jones.
Of all the possible names in the world, she ended up with the one
associated with her first kiss with Nathan, with her greatest triumph on ice.

"Do you have anything else?" she asked, but he shook his
head.

"Not around your age," he said. "Not female."

She wondered how the real Isolde Jones had died. She
silently thanked her for her life as she sat down for the ID photo
and told herself she could always go by Izzy.

THE BABY WAS born in a Travelodge. Karen was scared to go to
the hospital, scared to give anyone her new ID. But she was
scared to go it alone, too. She called Tansy, her boss at the diner

where she had been working; Tansy had said her sister was a mid-wife. She worked at a place called The Farm, but she also went to people's houses and let them give birth on their own beds, in their own bathtubs. Tansy had asked Karen if she wanted to meet with her for all the prenatal workups, but Karen said no; she had no money, no insurance. She read *What to Expect When You're Expecting* in the library and took notes in a spiral notebook; she made sure she was eating protein, taking the cheapest vitamins she could find. She was sure she could do it on her own. Women give birth in fields; she could surely do it holed up in a hotel room. Women in history didn't have ultrasounds, amniocentesis—why should she?

Once the labor started, she wasn't so sure anymore. She wanted someone to grab onto, someone who could cut the umbilical cord with something other than her teeth. She called Tansy.

Dawn arrived with her birth kit full of tubes and syringes and oxygen. Her hands were red and chapped from frequent washings, her fingers long, fingers that looked like they knew what they were doing. She looked different from Tansy—taller and thinner, hair cropped short, a little sapphire glinting on the side of her nose. She looked like a dancer, not a midwife. But she rubbed Karen's back, she made herbal tea in the hotel coffeepot; she showed Karen the railing in the bathtub that would be good to hold on to while she squatted and pushed; she listened to the baby's heartbeat and let Karen listen to it, too. It was the first time she had heard the heartbeat, the first time she really let herself realize there was another life inside her, and she cried with joy and fear all through the labor, until Dawn put sticky, bloody Quinn in her arms, and then she cried even more.

"HE'S OUT, YOU KNOW," SAID BEN. "NATHAN MAIN. HE got out of jail last week—it was all over the media."

I felt a chill just hearing the name. "I think I may have seen him, across the slough," I said. "I think he may have been the one who broke the bottles."

Ben closed his eyes.

"You should probably turn yourself in," he said quietly.

"I can't turn myself in." I jumped out of the chair. "They'll take Quinn."

"What are you going to do, then? Wait for him to poison you both?" He stood up, too, took a step closer to me.

"I don't know . . ."

"Do you want me to help you hide? Your face is all over the media now, too."

"Is that how you knew who I was?" As much as I hoped no one else had recognized my face, I felt something deep inside my chest relax. Ben had seen me. He had really truly seen me, all the way to the darkest corner of my heart. And he hadn't run away; he was still right there.

"I always thought you looked familiar." His eyes were soft, pained. "When I saw the news last week, something clicked. I even asked my dad if he thought you looked like that skater girl, but he said I was crazy, so I put it out of my mind. Tried to, at least. Then I saw you skate . . ." He let out a heavy sigh. "We really need to get you out of here, Izzy."

"You'd be an accomplice."

"An accomplice to an accomplice." He chuckled softly. "That probably isn't so bad. One year, maybe? Five? I'll get off on good behavior."

"If that's what does it for you." I couldn't seem to help myself.

He shot me a look and I started to laugh until I started to sob, and he took me into his arms. I wondered if he was thinking about how he was holding the same body from the video he had seen, if he got some charge out of that, but he shouldn't, it wasn't; it wasn't the same body. A body's cells are replaced every seven years. He was holding someone new.

IT WAS ALMOST 4 a.m. by the time I went back to my room.

"Did you get lucky?" Abcde mumbled as I walked past her bed. I didn't answer, let her drift back to sleep. I wouldn't call it getting lucky so much as getting clear. Coming clean.

I crawled into bed with Quinn and hoped she wouldn't be able to smell Ben all over me, but I relished the smell myself, breathed it in deep.

If a leaf touches a pear as it's growing, even just after the blossom has fallen, it leaves a mark. Sometimes you don't see it right away, but as the pear ripens, a dark spot will rise on its skin.

If I could see all the past touches on my body, I'd be one big bruise. Nathan's handprint would appear on just about every inch. Quinn's fingers would carve a deep, sweet shadow into my palm. Wherever Ben touched me, it felt as if he left a smear of light. I could almost feel myself glowing beneath the sheets.

QUINN AND ABCDE woke me much earlier than I would have liked. "Can we go swimming, Eema?" Quinn asked. When I opened my eye a crack, I saw she was already in her bathing suit. There was a small pool in the back of the hotel, the concrete pool area covered with a canopy of netting, presumably so people wouldn't try to dive in from the second floor.

"I guess so," I said. "Just be careful." I slipped easily back into sleep.

"EEMA." WHEN I opened my eyes again, at first I thought I was still dreaming. Quinn's lips were swollen, like some Hollywood starlet's. The smell of chlorine made me realize I was actually awake, that time had passed. And something crazy was happening to Quinn's face.

"Did you get stung?"

"I don't know . . ."

"I didn't see anything," said Abcde. "Her lips just starting blowing up. And she has a rash on her chest . . ."

I fumbled for the EpiPen. I thought I had left it on the nightstand, but it wasn't there. I jumped out of bed to search and finally found it in the drawer, next to the Gideon's Bible. I removed the gray locking cap, and willed my hand to stop trembling as I swung my arm back, then jabbed it against the side of her thigh. It bounced right off—the needle didn't come out like it was supposed to. I tried again, as Quinn said, exasperated now, "Eema." Nothing.

"Should we take her to a doctor?" asked Abcde.

"Probably," I said, but then I realized I probably shouldn't go to such a public place—not with fake papers. Not with Nathan looking for me, maybe advising other people to be on the look-out, too. "Can you go get Ben? He's in room 234."

"Sure thing." She raced off in just her bathing suit, haunches jiggling majestically.

"Can you breathe okay?" I asked Quinn.

"I think so," she said, her voice impeded by her inflamed lips.

"Your throat isn't closing up, is it?"

She shook her head.

Abcde and Ben burst into the room. I wanted to run straight into Ben's arms, but I also didn't want to leave Quinn's side.

"Hey, Angelina Jolie," Ben said to Quinn, and she smiled, even though it looked painful.

"She needs to see a doctor." I clicked the EpiPen mindlessly in the air—this time it worked, but it sent its cache of medicine out into the room.

"You shouldn't go." He understood immediately.

"Why not?" asked Abcde.

"I'll tell you later," I said.

"Izzy!" I could tell she was ready for some juicy gossip.

"Can Abcde come with us?" Quinn asked.

"Of course, sweetheart." Abcde tossed a filmy sundress over her bathing suit. "But that doesn't mean your mom's off the hook."

On the hotel stationery, I quickly scribbled a letter giving Ben and Abcde permission to make medical decisions for Quinn on my behalf, gave Quinn a huge hug that made her squawk, made sure they all had my cell number, and they took off for Ben's truck. I ran out to the balcony and watched them drive away, waving until long after they were out of sight.

I DIDN'T KNOW what to do with myself in the hotel room. I paced and paced, my limbs frantic with worry, and finally called Ben on his cell and asked him to hold it up to Quinn's ear. She wasn't comfortable talking, but I was happy to listen to her breathe, to hear Abcde and Ben joke around in the background; their laughs made me less concerned—they wouldn't be laughing so hard if she were in dire trouble.

Ben finally got back on. "We're in the ER," he said. "We can't use our cellphones inside, but I'll come out to give you updates."

"Thank you so much, Ben," I said.

"No problem," he said. "Just watch out for yourself."

I CONTINUED TO pace around the room, restless, bereft. It made me feel crazy to think of Quinn being so far away from me, especially with something scary happening. I made myself a cup of tea to try to settle down and noticed the pen and stationery still out on the table. Abcde had said we all wanted to write about the whales—I figured I might as well take a stab.

A whale is surfacing, I wrote. *Breaching, really. Comice has whales—who would have thought? Daughter, don't be afraid. Everything will be all right. Fear has a way of shutting us down—don't let it. Grow toward courage. Here, there are whales. It's almost a miracle, if you think about it. Just amazing. Kiss the air when they spray and it's almost like kissing the inside of their bodies. Let yourself imagine the inside of their bodies—you are Jonah, you are Pinocchio, but a girl, the first girl inside the belly of a whale. Maybe inside the heart. Never fear, my girl; even giants have hearts under their skin. Only we get to see them—aren't we lucky? Prepare yourself for amazement, my sweet one. Quinn, I know I sound crazy, but it's true. Ripe pears are all around us. Serious beauty there. Trees full of beauty. Under the Delta sky. Vivid vivid blue. Whether the whales are here or not. X marks this spot, right here, right now. You need to live this moment, Quinn, live it fully. Zero fear, that's all I ask of you, of us; zero fear.*

I FELT EXHILARATED when I put down the pen, as if I had just swum with the whales myself. I wondered if Abcde ever had that feeling when she wrote, that feeling where you think you're writing to someone else, but it turns out you're really writing to yourself. It turns out you're really writing to teach yourself what you need to learn.

THE CELLPHONE RANG.

"It's an allergic reaction," said Ben. He sounded calm, which comforted me. "They're not sure to what—something in the water, probably."

"Is she okay?"

"She's doing great. They're giving her Benadryl by IV—her lips are going down already, but they want to keep her here a few hours just to be on the safe side."

"I wish I could talk to her," I said.

"I wish you could, too," he said. "Maybe there's a hospital phone we can use—I'll find out. But she said to say hi, for now. Oh, and she wants you to find her Norse mythology book. She said she left it on the boat, but I don't think you should go over there by yourself right now, Izzy. I can look for it when we get back."

I KNEW BEN was right—I shouldn't go back to the Vieiras' by myself, but I was going stir-crazy in the hotel room. I tried to write a second piece, but I couldn't concentrate. I needed to get out, to do something that would help Quinn, even in the tiniest way. I knocked on the door of Mrs. Vieira's room, the room next to Ben's. I hoped she hadn't been able to hear too much the night before.

"Would you like to go back to the orchard for a little bit?" I asked her. "I have to get something in the houseboat."

She was wearing the same loose floral dress she had worn the day before. She nodded.

IT WAS COMFORTING to have Mrs. Vieira in the car with me, even though she didn't speak, even though she looked as if she had been crying all night, her lopsided eyes red and inflamed, her hair a mess.

The distillery was surrounded by police tape, but no police cars were in sight.

"Do you want me to go into the house with you?" I asked Mrs. Vieira, but she shook her head. "Do you mind if I go down to the houseboat to get my daughter's book?"

She waved me forward.

The levee was covered with spectators—the Vieiras hadn't been there to take the entry fees, to control the numbers. Thankfully, the whales were a few hundred yards to the west of my boat, so there wasn't anyone hanging out right where I parked.

I sat in the car, heart pounding, while I scanned the crowd, looking for any familiar body language. It seemed as if there were more men than usual, which made me nervous, especially since some of them had big cans of beer, but they didn't pay any attention to me. There was too much going on with the whales.

THE MOTHER WHALE looked like she was having some sort of fit. She was slapping at her baby, the white underside of her long fin making a resounding smack against the baby's skin, a resounding splash in the water. The baby tried to nurse, but this time, the mother shoved it away, a more gentle shove, but a firm, insistent one. She kept shooing the baby off, her motions increasingly frantic, until the baby did leave, its body a dark submarine torpedoing down the Delta. Faster than I'd ever seen her move, plowing forward with clear determination, hopefully toward the sea. A group of young men raised their beer cans and cheered.

I saw the people on the other side of the slough lean toward the water, craning their heads to watch the baby enter the Sacramento River. The mother whale turned onto her side, her fin straight up in the air, a stiff white flag. Surrender more than farewell.

When the rumbling began, I thought it was from the whale, her giant organs churning, a wail of grief rippling through her body as her baby swam away. But then the screaming started, the very human screaming, and the levee across the slough crumbled liked dry bread, the whole twenty-foot face of it falling into the water—stones, dirt, all the people on it tumbling down, toppling into the slough, water racing over the levee, flooding the much lower field of dead pear trees in a great whoosh, carrying people with it, the Coast Guard boat with it, the whale with it, sliding sideways over the old orchard like a train off its rails.

I ran to my edge of the levee, wanting to jump into the water, help the people bobbing, crashing into the piles of wood, crashing against the side of the whale, who was stuck up against a heap of trees herself, but I knew if I jumped in, I would get swept away, too.

My houseboat strained at its anchor below, like a dog pulling at its leash. I ran down the metal steps to the dock, unlashed the rope from its post, and jumped onto the deck. I had never driven the houseboat before—I didn't even know if the engine worked—but it didn't matter; as soon as the boat wasn't anchored, it started to move, sweeping across the slough, over what used to be an orchard. I tried to steer as best I could, but the current was too strong. The boat sped toward the whale, its fin still up in the air, waving weakly now. I tried to crank the wheel, but the boat kept barreling forward, and the whale kept looming larger. There was nothing I could do but drop to the floor of the cabin, curl into a ball, brace myself for impact.

———

THE BOAT HIT the whale with a *thwomp* that sent me reeling, my back crashing against the wall of the cabin. I got up and stumbled to the window; the bow had left a gash in the whale's side, pink and white beneath the dark skin. I walked onto the deck, slipping on her blood as I made my way to the railing. People were thrashing in the water, some floating facedown. I pulled two life preservers off the side of the boat—they had probably been affixed there for decades—and heaved them over the edge. I hoped they weren't crumbly inside, like old Styrofoam.

A woman, coughing, sputtering, grabbed onto one, and I pulled the raspy yellow rope to bring her toward the boat. It cut, burning, into my palms.

"Are you okay?" I yelled down at her, but she didn't appear to hear me.

"Can you climb up the ladder?" I asked. She looked up at me, dazed.

"Just hold on to the ring," I told her, and thankfully she did.

A man and woman fought over the other life preserver, trying to push each other away.

"You can both hold on to it," I shouted, even though I wasn't sure it would support both their weight.

I remembered the life vests inside the box built against the wall; I lifted the hinged lid. The orange vests were dusty, covered with spiderwebs, with spiders, but still might have some life inside them. I tossed them into the water, watched them bloom back into bright orange, watched them bob away from the people who needed them. I grabbed a broom and tried to push the vests back with the handle—they felt heavier in the water, like sweeping wet laundry. I gave the broom a big slogging push and the vests started to drift in the right direction.

And then I saw him. Pushed up against one of the piles of wood, limp. The collar of his T-shirt hooked onto a branch, holding his head above the water. I couldn't tell if his eyes were open, if he was awake, conscious, alive.

"Nathan!" I yelled, but he didn't seem to be able to hear me.

I called 911 on my cellphone. I'm sure others from our side of the levee had, too, because the operator said, "We're on it. We're on the way."

The life vests were finally reaching people, who clung to them desperately, some of them struggling to get their arms through the holes. I could see the Coast Guard tossing more life vests out a few hundred yards away. A couple of the pickers who had stayed at the orchard appeared in Mr. Vieira's metal fishing boat. I watched as they pulled a couple of people, including Roberts, from the water onto the boat.

The emergency vehicles began to arrive—helicopters, more Coast Guard boats, ambulances on the levee road, sirens everywhere. The back of my head started to pound; I had banged it fairly hard when the boat crashed into the whale. The whale whose blood continued to flow onto the deck. I managed to slosh through it to the railing, and pressed my face against the whale's side. Its skin was cool and smooth. I rubbed my hand along it, and could feel the giant heart drumming; it thrummed through my entire body. I felt the rhythm stutter, felt it slow, felt it stop, until all that filled my ears was something that sounded like wind.

"MA'AM," I HEARD someone call. "Are you okay?"

I opened my eyes. I felt dazed, drunk.

"You're covered in blood." It was a member of the Coast Guard. Their boat idled next to mine now; it was already full of people, some lying on the deck, some sitting, looking stunned.

"It's not mine," I said.

"Come on," he said. "We can give you a ride to the hospital."

"I don't know," I said, but when I stood up from leaning against the whale, I got so dizzy, I had to plunk down on my butt on the deck.

"Come on, ma'am," he coaxed.

"I have to get something first," I said, and slipped through the blood into the cabin, where I found Quinn's book. I hugged it to my chest with one arm as I reached out to the coastguardsman with the other and he pulled me over onto his boat. I could see Sam tending to someone else, someone who no doubt would see her as a heavenly angel swooping down to save their life.

I TRIED TO avoid the bodies that someone had covered on the deck. I sat down and closed my eyes, my head throbbing like crazy now.

"My mother killed herself, you know," said a familiar voice. I looked over; Nathan was lying on the deck next to me. His legs were bent at unnatural angles; his eyes looked as unfocused as mine felt.

"You never told me that," I said. It felt weirdly normal to talk to him after so many years, under such strange circumstances, even though both of our voices were tired, strained.

"I was ten," he said. "She couldn't take it anymore—my dad's drinking, screwing around."

"I'm sorry."

"When I heard you killed yourself, I wanted to die, too." His speech was starting to slur.

I looked around to see if anyone was listening, but most people around me were either crying or catatonic. Part of me wanted to comfort Nathan and part of me wanted to push him over the edge of the boat.

"And then I see a picture of you in the paper, nine years later, after I get out. And I am so happy and so fucking angry, so happy and so angry all at the same time."

"What were you planning to do when you found me?" I clutched the book tighter to my chest, the blue cloth cover mottled now with water, with blood.

He didn't answer, although his fingers lightly brushed my arm.

"Nathan," I said. "What were you planning to do?"

I looked over, even though it hurt my head to move. Nathan's eyes were closed. He must have passed out. I tapped his cheek a couple of times with the back of my hand; the bristles of his stubble prickled my skin, but he didn't wake up.

MY CELLPHONE RANG.

"Quinn's going to be discharged soon," said Ben before I even said hello. "They said they need the beds. Plus she's doing great."

"I need one of those beds," I said.

"Sounds good to me," Ben said playfully.

"No, really," I said. "I hit my head. They're bringing me in."

"Oh my God, Izzy. Are you okay?"

"The levee broke . . ."

"What were you doing at the levee?"

"Quinn's book . . ." Talking suddenly felt too difficult. "Just wait for me," I said. "I'll be there soon."

THE HOSPITAL WAS a mad rush as they wheeled me and other people in on gurneys. I seemed to get extra attention because of all the blood, even though I kept insisting it wasn't my own.

Ben, Abcde, and Quinn caught sight of me and ran next to the gurney as they took me back into the ER, all their faces concerned, Quinn's mouth thankfully back to its normal size.

"I'm okay," I tried to convince them. "It's the whale's blood."

"The whale was bleeding?" Quinn suddenly looked even more concerned.

"Seckel is fine," I said, blinking from the bright fluorescent lights. "She swam off. But Bartlett, not so much. I'm so sorry, honey."

Quinn wailed. I was glad Abcde was there to hold her.

I did my best to describe what had happened at the levee.

"It sounds like Ragnarok," said Quinn, snuffling. "The final battle between the gods and the giants."

I handed her the bloodstained book and wondered if I had yet to face my final battle.

AFTER A CT scan, an MRI, a good old-fashioned head X-ray, plus some sponging off, it was determined I had a concussion, some whiplash, a few contusions, but nothing too serious. The doctors wanted to keep me overnight to observe me, so they moved me into a room upstairs. Quinn went back to the hotel with Abcde and Ben—who had brought me some pajamas from my luggage—after visiting hours were over.

They unhooked my IV long enough for me to take a shower; after they hooked me back up, I wandered around the hallways in my flannel cupcake pajamas and slippers, pulling my IV pole, to see if I could find anything out about Nathan's condition. A nurse pointed me to his room after I said I was an old friend; I was grateful she didn't seem to recognize me.

When I poked my head inside the open door, I was shocked to see my mother sitting on the chair next to the bed where Nathan was sleeping or unconscious. She wore a gold sleeveless V-neck top, ivory slacks cinched with a thin gold belt, high-heeled sandals. Her arms were sinewy, her cleavage rising up to her throat. The breasts were new and startling, tan skin crepey between the hard-looking orbs. Her face appeared to be freshly tightened, her hair a brassy auburn, arranged in carefully blow-dried layers.

We stared at each other for a moment, all the air sucked out of the room.

"Well, you've certainly let yourself go," she said. Almost ten years, and this was the first thing out of her mouth. But there were tears in her eyes, a softness in her voice.

I wanted to tell her it felt great, she should try letting herself go sometime, but the words didn't reach my lips. My head pounded. I couldn't seem to find my voice. Besides, she was wrong. I hadn't really let myself go. I had let her idea of me go, which was a totally different thing. I had let her idea of me go so I could figure out who I truly was, myself.

"It's good to see you, too, Mom," I said. When I hugged her, she felt brittle, as if she might shatter in my arms, but her perfume smelled the same as always, and it took a long time for us to let go.

Nathan was still unconscious. He looked older in the hospital bed; I could see the silver threaded through his hair when my mom pushed it back at his temple, the lines etched next to his eyes.

"They're not sure he's going to wake up," she said. "Or if he'll have the use of his legs if he does."

He was in casts up to his hips, a catheter snaking out, leading to a bag filled with pee strapped to the side of the bed.

"I was working on getting him some shows, some interviews," she said. "We were talking about getting married."

I was surprised by the stab of jealousy I felt. I remembered the way she had kissed him that New Year's Eve. Maybe they had been together all along. Maybe they had plotted out our first kiss at Nationals; maybe my mom had thought getting me laid would loosen me up on the ice, would get us more publicity. I was ready to confront her, but then I saw the pain on her face, the love on her face, as she stroked Nathan's hair.

"I'm so sorry," she said over and over again, and even though she was looking at Nathan, I could tell she was saying it to me.

I HELD MYSELF together until I got back to my room and all my limbs turned to water. I lay back on the pillow and wept until I was empty.

"You okay?" the woman on the other side of the drape between our beds asked. "You need me to page the nurse for you?"

My head ached so much, I thought it might split open.

"You know when you graft a pear tree?" My mouth seemed to have a mind of its own now. "You graft the branch of a new tree onto the roots of an old tree? And you think you're creating something brand-new, but the old tree is still there, down to the roots?"

"Come again?" my roommate asked.

"You know that skater?" I took a deep, shuddery breath. "That skater who poisoned that other skater?"

I HAD TO tell my story over and over again the next few days.

To Quinn, who turned very quiet, so quiet I wasn't sure if she would ever forgive me for keeping such a huge secret from her, the person I loved most in the world.

To the police officers and FBI agents who came into my room in a steady stream, at some point handcuffing me to the bed.

To Lance's parents and sister, who flew out from Utah. They were in tears as they came into my dim room. I was so startled by their sudden presence, my pulse almost strangled me. It was strange to see Cindy as a grown-up—she looked almost the same, just taller, filled out. The years had dulled her cuteness a bit; at twenty-four, she had a middle-aged vibe to her, a suburban housewife vibe with her sensible short haircut, her floral blouse buttoned to the neck. I could easily see how Lance would have looked if he had been given these nine years—he would have filled out, too, but his features would have gone from cute to handsome, maybe even rugged.

I started to say "I'm sorry," but they stopped me before I could even get out a syllable.

"We're here to say we forgive you," said Mrs. Finkel, sitting on the edge of my bed. She had aged a lot, her hair gray, her face worn. "We know you didn't mean to hurt our Lance."

I nodded, my cheeks drowning in tears. She took my hand. "We're so glad you're alive," she continued. "It would have been tragic for two young lives to have ended needlessly."

"I have a little girl now, too." Cindy pulled a picture from her wallet of herself holding hands with a toddler in a puffy pink snowsuit, both of them in ice skates. "Lancey. She'll be two in November."

"Adorable." I sniffled. She looked just like Lance and Cindy did when they were younger—fresh faced, eager. Trusting. A pang of grief and remorse shot through my chest.

"We know Nathan didn't mean to kill Lance, either," she said. "He couldn't have known Lance couldn't handle barbiturates. We didn't know it ourselves until the autopsy—a metabolic issue." Her voice, so eerily calm until now, started to break. Mr. Finkel put a hand on her shoulder, and the three of them started to tear up again.

"We've asked the police to drop any charges against you," Mr. Finkel said. "There's no need to punish you more than you've already punished yourself."

AFTER THE FINKELS left, the policemen removed the handcuffs. I grabbed a teddy bear from the nightstand and held it to my chest, sobbing. I wondered what I'd do with all the flowers and stuffed animals that had started to fill the room. As word got out, old fans had started to send gifts the way they used to throw them on the ice. I supposed I could donate the ones Quinn didn't want to the children's ward, just as I had done with the surplus years ago. The occasional angry letter and phone call came, too, people telling me I should rot in hell, I should be put away for life; the hospital apologized for letting these messages get through, but I was actually glad for them. They made the guilt flare inside me like phosphorous, the guilt I needed to let myself feel. Some part of me wasn't ready to be forgiven.

THE DOCTORS EVENTUALLY said I was free to go home. Wherever home was going to be. I felt completely raw inside, completely stripped bare. All the sounds of the hospital—the beeps and whirs and pneumatic wheezes, the footfalls and intercom bleats—felt amplified, making my nerve endings prickle and wince.

Sam came into my room, holding a vase of lilies, as I was waiting for Abcde, Ben, and Quinn to come pick me up. I wanted to be happy about her visit, but I was too exhausted.

"I wish I had known you were someone," she said, flashing her brilliant smile. She was wearing the blue sweater she had on at the party, the one that brought out the color of her hair and eyes, and I wondered if she had dressed up for my sake.

"Why?" I said. "So you would have been nicer to me?"

Sam laughed nervously. "It just would have been nice to have known." She tried to find a place to put the flowers, but every available surface was already covered with gifts.

"Everyone is someone," I said, and closed my eyes until she left the room.

ABCDE FINALLY SHOWED up with some clothes for me to change into while Ben and Quinn waited in the hallway. I was so happy to see her shaggy dreadlocks, her layers of gypsy clothing, a welcome contrast to the sterile hospital environment.

"I saw your writing in the hotel." She sat on the edge of my bed, patchouli wafting. "You can write, girl. You need to write your story."

"But it almost doesn't feel like mine," I said. "It feels like it belongs to two different people."

"Then write it that way," she said, stroking my hair. "Write it as if it's two different people."

AS I SLIPPED on my jeans, I wondered when I had really made the shift from Karen to Izzy. When I took on Isolde Jones's ID, I still felt like Karen inside—the new name felt like a mask for quite a long time, like something to slip over the real me, something to hide behind. When Quinn was born, I definitely became someone new, but it was a nameless newness, an ineffable change. Maybe it was when I took my first picking job, when I introduced myself as Izzy to the foreman at the broccoli farm in Mississippi, baby Quinn strapped to my chest. Maybe I became Izzy as I bent over those bumpy green plants, sun and exertion burning Karen out of my muscles; maybe I became Izzy when I realized this would become our life—the constant movement from crop to crop, state to state. When I thought if we kept moving forward, the past would never find a way to catch us.

BEFORE WE LEFT the hospital, I took Quinn to Nathan's room. I tried to hold her hand as we walked down the hallway, but she pulled her hand away. When we stepped into the room, I could feel her stiffen, could feel her start to reach for me, but then she steeled herself, arms straight down her sides, hands in fists. I had never been more scared for her, more proud of her, in my life.

Nathan was conscious, but drugged; his eyes were half shut, lids dark and puffy. My mother wore a pink blouse with a plunging neckline, the same ivory slacks and heels as the day before. Bringing Quinn near them felt like bringing her into the bar at Rogelio's, someplace unsavory, someplace children should not go. Still, these were her people. She deserved to know them. Whether they deserved to know her remained to be seen.

"This is Quinn," I said, and I could feel a tremor go through her. "Your granddaughter. Your daughter."

My mother looked her up and down, a move I was all too familiar with. If she had said Quinn needed to lose weight, I would have throttled her, but she grew teary and said simply, softly, "You have your father's eyes."

Quinn walked up next to Nathan's bed and peered at his face. Nathan looked terrified, bewildered, as if she had sprung from his chest like some sort of alien.

"You killed someone?" Quinn asked.

"Not on purpose." He couldn't bring himself to look at her.

Quinn turned to my mom and said, quite firmly, "I don't have his eyes. I have my own."

MY HEAD STILL ached as Ben drove us back to the orchard. Everyone had checked out of Rogelio's and moved back into the house, Abcde and Quinn sharing the guest room.

"I wore nightclothes, don't worry," Abcde assured me.

"You can stay here as long as you need to recover," Ben told me when we were inside his kitchen. His parents nodded. All charges had been dropped against Mr. Vieira, too. It appeared that he and Roberts had patched things up quite nicely since the levee break, even though the flooding had short-circuited Roberts's robot and destroyed a large swath of his orchard. Mr. Vieira had even vowed to help Roberts with the cleanup; Roberts had told Mr. Vieira he was sure he would have been a goner if my fellow workers Tomas and Vincent hadn't fished him from the water. The fact that he had used their names was a major improvement. I wasn't happy with how I had let all the workers at my various farm jobs blur together in my own eyes—I had ignored their individual stories, their essential someone-ness. Maybe now that I no longer needed to hide my own story, I could start to pay more attention to others'.

FOUR PEOPLE DIED in the levee break: three spectators— Carrie Angstrom, a forty-two-year-old hairdresser from Guerneville, Timothy Hu, a twenty-eight-year-old math teacher from Sacramento, and Maxine Bayliss, a seventy-three-year-old retiree from Oregon—plus Miguel Lopez, a thirty-five-year-old worker from Oaxaca, one of Roberts's men. I wanted to attend the public memorial service for all of them at the community center where the *festa* had been held, but didn't want to be a distraction; I wanted any press coverage of the event to focus on those who had lost their lives, not on me. I was receiving enough coverage as it was, even though I hadn't agreed to talk to any reporters yet. Ben tried to show me some of the articles, but I wasn't ready to read them. I sent lengthy condolences to the families of the victims. I knew I hadn't done anything to harm the four who died, but I hadn't saved them, either, and this gnawed at my gut. When I thought about the whale, I just about doubled over.

Bartlett had been carried away on a cargo freighter. Biologists determined she had died from a heart condition, not the wound from the houseboat, which, despite the copious amounts of blood, had turned out to be fairly superficial. Still, I couldn't help but feel responsible. I wasn't sure if it made me feel better or worse to imagine she may have died of a broken heart as her baby swam farther and farther away. Seckel had last been spotted gliding under the Golden Gate Bridge, headed out to sea.

OUR OWN NEXT move was a big question mark. Ben had started to field offers for me from magazines, talk shows, cable networks, publishing houses, even ice shows, people wanting to pay me obscene amounts of money to give them the rights to my story. Ben joked that I should hold off and join the celebrity boxing circuit, like Tonya Harding. My mom offered to be my agent, but I told her no thank you; I was going to do this on my own, on my own terms.

"It's your story," said Abcde before she left for her workshop in Squaw Valley. "Make sure you find the right venue. Don't let anyone sell you out."

"Maybe you can come back when you're done." Quinn was inconsolable. She had started talking to me again, but still hadn't forgiven me entirely.

"I'm going back to Perth, love," said Abcde. "Going to try to see my boys. But we'll see each other again, I know it." Abcde gave Quinn a huge hug. "Always be cheerful, dig?"

"Dig." Quinn smiled through her tears. "Exactly."

I TOOK ABCDE'S advice and started to write my story, Karen's story, dedicating it to Lance's memory. I held off selling the book until I knew I could actually write the whole thing, myself—I didn't want any ghost writers, didn't want anyone to shape my life to their liking. The Vieiras were kind, letting us stay in the guest room as I recuperated and wrote, though I tried to help out as much as I could around the house, around the orchard. The future of the orchard was still uncertain—the Vieiras had taken a real loss, but they had some insurance to tide them over, and talked about replacing part of the orchard with corn to keep up with the growing need for ethanol.

"Not that it's the best renewable fuel source," said Ben, "and not that I want to be part of the whole corn industrial complex, but it could help us get over the hump." He talked about setting up some sort of subscription service so green-leaning yuppies could buy a share in the orchard, get bushels of pears when they were in season, maybe come help pick with their families. He talked about joining with other farmers in the Sacramento area to create a community-supported agriculture co-op, assembling weekly boxes of produce for people who wanted to eat local and organic. I knew that once I was ready to sell my story, I'd be able to help Vieira Pears, too.

In the meantime, Ben stayed home to do whatever he could to get the farm back on its feet. I moved into his room with him a few months later, giving Quinn her own room for the first time ever, enrolling her in the local school. She was so thrilled to have a lunch box, a backpack, a school bus to step onto each morning. We visited my mom and Nathan, who had moved to Los Angeles, a couple of times; it was awkward, and Nathan was frustrated with his rehabilitation, but Quinn seemed grateful to know she had more family in the world than me.

I started to long for my own roots, as well, my muscles aching for movement, for speed. I could hear the ice calling me.

It wanted my blades to scratch its long smooth back. It wanted to feather into soft clumps under the sideways swish of my hockey stop, break into snowflakes that melt quickly against the steel. My beautiful masochist, the ice, open as a heart, willing to give itself over again and again. It forgave me, it forgives all of us, the Zamboni sealing up the wounds, smoothing over the abrasions, restoring its placid dignity.

I did some searching and found a rink in Stockton, just half an hour away.

"I can't wait to see you skate, Eema," Quinn said as Ben drove us past one cornfield after another, past one marina after another. I had shown her a couple of competition videos online; she could barely believe I was the person on the screen.

"I won't be able to do what I used to," I warned her. "Especially not on rental skates."

When we walked into the small rink, the clean, sharp, unmistakable smell brought tears stinging into my eyes. The ice was blindingly white, only a few kids lurching around its surface. I was glad there wasn't a big audience for my comeback.

"We don't have to do this," Ben said.

"No, it's okay." I blinked the tears away, felt the give of the rubber floor beneath me, the chilled air against my skin. "This is home."

WE TIED UP our brown floppy-ankled rental skates, my fingers thrilling at the familiar rub of the laces. I knelt before Quinn to make sure her skates were tight enough. As soon as I was done cinching her up, she saw a friend from school. "Can I go skate with her, Eema?" Quinn asked.

"Of course," I said, and Quinn took off, stumbling a bit, ankles bowed, but managing to stay upright. My sweet Delta girl.

"You ready to do this thing?" Ben asked, and I suddenly had a flash of Nathan asking the same question before Nationals.

Nathan, when his legs were still strong. Nathan, who was slowly learning to walk again, slowly learning how to be a father.

I let out a long breath, a breath I must have been holding for years. This time, the decision to skate was my own. This time, I had chosen my partner, my pairing. Even with dull blades, flimsy boots, I felt more ready than ever.

I smiled and grabbed Ben's hand and we stepped, together, out onto the ice.

ACKNOWLEDGMENTS

Huge heartfelt thank-yous:

To Stephan Silveira for telling me about growing up on a pear farm in the Sacramento Delta; I never would have known about the area if it hadn't been for you.

To Tim and Laura Neuharth for so generously sharing the ins and outs of running an organic pear farm—my time with you at Steamboat Acres helped bring Vieira Pears to life.

To Colin Page for mentioning his mom had a student named Abcde and sparking a whole character. To Cati Porter for letting Abcde borrow part of her amazing double abecedarian poem, "A Feline Fine, Oh Kitty Kitty Mine" (from her equally amazing collection *Seven Floors Up*).

To Brian Henne, for all the great houseboat information.

To Elizabeth Brandeis and Laraine Herring for giving such helpful feedback on early drafts of the novel. This book has your lovely, wise fingerprints all over it!

To Anika Streitfeld for being such a fabulous editor in the early stages of the novel. To Lea Beresford for being such a fabulous editor for the next leg of the journey. I am grateful to both of you and your thoughtful, enthusiastic, whip-smart notes. Everyone at Ballantine has been wonderful. (I need to give a special shout-out to Kerri Buckley for swooping in like a superhero toward the end of the process!)

To Arielle Eckstut for first bringing me to Ballantine. You rock (and not just socks)! To Ellen Geiger for being in my corner now—I am very lucky indeed.

To all my friends, family, students, and colleagues who have given me so much love and support over the years, with special thanks to my parents, Buzz and Arlene Brandeis, for always encouraging me, never pushing me (and for giving me a lifetime love of skating, writing, food, and whales); to my kids, Arin and Hannah Brandeis-McGunigle, for being patient with their flighty writer mom; to my husband, Michael Brandeis, for all our Pear Fair memories and all our memories to come. And to Asher Brandeis, the brand-new fruit of our love.

DELTA GIRLS

GAYLE BRANDEIS

A Reader's Guide

A Conversation Between the Author at Age 41 and Her 13-Year-Old Self

Gayle at 13: So you actually became a writer.

Gayle at 41: I did, indeed. Are you surprised?

Gayle at 13: Not really. Do you remember when our second-grade teacher, Mrs. Koch, told our parents that I would be a writer when I grew up? They came home from the parent-teacher conference and shared what she'd said, and I was, like, "No duh." I mean, I've been writing poems and stories since I was four years old. It's cool that it really happened, though.

Gayle at 41: I feel very lucky to be able to do what I love. What we love.

Gayle at 13: Do you remember lying on your stomach on the living room rug and making up titles of stories you wanted to write?

Gayle at 41: Oh, yes; I remember writing them in crayon on the cardboard from Dad's dry-cleaned shirts. Long lists of titles, each one so full of possibility.

Gayle at 13: Is that how you came up with the idea for *Delta Girls*?

Gayle at 41: Ha! I can't say it is. The first seed of the idea came after my friend Stephan told me about growing up on a pear farm in the Sacramento Delta. I never even knew there was a Delta in California until he told me about it, and I was intrigued by the lush, strange setting. Then I began to see stories about the two whales who swam up the Sacramento River, and a story started to form in my mind of a mother and daughter who end up in the Delta around the same time as the whales, all four of them searching for home.

Gayle at 13: How did skating come into the story?

Gayle at 41: I had been dreaming about skating every night—I think part of me really missed it. I even started taking lessons again, thinking that's what the dreams were pushing me to do. It was great, but I got really dizzy doing the spins, and I realized that maybe I should be writing about skating more than I should actually be skating. At first Karen was a solo competitor, but then it dawned on me that I could play with the echo between "pears" and "pairs," and the whole story with Nathan emerged.

Gayle at 13: I can't imagine not skating.

Gayle at 41: I know—it's such a part of your life right now. Almost every day after school, some days before school. I'm curious—what do you love most about skating?

Gayle at 13: Don't you remember?

Gayle at 41: I remember a lot of it—the feeling of soaring, the cold wind on my face as I stroked around the rink—but I want to hear it from you while you're still in the thick of it.

Gayle at 13: My favorite part is when I step onto the ice during a competition or an ice show and the choreography melts away, and I just start skating to the music in whatever way my body wants to move right then.

Gayle at 41: I remember our coaches were not very happy about us doing that, throwing away all the hard work of their choreography so we could go with the flow. Deena certainly never would have stood for that if Karen started to improvise.

Gayle at 13: I can't help it, though—it's like something else takes over.

Gayle at 41: Writing a novel is like that, too—I love when the characters take over, when they do completely unexpected things that surprise me. I don't like to choreograph my stories in advance.

Gayle at 13: That's cool. I'm glad I still like to improvise, even if it's off the ice.

Gayle at 41: Am I how you imagined you'd be at forty-one?

Gayle at 13: I never imagined myself at forty-one. I never wanted to grow up, remember?

Gayle at 41: I remember very well. I thought I would live in the apartment across the hall from our parents—that was the farthest I wanted to move away from childhood.

Gayle at 13: Why should I want to be a grown-up? Grown-ups wear panty hose and carry briefcases. Grown-ups are way too serious—they forget to have fun.

Gayle at 41: Guess what? I don't even own panty hose or a briefcase, and I definitely don't take myself too seriously. In many ways, I feel like the same person inside as I did when I was you.

Gayle at 13: Karen and Izzy are such completely different people, but I guess you do still seem like me, just with a few wrinkles, a little white hair.

Gayle at 41: I didn't have to run away from my life the way Karen did. I didn't have to create a brand-new identity like her. But I've had moments when I've started fresh in life—just a couple of years ago, I made the incredibly difficult decision to leave my first marriage—and those experiences have definitely changed me. Still, I feel like the deepest part of me is the same that it was when I was your age.

Gayle at 13: I never thought I'd get divorced. Then again, I never really thought I'd get married.

Gayle at 41: I never thought I'd get divorced either, but life is full of surprises. And now I'm remarried. And pregnant.

Gayle at 13: At your age? Ick.

Gayle at 41: I think that's what my older kids thought at first, too.

Gayle at 13: Your older kids?

Gayle at 41: They'll be nineteen and sixteen when this interview comes out. Older than you are now.

Gayle at 13: Weird.

Gayle at 41: I agree—time moves so fast.

Gayle at 13: Do they care that you write about sex?

Gayle at 41: There's really not a lot of sex in the book.

Gayle at 13: But it's there.

Gayle at 41: It's part of life. I want to write about all aspects of life.

Gayle at 13: It's a gross part of life.

Gayle at 41: You'll change your mind about that, trust me. Besides, as I recall, you searched for all the "good parts" in Judy Blume's *Forever* not that long ago.

Gayle at 13: That's different. I was curious.

Gayle at 41: And I'm still curious. Writing is a way to explore what makes us curious, don't you think?

Gayle at 13: I guess so. But you never answered me before—how do your kids feel about this?

Gayle at 41: I have to admit, my daughter once asked if I could write some more "family-friendly" material. I dedicated my first young adult novel, *My Life with the Lincolns,* to her to honor that wish. But I think they also understand that it's important to me not to censor myself when I write.

Gayle at 13: Is your relationship with your kids like Izzy's relationship with Quinn?

Gayle at 41: The circumstances are vastly different, so it's hard to say. I certainly have the same fierce love for them that Izzy has for Quinn.

Gayle at 13: I was happy to see how much Quinn loved mythology. Are you still crazy about Greek myths?

Gayle at 41: I still love them, but I'm not as up on them as you are—the pantheon and the stories are a bit fuzzy to me now.

Gayle at 13: How could that be? I am constantly reading Greek mythology. I even made that Mount Olympus newspaper, do you remember?

Gayle at 41: I do indeed. It told the Greek myths in journalism form.

Gayle at 13: I spent so much time on that newspaper—figuring out what stories to tell, using rub-on letters for the headlines, finding images from different mythology books to copy. How could you let that go?

Gayle at 41: I didn't let it go, exactly. I've just had many enthusiasms over the years. Norse mythology is a newer interest of mine.

Gayle at 13: But you never stopped loving words and writing, right?

Gayle at 41: Very true. Do you remember our favorite vocabulary word in third grade?

Gayle at 13: I do! It was "succulent." We came home from school that day, and had a piece of fruit, and said to our mom, "My, what a succulent pear."

Gayle at 41: I've loved pear words ever since.

Gayle at 13: Abcde loves pear words, too.

Gayle at 41: Yes, she does. It was a blast to be able to write about a slightly unhinged poet; I have such fondness for Abcde. She was actually inspired by one of my poetry students, who told me that his mom had a student named Abcde. We were writing abecedarian poems in class; something just clicked, and my character Abcde was born.

Gayle at 13: I want to try to write an abecedarian poem now.

Gayle at 41: You should—it's great fun!

Gayle at 13: All boys cooties deliver . . .

Gayle at 41: Aren't you a little old to be talking about cooties?

Gayle at 13: I don't want to grow up, remember?

Gayle at 41: Ha! I like how you twisted around the grammar, though. Very Yoda of you. Speaking of twisting, did you figure out the twist in the story before it was revealed?

Gayle at 13: Yeah—did you want me to?

Gayle at 41: Not exactly, but I was hoping that if people did figure it out, it wouldn't upset their reading of the rest of the book. Did it for you?

Gayle at 13: Well, it kind of made me feel smarter than you.

Gayle at 41: In some ways, you probably are!

Gayle at 13: But it didn't ruin the story.

Gayle at 41: That's good to hear.

Gayle at 13: So is there anything you think I should know about my future? Any words of advice you want to give me as I grow up into you?

Gayle at 41: I am hesitant to tell you too much, because I want life to be full of discovery for you. And I hate to give you too much advice, because you need to figure things out on your own. I will say that you have a couple of difficult years ahead of you, and part of me wants to protect you from them, but you'll ultimately be fine. You'll grow and learn and those years will be part of what makes you who you are. Who we are.

Gayle at 13: Now I'm scared!

Gayle at 41: I remember being scared of so many things when I was your age. When I was you. But please try not to be. It's all part of the journey.

Gayle at 13: That's what Izzy said to Quinn, too, right? "Zero fear."

Gayle at 41: No one can make fear go away completely, of course. But you can choose how you react to it. Just try to be as brave as possible—in your skating, in your writing, in your life—okay?

Gayle at 13: I'll try.

Gayle at 41: And I'll try, too. Is it a deal?

Gayle at 13: It's a deal.

Gayle at 41: Well, then . . . enjoy the next twenty-eight years! I look forward to seeing what adventures still wait for us.

Gayle at 13: At least we know there will be more writing.

Gayle at 41: That we do know.

Gayle at 13: And many succulent pears.

Gayle at 41: Yes. Many succulent pears.

Questions and
Topics for Discussion

1. Discuss the themes of gestation, growth, and motherhood in *Delta Girls*. In how many different ways do these themes apply to the story?

2. Before you realized that Izzy and Karen were the same person, how did you think they might be connected? At what point did you realize that Izzy was an older version of Karen? Which clues tipped you off? Were you surprised?

3. Is Izzy a good mother to Quinn? What missteps does she take? How do Deena and Izzy differ as mothers? How are they alike?

4. Consider this line from page nine: "Better to pluck it when it's green, store it someplace cold, let it forget where it came from." Izzy is talking about more than pears here. Do you agree with her? Has trying to forget her past helped or hindered Izzy? Quinn?

5. Abcde is able to provide something for Quinn that Izzy is not. What is it, and why can't Izzy fulfill this role? What does Abcde give Izzy? What do Vieira Pears and the community of Comice offer Izzy and Quinn?

6. Why does Izzy want to keep the whales secret?

7. How does Quinn's study of Norse mythology affect her own story?

8. Why is Nathan so jealous of Karen's friendship with Isabelle? Her innocent interactions with Lance Finkel? Do you think it's possible for a young person with serious goals—in dance, skating, music, acting, sports—to lead a somewhat normal life with fun and friends?

9. When Karen becomes Izzy, she feels like a different person. Do you ever feel like someone else entirely when you look back at your childhood self, your teenage self, your young adult self? What about you has changed, and what events in your life fueled those changes?

10. Why is Izzy so drawn to Sam when Abcde has proven herself to be such a loyal friend?

11. Do you think Deena engineered the relationship between Nathan and Karen for publicity? Was Nathan seeing Deena all along?

12. Try writing your own abecedarian poem. How does the form restrict your creativity? Release it?

Photo: Brooke Garcia

Gayle Brandeis is the author of two novels, *The Book of Dead Birds*, which won the Bellwether Prize for Fiction in Support of a Literature of Social Change, and *Self Storage*, as well as a young adult novel, *My Life with the Lincolns*, and a writing guide, *Fruitflesh: Seeds of Inspiration for Women Who Write*. A former figure skater, she lives in Redlands, California, and has one child in college, one in high school, and one new baby.